The Rose

REDEMPTION DUET BOOK 1

SHERITTA BITIKOFER

MOONSTRUCK WRITING

Cover art by Angela Quincoces Rivera at http://www.dream-designz.com

EBook ISBN: 978-1-946821-38-6

Print ISBN: 978-1-946821-39-3

Contents

To those fighting a battle that no one understands or knows about. Stay strong and keep going. You are never alone.

Chapter 1

For the first time all day, Belle could finally breathe. As she curled up her feet on the sofa, a steaming cup of lemon jasmine tea between her hands, she basked in the comfortable silence. The rain outside had picked up and she had already spotted a few flashes of lightning through the speckled windowpanes, but that didn't bother her. The thunderstorm added just the right ambience to help her relax.

The last hour had been spent actively trying not to go over the events of the day. She didn't want to rehearse every word, every action, or overanalyze all that had happened to her in the bookstore. All she wanted to do was let her mind go blank. With the christening sip of her tea, its aroma soothing her anxious mind, she resolved to do just that.

On the coffee table sat her laptop and a lit lavender candle that added to the whole calming atmosphere she strived to create. She glanced to the screen and watched the four security camera windows with the black and lime-colored images of her animals in the barn. Three horses and a small flock of sheep all rested peacefully through the storm. There was the occasional stirring from an ewe or head toss from one of her mares, but nothing alarming. Just how she preferred it. A quiet night recuperating from the chaotic, stressful day.

Belle sunk lower against the mass of pillows and let the tea take effect on her rattled nerves. This was just another end to a long day that, to anyone else's eyes, went off without a hitch. But to Belle, clad in her soft pajama bottoms and baggy Longhorn shirt, it was one of many that left her tired, drained, and in need of recharging.

All day, every day, she put on the mask. The one that gave a friendly smile to everyone, the one that spoke the right words every time, and never showed how truly terrified she was to be facing a perfect stranger. She spent so much energy keeping that mask firmly in place to hide her true self that at the end of the day, all she could do was crash on the couch with her tea and wonder if this would ever get easier.

Here, in her home, she was safe to be herself. It was her haven, her port of call. Her nearest neighbors were at least half a mile away on either side of her expansive farm, the one that had been passed down through her family for generations.

Everything in the barn and her two-story little farmhouse whispered the cherished memories of her childhood and a dozen childhoods before her. From the dining table in the kitchen that was made by her great-grandfather, to the wall of bookshelves in the living room packed with novels that had been collected over decades. Not to mention the three upstairs bedrooms that stored precious heirlooms dating back to her great-grandfather's time when the house was first built. All of it embraced her and welcomed her into a safe place she would never trade for the world.

She might have been alone here, but she was happy. Here, she was able to let down her long brown hair, freeing the waves and curls she tamed back every day in a ponytail. Here, she could let loose and be who she wanted to be and not have to fake her own existence for the sake of being polite and normal.

Once she had drained her first cup, Belle begrudgingly stood from the sofa and made her way into the adjoining kitchen to pour herself another. Two more and she'd be ready for bed soon, the pacifying effects of the brew thoroughly cleansing away her anxiety. Her socked feet strode across the black and white checkered tiles, the ones her grandfather had laid when he first brought his new bride home. Her father once told the story of how she took one look at the patterned vinyl and demanded it be replaced. The project was completed in just two days before her grandmother made some comment about the cabinets, and they were replaced too.

Now, dark wood offset the green countertops, giving the rustic kitchen a mis-matched look that Belle couldn't bring herself to remodel. There was too much character here, and even the thought of replacing the old appliances made her feel a little sad. So, she tolerated the dryer that had a mind of its own in the corner with the washer, and the gas stove that didn't always want to start, and the refrigerator whose icemaker broke when she was ten years old.

No, she wouldn't change a single thing about any of it.

As she poured hot water from her overused kettle over a fresh teabag, she heard a loud crash followed by a peel of thunder. Belle glanced over her shoulder to the darkened window but saw nothing except the pattering of raindrops against the glass.

She went straight to her laptop table and peered at the surveillance videos. She couldn't see anything obviously wrong until one of the feeds showed that the barn door had come unlatched and banged furiously against the outer wall. This startled the horses and though there was no sound on the footage, she could hear all three mares knicker and the loud cries of the ewes over the pouring rain.

With a sigh, she knew she'd have to wait to start on that second cup of tea until she fixed the door. But just when she was about to turn away, Belle caught sight of something in the camera. For just a moment, she thought she saw something moving outside of the animal pens. It was too big to be a sheep and stood upright like a person.

She stared at the screen longer, her pulse racing as she tried to make sense of what she saw. Nothing moved again, but that didn't keep her from spiraling into a panic. Maybe someone had broken into her barn. Her entire body went ice cold at the thought.

Another clash of lightning made the power flicker and she could see the bright green glow of the string lights flicker and die in the live video feed. Belle had convinced her father years ago to rig the barn with electricity so they didn't have to take a lantern or flashlight with them if they had to check on the animals at night. However, that power had always been glitchy and unreliable at best. She had left the lights on to give some comfort to the animals during the storm, but who knew if they would turn back on.

Donning her rubber boots and raincoat, she grabbed a flashlight from the hook on the wall and dove out into the storm as she tried to ignore every instinct to stay inside where it was safe and dry.

Mud sloshed all around her pant legs, soaking them through until she felt the water chill her ankles and seep into her socks. Not even her boots could keep out the torrential downpour. Plump, cool drops splashed on her face, thoroughly dampening it despite the hood that concealed much of her head.

The rain fell across the yellow beam of light, almost obscuring her view. Somehow through the darkness and haze of rain, she saw the barn door slapping against the front side of the barn with every gust of wind.

Belle stopped to examine the damage, her shoes sinking into the deep puddles that had already formed on the ground. She knew for a fact that she had locked up the barn before going back inside that night. The padlock couldn't have been knocked off by the wind and the key was still sitting on the kitchen counter. It had to have been broken by something. Or someone.

Fear rose up in her throat, but she tread softly toward the barn doors. Belle swallowed hard as she inspected the lock and found that it, along with the latch, had been ripped completely off, and lay in the mud just in front of the entrance. Whoever had gotten in was either incredibly strong or had a tool sturdy enough to rip off the lock.

When she shined her flashlight around the opening, she saw what the intruder must have used. An iron crowbar lay in the dirt just inside the threshold. It hadn't been there before, but Belle recognized it as her father's. His initials had been etched into the handle when he forged it himself for a school project.

Belle picked up the crowbar and swung the door shut behind her. She pushed back her raincoat hood and shined her flashlight around inside of the barn, willing for the beam to stop bouncing as her hands continued to shake. She swept it along the horse stalls, then to the sheep's pen to the far back right corner, then to the old run-down Volkswagen opposite from them.

There was a thickness in the cool air that confirmed her suspicions that something wasn't right. Whoever had broken into her barn must have still been there, lurking in the shadows where her flashlight couldn't penetrate.

After another quick check with her light, she roamed to more closely inspect the barn. Nothing appeared to be missing in the way of supplies or animals. Yet, there was still an unease that filled her spirit. It just didn't feel right, and she hated the way her heart pounded against her ribs with painful urgency.

Thinking that it might have been the storm making both herself and her animals nervous, Belle turned to leave, willing to dismiss what she saw on the camera feed as a moth or bug that got in the way of the lens. Maybe the wind had picked up a sturdy piece of lumber and knocked it against the lock to make it fly off instead of the crowbar she found. The wood of the barn door wasn't new by any means and probably bore the beginnings of dry rot anyway. She couldn't remember the last time the latch had been replaced, so it was possible that there was no intruder after all. That's what she wanted to believe.

Then, she heard a sneeze. It wasn't an animal sneeze, as she knew them all too well. This was a human sneeze and it sounded distinctly male.

Belle whipped around, crowbar poised and ready to throw or beat down whoever came near her. Her flashlight darted to all the corners, but still found nothing.

Finally, she called out in the strongest voice she could muster, "Show yourself now or I'm calling the cops!"

It took a moment, but there came some movement from the stack of hay bales near the back wall. Belle, as shaky as she was, stood her ground and gripped her weapon tighter. Though her teeth were clamped tight, her ragged breaths came sputtering out from her nostrils. There was no hiding her fear, no matter how she tried.

A man came forward with his arms raised in submission. He was shirtless, only clothed in a pair of battered jeans, torn and stained. His body made the air in Belle's lungs freeze. Residual rainwater dripped from his barrel-chest down his toned, rippling abs and curving along his narrowing waist. He had broad shoulders and beefy arms as thick around as her thighs, all muscle and power.

Her flashlight stopped at his neck, but her eyes continued to roam upward. A pair of pure blue eyes sparkled from beneath dark brows. A beard covered his jaw and around his mouth, as black as the night sky. His equally dark, damp hair was slightly flattened and tangled by the storm, its tips grazing against the bare skin of his collarbone.

But it wasn't the striking contrast of his hair and eyes that stunned her. It was the way he looked directly at her, ignoring the weapon she held, and the harsh light shining on his torso. He wasn't afraid, but neither was he on the offensive. There wasn't a hint of malice anywhere in his expression. There wasn't a hint of anything. He met her stern gaze with a steady, gentle one that both intrigued and unnerved her even further.

Yet, somehow, she couldn't look away, even if she wanted to. She would have given anything to drop her eyes in submission. Her mask wanted to come up, to protect her from this man and his hypnotic gaze. But, it couldn't. Why couldn't it? Maybe it was the long day or the tea she had drank earlier. It put her at a disadvantage, and she wasn't prepared to face another person that evening. Exposed, caught off-guard, and terribly vulnerable. Anything could go wrong here, and she needed to be brave and detached. But the mask wouldn't stick as long as this man was looking at her like that.

They stood there, in a stalemate for what seemed like several minutes before he spoke in a deep voice that rattled her bones. "Are you still going to call the police?"

Belle blinked and realized that her eyes were burning from the strain of the stare. He had an accent that certainly placed him out of Arkansas. English, perhaps? No, it was closer to Irish or maybe Welsh. But it wasn't thick. It had a watered-down quality, like he had been in the states for too long.

Instead of answering his question, she shifted her stance as if it would help her. "Who are you?"

His lips parted, ready to speak, but no words came out right away. For a second, it almost looked as if he were confused or thinking hard about something. "My name's Leo Thompson," he replied in a lilting voice, though she could detect a quiver in it as if he were shivering in the cold.

"What are you doing in my barn?" she demanded.

He blinked a few times as if he were trying to keep up with the conversation and gave a subtle gesture toward the doors. "I needed someplace to stay while it rained."

"That's what homes are for," she snapped, feeling the stress of the situation finally override her fear. This man was obviously unarmed, otherwise he would have attacked by now. That is, if he wanted to. "You can't just crash into people's barns like this!"

Leo looked mystified by her outburst as a thin line formed between his dark brows. "Well, I didn't plan on being found either."

Belle bounced the crowbar in her hand to remind him that she was still in control. "I demand you leave immediately!"

"Will you still call the police?"

"Not if you leave peacefully."

Leo kept his hands raised to show that he wasn't trying to pull a fast one, and took long sinuous steps toward the barn doors, keeping his eyes fixed on Belle and her crowbar. When he came closer, Belle's heart began to pound at the realization that he was quite tall and even more muscular than she first assessed.

Anyone else might have been intimidated. Of all people, Belle should have been intimidated too. Compared to her short and thin stature, he was a giant. Suddenly, her crowbar seemed like a useless weapon. If only she had a gun or pepper spray. This man could crush her with his bare hands, yet he submitted to her wielding a crowbar that might have only bruised him.

As Leo came unbearably close, just a few feet away, Belle skittered backward. He had violated the carefully formed social bubble she tried to maintain, but her notice of it was slightly delayed, much to her chagrin. He seemed to take notice of this and stopped just as he was about to pass her by.

"If it's any comfort to you, I took nothing."

Belle nodded. "I appreciate that."

Leo slowly lowered his arms to his sides and finally broke eye contact to turn toward the doors. As soon as his eyes, two perfect sapphires in the dark, had peeled away from her, Belle sensed an ache inside that she couldn't explain.

For some reason, she felt a prodding in her soul. This man must have had nowhere to go. Why else would he be breaking into her barn? She had been too quick to judge. She didn't know whether it was the need to feel those eyes on her again, or the subtle nudging to help this man who was so obviously in need, but Belle knew she couldn't let him go just yet.

"Is your home far from here?" she asked quickly before he had a chance to open the barn doors. "I can drive you there, if it's too far to walk."

Leo turned to face Belle. Once more, she was taken breathless.

"I have no home to go to," he stated rather plainly, as if it weren't a tragic thing to be destitute.

"So, you're homeless?"

He shrugged his broad shoulders. "In a manner of speaking."

Belle felt irritation rise up in her and there was little stopping it from spewing out now. "Do you have a home to go to or not?"

A flash of amusement came across his face and Leo shook his head. "No, I have no home."

Belle shifted weight from one foot to another and realized that she had lowered her crowbar. If this man had no place to go and she wouldn't let him stay in her barn, he was likely to go to one of her neighbor's barns and take shelter there. Some people around Levi would not take kindly to intruders. Mr. Johnson would shoot first and ask questions later. Either that, or he would freeze to death in the woods. Summer was coming to a close and even if it wasn't raining, nights were growing colder and colder.

Belle didn't want to take responsibility for any harm that came to Leo if she could help it.

But, what was there to do? She couldn't let him stay on her property, even if he just slept in her barn for the night before moving on to the next place. Looking him up and down one more time, he didn't strike her as the homeless type. The thick stubble around his face was well trimmed and his hair was not unkempt besides what the rain and wind had done to it. His pants were worn out, but she had seen many laborers and ranch hands wearing jeans in worse condition.

After a few silent moments of deliberation - Leo waiting patiently for her to continue - Belle sucked in a breath and nodded at her decision. "There's a homeless shelter in the next town over. It's about twenty miles... Are you hungry?"

Leo's eyes diverted to some unknown spot behind Belle before he replied, "As a matter of fact, I am."

"I have some food up at the house. You can dry off there. I also should have a shirt you can try on. If it fits, you can keep it. The shelter might not give you clothes."

At first, Leo said nothing. He seemed puzzled, as if he didn't understand exactly what she was offering. Belle moved toward the door anyway, keeping a tight hold on her crowbar in case he had a change of heart. She wasn't about to wait around for him to figure it out. "Come on."

She flipped her raincoat hood up. The high winds outside tugged at the door, but Belle held it fast until Leo joined her, standing so close she could smell the raindrops and earthy scent of soil on his jeans.

After Belle let the wind throw the door open, Leo darted out into the storm toward the general direction of the house. She stayed behind to latch the doors together with a bit of spare rope from inside the barn, but found it difficult to keep a hold on both her flashlight and the crowbar.

By necessity rather than logic, she dropped the piece of iron into the mud and lashed the doors together. When she turned, she saw Leo standing by the back door, drenched in the rain with the soft amber glow of the kitchen light shining through the windows to illuminate his outline. He didn't even bother to shield himself from the effects of the storm as he stood tall like a sentinel and waited for her.

Knowing she had his attention, she waved him around to the front of the house where the porch would give them adequate shelter. Belle jogged across the stretch of grass between the barn and the house. Leo obeyed her signals and followed.

Glancing over her shoulder, she saw Leo standing just at the top of the porch steps, a wall of raindrops pouring down behind him like a waterfall backdrop.

"Stay out here. I'll bring you everything."

He took a step forward, and looked like he was about to protest, but thought better and nodded. Belle wasn't about to let this strange man into her home, ruggedly handsome or not. Too many things could go wrong and she wasn't about to take that chance.

Belle ducked into the house, stripped off her muddy boots and dripping raincoat, and hurriedly fixed a plate of the same spaghetti leftovers she had earlier that evening. While the meal was reheating in the microwave, she went upstairs to find him a shirt.

She kept many of her father's personal possessions after he passed away and there was bound to be something that could fit Leo's burly frame. Inside her bedroom closet was a box filled with photo albums, trinkets, and a few shirts and polos he used to wear to church on Sundays.

With nimble fingers, she combed through the stack and found a suitable black, button-down shirt. She tried not to breathe in too deeply, knowing the scent of her father's old cologne still clung to the fabric. The microwave dinged downstairs and she scuttled her way back into the kitchen with the shirt and a bath towel draped over her arm.

Even as she was pulling out a fork and spoon, Belle began to wonder why she was doing this at all. He was a stranger, and potentially dangerous. Even if he was homeless, it might have been easier to drop him off at the shelter with a twenty-dollar bill and let him figure it out from there. But, for some reason, she was willing to sacrifice her own food and a priceless sentimental keepsake to this man who had barged into her life so suddenly.

Maybe it was how he had looked at her in those first few seconds. Or maybe because, deep down, she felt sorry for him. An old scripture from her childhood came to mind. The one about feeding and clothing the poor. Did she do this out of good Christian charity? Or did a more lustful element play into her decisions tonight? She shook her head sharply at the notion. Leo was hot, but nothing trumped her anxiety these days. Not even charity. It had to be something else.

Stepping out with everything, she saw Leo leaning against one of the white posts, staring out into the stormy weather. A light mist was blown under the porch and gently played in his dark hair. Lightning flashed in the distance and startled her out of the daze she had fallen in while watching him.

She flipped on the light and Leo turned around. His eyes raked over her from head to toe, then locked onto her eyes. But, the subtle shrug of his eyebrows that might not have been intentional at all, was not lost on Belle. He had checked her out and a little color rose to her cheeks as she remembered her informal attire. She must have looked like she was ready to crawl into bed. Her raincoat and rubber boots couldn't hide her pajamas anymore. He seemed to completely ignore the food and clothing until she wordlessly handed them over to break the awkward silence.

The tips of his fingers grazed against her skin in the transfer. Belle was not a romantic by any stretch of the imagination, but she couldn't deny the electricity that pulsated from his touch. She swallowed hard and crossed her arms over her chest as she watched him set the plate down on one of the deck tables and dry himself off.

Her eyes roved over his body, watching the way the porchlight shined against his smooth, tanned skin. With better light to see him by, she began to notice more things.

Such as, before he slipped on the shirt, she saw numerous faint scars along his arms and torso.

Without thinking, she asked, "Where did you get all those scars from?"

She winced. Not only was she getting too personal with this stranger, but now he knew where Belle had been looking.

Leo glanced at her while fastening the buttons, leaving the top few open to leave half of his chest exposed. It was a tight fit around the arms, but after he tucked in the tails into his damp jeans, the shirt appeared to suit him well. As he rolled up the sleeves, he replied, "Various places."

Belle accepted that, even though she desperately wanted a better answer. Leo took up the fork and began to twirl noodles on the plate as he slowly ambled away to lean against the porch railing again.

"Do you want something to drink to go with that?" she asked, desperate to fill the silence.

Though he might have been starving, Leo ate rather slowly, taking his time to chew and twirl his fork. Once his mouth was empty, he said, "No, thank you."

Belle couldn't help but make note of how calm he was, as if he were completely contented. He behaved as if he had visited her farm several times, leaning against the railing so casually like he belonged here. A few neighbors came and went, like Mr. Johnson who helped her with her sheep or Mr. Levinson when she needed repairs to her barn. But few lingered as Leo did. It was like he had leapt from being a stranger to a friend over a plate of spaghetti.

Then, it dawned on her that she knew his name, but he didn't know hers. That might as well have been a good thing. She didn't want him taking her name and using it to his advantage somehow. Her family name held so much weight in Levi because of her father that anyone would willingly offer up favors if she so much as hinted at it.

While Leo ate, Belle turned her attention to the storm around them. If she was correct, the downpour seemed to be lightening up already. But the hush between them was too much. Belle felt her nerves tighten like a wound-up spring.

"How long have you been homeless?"

Once more, Belle knew she had crossed a line. But she began to realize that a strange thing happened sometime between this moment and when she had stepped into the barn. The consciousness of her actions was there, but there was little to no filter to keep her from blurting out the things she knew should not be said. It was as if, for several minutes, she had been her candid self with Leo. What was worse, she couldn't stop.

Leo paused, mouth full of noodles and ground beef, and looked up to her with raised brows, as if he hadn't expected her to ask such a probing question. Belle hadn't expected it either. Once the words were out, she wanted nothing more than to duck inside the house and hide.

Yet, she stood firm with her arms crossed defensively and waited, her gaze locked onto his with a boldness that she rarely exuded.

Leo swallowed down what he had in his mouth and replied, "A long time."

"You don't sound like you're from around here."

He seemed to recognize the question in her statement and nodded. "I was born in Scotland."

Belle had been close when she assumed Ireland and that gave her some satisfaction. "When did you come to the states?"

Leo eased his shoulders back from the hunched position over his plate. "A long time ago."

"How long is that?" she inquired, knowing full well that she was stepping over the border between curious and interrogative.

A shadow passed over Leo's eyes, giving him a dark and brooding look without a flicker of facial muscles that Belle could consciously detect. "A long time," he repeated.

Belle was getting nowhere. The way he had totally shut her out did not startle her, but it did deter her from asking anymore questions, however much she wanted to.

This man intrigued her on a level that she had never known before. Yes, he was handsome, but there was something more to it than just attraction. He had an air about him that made her want to know more, to peel back the layers he was so obviously strapping down. She couldn't recall a time when she cared this much about anyone.

Most of the time, she was too scared to get close, too scared to talk and ask. There were still plenty of things she didn't know about the coworkers she had been with for years, because she couldn't gather the nerve to get past the little things.

"The shelter is a good place," she stated. "Members of my church volunteer there a lot."

Belle watched a tendon in Leo's jaw jump at the mention of the shelter. He resumed eating and lowered his gaze to his food, giving her nerves a reprieve. She turned away to watch the rain once more, mostly to prevent herself from staring at Leo.

"I've been to shelters before," he said, drawing her attention back to the mysterious Scotsman.

"Where?" There she went with the questions again. What had come over her?

He aimlessly pushed around a few bits of beef on his plate. "Many places."

Belle blinked and leaned all of her weight on one leg, making herself look particularly sassy. "Forgive me for saying this, but you don't look like a homeless person at all."

Leo glanced up briefly. "Oh?"

"I imagine homeless people as being dirty and shabby. You don't look like that. I mean, you are kind of dirty, but not as dirty as I would have thought."

One corner of his mouth tilted up. "Aren't you stereotyping a wee bit?"

Belle wanted to laugh at his choice of words. She had never heard anyone use "wee" in a sentence without mocking intent.

"I might be. But if you've been homeless for a long time, how do you stay clean cut? I would think your beard would be pretty long and scraggly."

Leo chewed and gulped down the last of the spaghetti. "They do have shaving supplies at most shelters, as well as showers."

Having never stepped foot in a shelter or offered to volunteer, Belle learned something new. If homeless people were provided the basic hygiene amenities, why did she see so many men on the side of the road looking like bums?

She nodded and took the empty plate from him. "I guess I learned my lesson about judging a book by its cover."

When she met Leo's stare, she felt her insides churn again.

"I suppose you have," he replied softly before she turned to disappear into the house.

Belle was filled with conflicting emotions as she grabbed her keys that were sitting on the kitchen table. Even though Leo's presence made her so undone, she didn't look forward to dropping him off at the shelter.

It didn't seem right, somehow, to just ditch him there. If what he said was true, and that he had been homeless for a long time, he didn't need another shelter. He needed a job and stable situation. She wondered if there were any companies in town that were hiring.

Not only that, but something in her spirit didn't want to let this man go. She wanted to know more. Why was he in the states? How did he come to Arkansas? And why did he affect her so strongly, this man that she barely knew, but felt so comfortable to be around. Belle had never felt that way with a stranger.

She wanted to know how Leo had cracked her defenses. Was it coincidence or was there more to those beautiful blue eyes than he was letting on?

Chapter 2

After half an hour of riding shotgun in the girl's pickup truck, they finally arrived to the homeless shelter. The ride had not been a smooth one and Leo didn't have to look at the odometer to know this truck had seen better days. From the noise coming from under the hood, he could tell the engine needed work. Or better yet, scrap the whole thing and replace it with something new that didn't knock and grind so hard.

From the looks of it, the shelter was like many Leo had visited over the years. He'd been to big city shelters and small local operations, experiencing the best charity and the worst scrutiny from their volunteers.

It had been a couple of weeks since his last visit to a shelter. If it weren't for the rain and this woman's desire to help, he would have gone much longer. Leo wasn't sure how to feel about that. This region of the country didn't lack in barns, abandoned or not. If he had been a little more careful with that lock, he would have been able to stay the night on a comfortable pile of hay and slip out at dawn when the weather cleared.

Yet, he was almost thankful for the way things worked out. He slid a glance in her direction as she parked the truck along the curb.

When he first saw her in the raincoat, hair disheveled from the wind and rain, and angry scowl fixed on her face, he thought she was strikingly good-looking. When they came to the house and he saw what had been concealed under the coat, he was even more impressed, and pleasantly amused.

She was short, like a skinny adolescent, but he hadn't imagined she would be so unlike the child he had suspected her to be. No, she was all woman with the right curves in the right places to make his heart beat a little harder in his chest. He had seen more voluptuous women in his time, but no other ever pulled it off with grace, making each movement alluring without even meaning to.

He was especially taken by her green eyes. Even in the dim glow of the dashboard controls of the truck, he could make out the beautiful emerald, rimmed in a slightly darker shade. Her eyes reminded him of the rolling hills of pasturelands in Scotland, the only thing he missed from the home he could never return to.

Her personality aroused his interest as well. The way she tried to defend herself with only a crowbar was laughable. He had faced down plenty of opponents with more dangerous tools and come out without a scratch. She posed him no threat. Her mild reprimands about him breaking into her barn didn't faze him in the least.

What caught his attention was the way she changed her mind so suddenly. He had been content to leave that barn and walk for a few more miles in the rain until he found another. But, she wouldn't let him. He wasn't the type of man to argue against a hot meal and fresh shirt when it was offered.

He wondered what might have tipped the scale in his favor, if he had anything to do with it. The way she badgered him with questions was bothersome, but hardly anyone had asked them before. No one cared. The men who paid him under the table for odd jobs sometimes showed this kind of curiosity, but they didn't seem quite as concerned as she did. They asked, because they didn't want to be slapped with fines or a lawsuit. She asked, because she genuinely wanted to know.

Yet, he couldn't determine - besides in the way that she had blushed only once - if she was attracted to him in the same way. Leo hadn't seen her truly smile yet and she made no effort to flirt or make her feelings known the way women did when they were around him. It was refreshing, yet disappointing, that this girl didn't even try. Part of him wanted her to.

More than any of this, Leo felt something when he was with her. She somehow muted the constant white noise of rage and hatred, leaving him in a silence he hadn't experienced in years. He could breathe, think, feel. He didn't want to climb out of this truck as long as she was in it. He had a feeling that the moment he did, everything would come crashing down again.

The lass let out a puff of air as if she were preparing herself for a difficult task and pulled out a small notepad from the middle console. He watched her take a pen and scribble down a name and telephone number.

"I know the shelter will take good care of you," she began, "but if you need anything else while you're in the area, give me a call."

She folded up the sheet of paper and handed it to him. As before, he purposefully let their fingers touch as he took it from her. He then unfolded the paper and read her name.

"Belle," he said. It suited her well.

She shrugged. "It was my dad's choice. Annabelle Rose is my full name. My mom picked my middle name and she said it always had a sing-song kind of ring to it."

He wasn't sure why she shared that with him, but folded up the paper and gripped it tightly in his fist, afraid to put it in his damp pocket where it might get ruined. He wanted to keep that number, if for nothing else than to remind him of her kindness.

"I appreciate everything you've done for me tonight."

Satisfaction bloomed in his chest when he made her blush for the second time since they'd met.

"You're welcome." Belle lifted her chin and gave him a nod. "I wish you the best of luck."

He gave her a friendly salute and climbed out of the truck. The storm had moved on, leaving the air humid with a hint of fuel exhaust from her truck. The sound of the old, rattling engine drowned out the traffic noise roaring through the streets.

He stepped onto the sidewalk, but didn't hear her zoom off into the distance like he half expected her to. Turning, he saw that she had been watching him leave, probably to make sure that he was actually going to go inside the shelter. Even at the last minute, she displayed her unease.

A few cars sped around her truck and blared their horn to complain that she was blocking traffic. Leo hurried to the shelter doors and waved to her one more time.

Watching her pull away from the curb, red brake lights shining through the dark, Leo felt a strange ache that he hadn't felt in many years.

People came and went in his life, but he never permitted them to stay. He wasn't the man to keep attachments. It was safer that way for himself and for those around him. If he ever made friends, it was short-lived before he moved on to the next town. He was a nomad and always would be. There was no other way.

Yet, Belle had gotten to him somehow with her spunk and tender gaze. She was ready to take on a man twice her size with a flimsy crowbar, then turned around and gave him a shirt. He assumed the previous owner of the shirt was her brother or maybe a boyfriend that didn't live with her. That latter guess twisted the knife in his gut and sobered any potentially romantic thoughts he might have had.

Out of all the women he had known, she would forever stand out, boyfriend or not.

Leo waited until he could no longer see her tail lights and turned to the shelter. He tugged on the handle, but the locked door wouldn't give way. Peeking through the glass pane, he saw the lights were on in a room far down a narrow hall beyond a reception desk.

A shadow passed and he banged on the door, making the glass rattle. A few seconds later, an older woman came and poked her head out.

"I'm sorry, sir. We're full for the night and it's past our check-in time."

Leo sighed and looked past her as if to check if she were lying. He nodded and turned away back to the street. This wasn't totally unexpected. It had happened to him several times. He waited until the volunteer shut and lock the doors again before shoving his hands into his pockets.

Glancing up and down the street, he saw plenty of closed retail stores, restaurants, and other establishments, but no hotels. Upon a second sweep, he saw neon lights about half a mile away, blinking red and blue, and advertising for good times and good beer.

He reached down into his back pocket and pulled out a fistful of cash. Leafing through the moistened hundred dollar bills, he reasoned he might have enough to do what he did best nowadays.

Leo had amassed a sizable crowd around the table. It was poker night at the bar and evidently, it was a community event. Out of the six men who joined the game in the beginning, nearly four hours ago, only one more remained who was willing to deal another round with him. The other five were still in the bar, but had folded and chosen not to play him again. The only reason they stuck around was to see if anyone else could beat the stranger.

Leaning back in the rickety wooden chair, he fingered the five cards in his hand, keeping their faces hidden from the others who crowded him on every side, especially from the woman who had her arms draped around his shoulders.

He had done a fine job of fattening his pockets even more than they already were. The man who sat across from him had lost the most. With a few thousand dollars sitting in the pot on the table, waiting for a winner to be declared, his opponent had a hard time keeping his cool.

In fact, they all - in one form or another - gave away their hands too easily. Leo had gone up against more seasoned players before and this crowd proved to be less of a challenge.

The man stared intently at his cards, raking his sweaty hand through his tousled hair. The way his eyes shifted between his hand and the pot, Leo knew that he was debating on whether to raise or fold. They had gone back and forth for a while now and Leo was growing a little more impatient with each passing moment that the man refused to act.

He took a sip of the beer he had been nursing while the woman slipped her hand past his open collar to stroke his bare chest. Leo was in no mood for her games. Not because she was a distraction, but because she had no chance of earning the money that sat on the table after he had won it. Leo knew these schemes all too well.

In addition to that, he could think of no other woman than the one who had dropped him off in this town earlier that evening. Checking the clock on the wall, he saw it was well past midnight. His thoughts wandered back to Belle and the farm. She must have been in bed by now. Or was she still awake and maybe thinking of him? He hoped that she was.

"Can I give you an IOU?" the nervous man asked.

Leo turned his attention back to the game and shook his head. "No IOUs." He leaned forward, gliding from the woman's hold and flipped his cards down, keeping their values hidden. "But, I'll make a deal. This is the last round. If your hand wins, I'll give everyone their money back." The man looked a little relieved. "If I win, you give me the keys to the shiny Harley outside in the parking lot and you can keep this pot." Leo had already won enough from the previous games that these winnings would be straight icing.

The man's eyes went wide. "My bike? You want my bike?"

Leo shrugged and leaned back again. "I need something to get around in. I fancy the bike. You can fold now and I take it, or you can stick it out and see if you can win it all back for your mates."

The crowd shouted their opinions on the matter, but Leo kept his gaze aimed on the man whose eyes darted wildly around the room. After a hasty deliberation, the man pulled out a set of keys from his pocket and tossed them into the pot.

Leo laid down another hundred-dollar bill from his original stash and leaned his elbows on the table again.

"Time to reveal, lad. What do you have?"

The man laid his hand down to reveal four of a kind in the form of nines. Leo nodded his acknowledgement of the hand while everyone else shouted for joy. Little could beat that.

Leo let them have their small victory before flipping his cards over in one smooth roll of his wrist. The crowd exploded in groans of dismay at his royal flush of hearts. The man who had lost his motorcycle bolted from the chair, shouting obscenities.

"You cheated! No one can be that lucky!"

Leo cocked his head, discovering that the man had a backbone after all. "No, lad. I don't cheat," he said as he plucked the keys from the pot. That was all he was interested in.

Leo saw the man reach around behind him and even in the smoky air of the bar, he saw the flash of something black in his hand. Before the gun could be pointed at him, Leo vaulted over the table, grabbed the man by his wrist and swung him around to plant his face into the smooth lacquered table top.

He wrenched the gun away and tossed it to the floor. Shouting erupted through the crowd as they realized what had just happened. Swinging him around again, Leo threw him against the wall. By now, people were scattering out of the way to avoid being dragged into the fight that wasn't theirs. The bartender kept a close eye, but didn't interfere just yet.

The man staggered a bit to regain his balance, the half a dozen beers he had guzzled taking its toll on his body. Leo wouldn't let him fall or run, and pinned him to the wall with his thick forearm pressed against the man's thin neck. He could feel the rapid pulse against his taut muscles.

Leo came in close, their noses almost touching. "You got a problem with me?" he growled.

The man gasped for breath as Leo crushed into him with the full force of his body. His eyes were wide with fear, his nostrils flared and Leo could sense the panic rising in his trapped opponent. The man did not fight back, but feebly clawed at Leo's arm that had him pinned.

Seconds ticked by, but the man wouldn't answer him except in pathetic stutters. Leo felt the vicious rage grow within him like a hot poison in his veins.

Kill him. He insulted you. Kill him.

Leo blinked and slowly let the man crumble to the hardwood floor, coughing and sputtering for breath. It took a good minute for him to cleanse the hateful venom from his chest. Losing his control wasn't uncommon, but that didn't make it any less unacceptable. Especially here.

He turned to see a spread of faces open in shock and horror. Leo strutted to the table and plucked up the keys that he had dropped earlier, ignoring the eyes that followed him.

Outside the bar, Leo took a few deep breaths, calming back the violence that he had almost unleashed on someone who wasn't worth it. No one in that bar was worth it. They weren't the ones to blame.

Leo looked up into the clouded night sky, gripping the motorcycle keys in his fist until the metal edges bit into his palm. At least he had a way to get back to the town where Belle lived. His plan had unfolded perfectly and now he wouldn't have to walk.

You can't stay there. Stay moving. Don't settle down. Don't get attached.

Leo shook the voices from his head as he mounted the bike. He wouldn't listen. Not this time. He wouldn't go to Belle, not right away. Maybe this place would be different than all the others in the same way that Belle was so different from all the other women he had known.

It might have been risky. It might have been a mistake and would turn out terribly wrong. The moment things turned sour, Leo knew he would need to leave. That was another thing he was good at. Leaving.

Belle bit her nails as she stared across the street. It had been ages since she bit her nails and Ivy, who stood beside her smoking a cigarette outside the bookstore, had noticed almost instantly. It wasn't like Belle to show her anxiety in little tics like everyone else. It made her more human and appeared less like the perfect flower that she had pretended to be for so long.

And it was all Leo's fault. Belle couldn't stop thinking about the night before when he'd broken into her barn. He had visited her in restless dreams and she saw his gorgeous blue eyes and ruffled black hair everywhere she went. Though she knew that he was long gone, she searched for him on the streets, hoping that by some miracle he would appear again.

It was foolish to want him back. What would she say? They spoke very little the night before. It was clear that Leo was not a talker and not interested in sharing.

The more she thought about him, the more she replayed the events in her mind, the more she so wanted him to be there. She thought that maybe they could start over and get off on a better foot. Belle would put on her mask and earn his trust. Then, they could be friends. But why would she want that at all?

"What's got you all wound up?" Ivy asked before blowing smoke into the air above their heads. She had always been considerate of Belle's aversion to the smell of cigarette smoke. It was a small way for Ivy to repay Belle for her company. Since she didn't smoke, Belle would have much rather have been inside, but she needed the break from their irritated boss just as much as Ivy did.

Belle had found an unlikely friend in Ivy. They met on the job, and Ivy's bubbly and outgoing personality ensured they became friends too quickly for Belle's comfort. On the clock, she was polite and talkative with the customers, striking up conversations at the drop of a hat that would last for an hour or more. Belle admired Ivy for her ability to socialize so fluidly. Ray, their boss, hated it when she became so distracted with getting to know everyone that walked through the door, that she neglected her own job.

Outside of work at the bookstore, Ivy was just about the same, but much wilder. Ivy was what Belle liked to call a Dixie Diva. She epitomized all the stereotypical country songs that played on the radio. Sassy, fun, and a little on the flirty side after a few drinks. They were complete opposites. Belle felt no compulsion to do the things that Ivy did, even if partying in honkytonks could have made her popular.

Growing up with a single father who was devoted to the church and community, Belle didn't have the time or the opportunity to hang out with kids her own age. And when she did, she found it too unbearable and draining. Even now, the thought of going out with a group of people made her stomach drop.

"Nothing," she lied with her thumb nail between her teeth.

Ivy propped her fist on her hip and gave Belle a look. "Come on. I know something's bothering you."

Belle let go of her nail and turned to her friend. "I met a guy last night."

The admittance surprised them both. Belle was not in the habit of sharing her innermost thoughts with anyone. In the time that she had known Ivy, Belle couldn't recall one instance when she talked about something anywhere near this personal.

Ivy's face lit up with delight. "Where did you meet him?"

Belle chewed on her lip in place of her nails and looked away, unsure if she should continue this conversation. It wasn't any of Ivy's business and Belle knew that Ivy had a propensity to gossip around town. If she told her everything, what was the likelihood of the story becoming twisted into something that didn't resemble the truth at all? She'd have all the ladies at church banging on her door asking for explanations.

Yet, Belle took a breath and let it out slowly before telling Ivy all about the storm and how this man had broken into her barn. In her words, she tried to stay as professional as possible. She didn't mention the fact that he was shirtless, and she didn't even go into detail about how his stunning eyes checked her out on the porch. A flash of heat crawled up her neck at the thought of him seeing her in that baggy Longhorn shirt. She had been in more embarrassing situations, but none recently.

Belle couldn't understand why she was opening up so unaccountably. Perhaps she needed to confide in another person about what she had experienced and, only then, could she rid herself of Leo's memory. Or it might have been a prolonged effect of his influence over her.

"That's so creepy," Ivy commented after Belle had finished her story. "What if this guy comes back and tries to break into your house or something?"

Belle shook her head. "He's way out of town and not likely to come back, I'm sure."

Ivy's shoulders shivered. "But what if he does? I mean, he knows where you live now." She turned to Belle with wide eyes. "He could have been some escaped convict."

Belle pressed her lips into a thin line. The thought that he could be a runaway felon never crossed her mind, but it might explain why he was so buff.

Yet, when she pondered it more, Leo didn't fit the mold of a criminal. He didn't seem violent and he didn't have that crazed look about him like he wanted an excuse to cut open her throat. He was polite, if not a little off-putting, but he didn't seem that dangerous, despite her initial fears. If Leo was a convict, he would have been the rare exception to the stereotype. Then she was reminded of what Leo told her about judging a book by its cover.

"I don't think he was a convict or a psychopath or anything," Belle replied, "and I don't think he'll come back."

As much as it pained her to say it, she knew that she was right. Leo was long gone and the only thing that she had to remember him by was a remarkable experience and an ache in her chest that hadn't gone away since she drove on from the shelter. She was sure that it would fade with time. All things did.

At least, for an hour or so, Belle got the chance to be completely candid with a perfect stranger. No, she didn't bare her soul, but she didn't put on a facade for Leo, which never happened. He got to see her in all of her uncensored glory. No mask, no shallow mingling, nothing fake. And it felt so right. Who knew when that chance would come again? When she would be so real with anyone.

A shout came from the front door of the bookstore. "Hey! You two have been on break long enough."

Ray, the owner and manager of the New Beginnings Bookstore, poked his bald head out from the doorway and glared at them with his dark eyes. His managing skills were unconventional. Both Ivy and Belle treasured the days they worked alone in the store without their supervisor. While Belle endeavored to think the best of everyone, Ray was a hard case. She blamed it on his ulcer or the rocky marriage that he went home to every night. Ivy, however, could never find an excuse and borderline hated the man.

But, Belle always put on a smile and did her job. As far as anyone else knew, she was a sweet little farm girl who was always polite and willing to please. None of them saw the edges of her mask. None of them could have guessed how much she lived for the moment she returned home to silence and solitude.

Ivy scraped the smoldering tip of her cigarette against the brick wall and flicked it into the trash. "Well, I'm glad he didn't kill you. Now will you take my advice and get a gun?"

For all Ivy's bouts of rebellion and carefree lifestyle, Belle liked the fact that she cared deeply for those she knew. That might have been their only commonality.

Belle rolled her eyes. "I guess it wouldn't hurt," she gave a mocking groan.

The two girls turned and stepped back into the bookstore just as Belle heard the heavy rumbling of a motorcycle cruising down the street.

Leo slowed down as he entered Levi and marveled at how small it seemed compared to other places he had been. He familiarized himself with the basic layout of the town. Half a dozen or so roads intersected in a grid pattern, all lined with locally operated stores and restaurants. A band of neighborhoods surrounded the edges of the town, and beyond that were the ranches and farmlands like Belle's. Only one supermarket, one hotel, one bar, no apartments, and nothing better to do on a Friday night.

But he wasn't here for entertainment. He traveled up and down every street and boulevard, eyes skimming for a home that was available to rent. He couldn't go through a realtor, knowing that he met absolutely none of their qualifications except enough money to pay the first and last month's rent.

Most of all, he needed a job and at least one person who was willing to take a risk on him.

Having not slept in over twenty-four hours, he was weary and his body ached for rest, but he couldn't until he had a place of his own. No barns or roadside motels for him now. The day had not been fruitful until Leo found himself parked in front of a series of vintage brick storefronts on one of the more historic streets of the town.

Leo pulled his new bike to the curb, more or less just to rest for a moment, and parked for what seemed the hundredth time that day. The kickstand was certainly getting a workout.

In the window of the shop he had stopped in front of, he spotted a handmade sign bordered in colorful swirl designs and feminine cursive reading, "Room for Rent" in the center. An old sewing machine propped up the sign and by the looks of the other display items in the window, this was some sort of craft or fabric store. It was worth a shot.

Stepping through the door, a tiny bell tinkled above him. The store smelled of dusty fabric and musty wood, ineffectively masked by a vanilla candle burning somewhere out of sight.

In the center of the store were tables, mounded high with piles of colorful bolts of fabric of all different patterns. Around the walls were bookcases that contained even more fabric and racks of pattern packages from the last few decades. Signs reminiscent of the mid-twentieth century and hand-patched quilts decorated the walls to give the store a homey feel.

Ahead of him was a doorway that led into another part of the store, and from what he could gather in his limited view, contained sewing machines. Leo wasn't willing to venture beyond the first room where a checkout table was set up, complete with old cash register and a bell to ring for service.

He reached out to do just that, when he blinked and all reality shifted. The sewing store was engulfed in fire, the fabric burning and reduced to ash. Flames rimmed the doorways and scattered furniture. He could feel the heat on his face and smell the soot. That's how real it seemed, but he knew it wasn't. He had learned that well enough over the last decade.

Leo stood perfectly still and waited until the hallucination died away. It was a warning. He had imagined plenty like them over the years, but this was the first in months. He had never made an effort to settle down like this, and he knew it had agitated the balance of things.

But he couldn't be run off. Not by the voices, visions, or anything else. He'd give it a try. If it ended in ruin, then at least he would have given it a shot.

He tapped the head of the bell, and the sound carried throughout the store, reverberating in his ears. He heard the creaking of floorboards under light footfalls.

Seconds later, a woman appeared from the other room. She was short and round, her face wrinkled with bags under eyes half hidden by a pair of horned spectacles. She even sported the old-fashion beaded chain draped around her neck and attached to the ends of the glasses. Her salt and pepper hair was pulled up into a loose bun behind her head, a few tendrils hanging down around her flushed, chubby cheeks. She wore what Leo might expect a woman of her age to wear, a flowered cotton dress that reached down passed her knees and tailored rather modestly around her collar.

As a whole, she reminded him of an old granny from children's storybooks, and he would have chuckled if he thought it appropriate.

She hurried forward, a little out of breath, and stopped a safe distance from Leo. He could see the hesitance in her face. It wasn't every day that she received a male customer to her shop, let alone someone who looked like him. His clothes were dirty from the road, and he probably smelled a little rank, because he hadn't showered since long before that night spent in the bar.

"May I help you, sir?" she asked in a wiry, but cheerful tone.

Leo jerked his thumb over his shoulder at the sign in the window. "I was wanting to inquire about the room for rent."

Having realized that this man did not want fabric from her, she relaxed and smiled sweetly. "Oh, yes. The room is still available. I haven't had many ask about it. Kids these days want the newest apartments with all sorts of amenities." She leaned forward as if to tell him a secret. "And more often than not, they don't agree with my terms."

Leo gave her a warm smile, lessening his intimidating appearance. *Just stay pleasant. Don't let them see what's underneath. You need this.*

"I'm sure they'll be reasonable for me. How much are you charging?" he asked. She told him and he nodded again. "That seems fair."

The woman held up her hand in warning. "My conditions are: no women, no pets, no late-night carousing, no cooking in the room, no loud music at any time, and I require half of the last month of rent as a deposit."

Leo nodded. "Done," he replied as he pulled out the wad of cash from his back pocket.

The woman watched him and then stammered a bit for him to wait once more. "I'm sorry I have to ask this, but can I see some form of identification?"

He paused before reaching into his other pocket to pull out an ID card that wasn't even registered in this state. It was the only thing he possessed from that span of six months in Wyoming. It hadn't ended well, but she didn't need to know that. Everything else listed was correct as far as anyone else knew. He came closer and handed the card to the woman.

"Will it be just you in the room?"

"Aye, ma'am."

She looked it over, her brows pinched together as she examined every part. "You don't have a driver's license?"

"Not yet. I'm hoping to remedy that soon."

"The DMV may be closed now, but it's inside the court house just down the road... Do you have a job here yet? I see this is from out of state."

Leo nodded and repeated what he had already told everyone else he met that day. "I don't have a job yet, but I have a lot of experience in labor jobs and I'm sure I can find something within the week."

The woman peered at him over the rim of her glasses as if she didn't quite believe him. Few did. Then, a light must have flipped on between her small ears. She lifted her chin and snapped her fingers at the idea. "You know what, I know for a fact that the lumber company is hiring. They're outside of town, but they clear out land for farmers and contractors in the county. I know one of the managers there and I'm sure he could use the help."

A room for rent and a job lead all in the same day. Leo hoped this streak of luck would continue. "I'm certainly open to hearing about it."

The woman grinned and offered his card back and then her hand in a deal-binding shake. "I'm Blanche Cravatt."

"Leo Thompson," he replied, mostly out of cordiality. She must have seen his name on the card. "It's nice to meet you, Mrs. Cravatt."

She flipped her hand at him. "Oh, dear, call me Blanche. Besides, it's Miss Cravatt. My husband passed on a few years ago."

"I'm sorry for your loss."

"It's all right. I'm over the worst and picked myself up again. Sometimes, that's all you can do. Since my kids have moved out to start their own families, it's been pretty lonely. I live in a house around the corner, so you'll have the entire upstairs to yourself. I'm afraid it's not much. Just the bedroom and bathroom, and a few store rooms that I'll ask you not to go into."

Leo nodded and listened to her other instructions before excusing himself to park his bike around the back of the store. The fire escape would be his one way in and out of the upstairs portion of the building. He had nothing but the clothes on his back, but he would soon take care of that.

The guest room was tastefully decorated and contained all the furniture he would need to make his stay in Levi comfortable. He had forgotten to ask what lease term she was expecting. Even six months might have been a little too ambitious for Leo. Still unsure if this would work, he didn't want to get Blanche's hopes up that he would be a more permanent resident.

He tossed his keys on the dresser and sat down heavily on the quilted mattress. The springs squeaked as his heavy body settled, but it was just the rest his legs needed after riding and standing all day.

Looking around, Leo tried to let it sink in. This would be his room for the indefinable future. He tried not to think about the other places he'd stayed. All the apartment buildings, the motels, the barns, and shacks. He wasn't sure if it was because of the town or who he knew to be living there, but this little room above the sewing store felt more special somehow. More homey and welcoming than any of the other places he had been.

Leo fished out the piece of paper that had Belle's name and number written on it. He was sure that Blanche wouldn't mind him using her store's phone until he was able to find some place that sold prepaid phones. Staring at the number, he debated whether to take that step.

Belle had given him no direct impression that she was interested in continuing what they started last night. Her conditions for using her number were if he needed anything. He did need something right at this moment, but it wasn't anything she could give him. His exhausted, burning eyes were the reminder that he needed sleep first. Building relations with the townsfolk and making a home for himself would come later.

For now, he folded up the paper and set it down on the nightstand beside the bed. Leo succumbed to a fitful sleep, filled with visions of dark creatures and fire. He had become so used to the nightmares that they hardly bothered him anymore.

Chapter 3

As Belle made her way across the gravel parking lot, she fortified herself for what would come. There were dozens of cars and many had no choice but to park on the lawn in front of the white country church. Its tall steeple loomed overhead, casting a long shadow across the rows of cars. It was a rather large turnout for prayer night for her congregation.

Her father, a former deacon, told her all about how New Hope Church was the first building for the town of Levi when it was settled in the early nineteenth century, before Arkansas even became a state. The building's rich history was written in every layer of paint that had been applied and reapplied over the last two centuries, and it was due for another soon, judging by the peeling flakes on the exterior wood planking around the windows. Its age also showed in the way the air conditioning unit malfunctioned almost every few months, leaving the congregation to boil inside the sanctuary during the summer.

Belle pushed open one of the large mahogany doors and shuffled into the sanctuary as everyone was taking part in fellowship. The musty, old smell acted as a balm to her nerves, but it wasn't enough to chase away the deeply set fears at hearing the murmuring voices of the parishioners. There was no reason for her to be afraid or nervous. These were her friends, practically family. They all loved and cared for her, but Belle wanted nothing more than to run home and be alone. The thought of small talk, of the shrill feminine voices raking against her ears, and the sudden booming laughter from their husbands, all made her anxious even before she got out of the truck. All of these people knew her and her father before he passed away. They were trustworthy. Yet, Belle still did not feel comfortable around them and she wondered if she ever would.

The church had two dozen rows of pews on both sides of the vast, spacious room. Belle turned her eyes upward, as she usually did, to the high ceiling lined with oak rafters that had never been painted or varnished. When Belle used to attend church on Sunday mornings with her father, clad in a frilly, lacy dress, she would love to prance through the pews and shout to the ceiling just to hear it echo back. Everyone thought the five-year-old was adorable, but Belle cringed when she thought of that time now. Why couldn't she have been better behaved?

As she looked out over the mass of people gathered around those same pews, she wished she had been that five-year-old again and had her father by her side. It might have made things easier.

Belle felt like a lone gazelle as it approached a watering hole filled with crocodiles and hippos. But, she reassured herself that this meeting - just like all the ones before it - would not end in carnage and it never would. As long as she kept her mask on, everything would go just fine.

"Annabelle!" a thundering voice called out over the crowd.

Belle's chest tightened when she saw the pastor of the church come barreling down the center aisle, as he always did, arms wide open to receive her.

Pastor Kendall was a stout, jolly man. A roll of fat usually hung over his belt, and his tie was knotted too tight. The pastor of New Hope Church had been close friends with Belle's father all the way up to his final days in the hospital. Some of her earliest memories were when the pastor and his wife would come over for dinner during the week. The older men would talk about church business while Mrs. Kendall would talk with Belle in the living room about Bible stories.

The years had been kind to Pastor Kendall. Despite the touch of grey around his temples and heavy bags under his eyes, there was a youthful vivaciousness about him that was infectious to all of the congregation.

Even though Belle had not always been fond of hugs, she let Pastor Kendall's meaty arms enfold her, because he might as well have been like an uncle. Belle could tolerate Ivy's lively personality, but Pastor Kendall went a bit over the top some days. "It's the joy of the Lord," he would tell people. And Belle believed it wholeheartedly. It was a joy that she wished she had.

"It's wonderful to see you!" the pastor exclaimed when he finally released her and placed his massive hands on her shoulders.

She smiled to him in the same way that she had smiled to the customers at the bookstore and nodded. "It's great to see you, too." She always said it, even if she didn't mean it.

"How was your day?" he asked.

Belle rattled off her usual answers, being careful to use different wordings each time to remove the risk of someone catching on that she had rehearsed these things to herself in the mirror at home. Everything had to be practiced. Speech, smiles, and posture. Her performance had to be perfect to be believed.

After Pastor Kendall moved on to bombard other members of the congregation with his exuberant greetings, Belle was met by others. Once again, she recited the answers to the questions they always asked. "How was your day?", "How's the farm doing?", "Have you met a man yet?", "How's your mother doing?".

Belle fell into a comfortable routine with them and the smile she had faked when she came in became unpretentious the more she talked and laughed with the people that thought they knew her. They didn't really know her. They knew the little girl that she used to be and the actress she had become.

This went on for nearly half an hour, running into the time usually dedicated for the prayer meeting. It wasn't surprising, as Pastor Kendall was often caught up in conversations. Sermons nearly always started and ended late. Only when his wife - a slender woman with silver hair - came to rest her thin hand on Kendall's forearm while he was in the middle of hearing an anecdote from another elderly man on the church's payroll, did the pastor realize what time it was.

Belle sat herself in one of the pews on the inside closest to the aisle. That would make it easier for a speedy getaway when the meeting was over, though it was highly likely that she would get caught between the pew and the door on her way out.

Pastor Kendall read through the list of congregation members who needed prayer for various problems, as well as some non-believing family members in the town who needed silent support during a difficult season of their lives.

Many members prayed together in groups. Others, like Belle, tended to pray by themselves. She bowed her head and folded her hands the way she was taught as a child and prayed fervently for those that needed it.

Like every Thursday, she prayed for herself as well. She prayed for strength, comfort and an end to a life of living on edge. She prayed for the confidence that she used to have and the courage to be herself again. The mask had become necessary to function, but she hated it as much as she hated her anxiety. She prayed one more time for something to help shatter that mask and end her constant struggle to be someone that she wasn't. At times, she looked in the mirror and wondered who it was that looked back at her. Belle wanted to know that person, to understand herself again and be the kind of woman that everyone wanted her to be. Brave, normal, and stable. One day, if she had enough faith, perhaps she could be.

When she thought she was finished, there came a deep stirring in her spirit. She wondered if a name would suddenly come to mind. Someone in the community who needed help, someone who was in trouble but couldn't reach out.

But only one name spoke into the quiet of her heart.

Leo.

Her eyes popped open as a flood of feeling washed through her. Feelings that she didn't think were appropriate to have inside a church. So she prayed, her lips quivering with the words. She prayed for Leo, his safety, his health, and whatever unspoken need that prompted this remembrance of him. She did hope that he had found some help at the shelter and that he was well on his way to becoming an upright citizen who didn't hide out in barns.

Before she closed with an amen, an impulse gripped her to pray that one day, their paths would cross again. Just once, so she'd know if her small act of kindness was worth it all.

It had been a week since Leo first arrived in Levi. Since then, he had landed the job with the lumber company that Blanche had referred him to, purchased a fresh wardrobe for himself, and received his first paycheck.

His boss had been agreeable about paying him under the table for his work. The fistful of bills was much less than he had earned in the past from other jobs, but it was enough to get him by for now. The kind of work that he did at the lumber company was something new, but as with everything else, he was catching on quickly. Living as he did, it paid to be a fast learner.

Leo donned the navy-blue ball cap he had gotten the other day and headed off to the supermarket. With Blanche's rule about no cooking in the room he was renting above the sewing store, he had to be mindful of what kind of groceries he could get and which he could not.

Most evenings, Blanche brought him a home-cooked meal, leftovers from her own supper that she didn't eat. Other nights, Leo grabbed some fast food on the way home from work. His landlady may not have allowed him to cook, but she set up a microwave in the small storeroom downstairs for him to use when he needed it.

The supermarket was only a few blocks away from the sewing store, so he decided to walk instead of taking his motorcycle. He discovered that many of the citizens owned pickup trucks and minivans as opposed to bikes or sedans. He wasn't sure what that said about the town in general, but whenever an old white pickup passed him in traffic, he craned his neck to see who the driver was.

Every day, whether he consciously did it or not, he looked for Belle – the girl who gave him food and a ride to the shelter. He failed miserably at getting her out of his thoughts. Her green eyes haunted his dreams and he began to forget what her voice sounded like.

Leo didn't expect to find her right away, even if this was a small town. He had thought about passing by her farm early in the morning before going to work, but decided against it. There was no telling how she would react to him suddenly showing up on her doorstep... again.

Almost every evening, he wanted to call her and each time he picked up her note, he shook his head and put it back down. There was no point in scaring her away by being too forward.

He still couldn't comprehend his own feelings. She shouldn't have mattered to him. Belle was just another girl, just another person that came in and out of his life. They were all like comets across his night sky and he stayed forever stationary, trapped... cursed. But he wanted Belle to be a constellation, something permanent to twinkle brightly in the darkness. Something to set his compass by and follow to the ends of the earth. Perhaps that's what he'd wanted all along. He wanted to know that feeling she had activated that long ago night. That feeling of warmth, comfort, security, of home. He had to know if it had been her all along or something else.

As he stepped inside the air-conditioned supermarket, he pulled down the cap's visor over his brow to conceal his face. He had no reason to hide and had done nothing wrong, but the act somehow made him feel better.

He went straight to the checkout line that sold cigarettes. It had been ages since he satisfied his craving for nicotine, and with the financial freedom to do so, he wasn't about to pass them up. Their calming affect promised him a little relief from the stress of all this change. When he was living on the run, Leo had to watch where and how he spent his money, unsure of when it would be replenished again.

The supermarket seemed crowded for a Friday evening. Families with rowdy children hustled down the aisles while single individuals were doing the same, only too preoccupied with staring at their shopping lists to bother looking where they were going.

Leo watched them all, taking record of faces and reading their body movements. Over the years, he had learned to be hyper-aware of his surroundings, discounting no one and their potential ability to give him trouble. He couldn't kick the habit, even here in Levi, where he was sure that no one would try to pull a knife or a gun on him. In his heart, he knew he was safe, but it took a while for his brain to catch up.

He stepped up as the line continued to move when his eyes caught the bobbing of a brown ponytail. His hands stilled, holding a bag of oranges over the belt as he stared.

She wore a pair of jeans and casual button-up blouse that showed off her trim waist, her hair pulled back tight and high so it didn't get in her face, which was softened by a serene, contented look. Her smiling green eyes were looking for an open aisle to dive into with her shopping cart full of groceries.

The night they met, she had been lovely. Seeing her in the day-light, the way her sun-kissed complexion seemed to glow, she was even more stunning. It had taken a week for their paths to finally cross in this small town.

Leo felt the breath stall in his throat as he watched her move so classily down the lane. Without a second thought, he slipped past the shoppers who were in line behind him and approached Belle, filled with baseless confidence.

Leave her be! The voices screeched. *Leave her and this town while you have the chance!*

But he didn't listen. He hadn't listened for days now, and defied them at every turn, no matter the cost later down the road. He looked forward to the laugh he would have at her expense when she laid eyes on him again and stumbled for words. Leo wanted to blow her away and maybe catch a glimpse of that bluntness that he had admired so much. More than this, he would see if he'd fall under her spell again. Then maybe, she would quiet the voices for him.

Belle pushed her weighted down buggy through the crowd, her shields up high and mask fastened on tight. To anyone else, she looked at ease in this public setting. Inside, she was screaming for an escape.

She had never like grocery days. Having her choice of going to church or shopping for potatoes, she would have gone to church during the late service when it was more crowded. At least at church, there wasn't this thick, busy energy that threatened to suffocate her.

Belle never professed to be sensitive to the feelings of others, but crowded places like this were too much, even on her best days. Too many people and too much stress. Everyone was buzzing around to grab their things and leave, whether it meant practically running over their fellow shoppers or cutting off someone else. She avoided the congested aisles as much as she could, but sometimes she had no choice but to try and squeeze past two soccer moms talking about their kids, or lean over to grab a few cans directly in front of another shopper. She always felt in the way, always hemmed in on every side and taking up too much space.

The knotted, panicked feeling in her stomach was a constant reminder that she shouldn't be there. She should have been home, recuperating from the rough day she had at work. Her boss took out some unknown frustration on his employees, barking orders and expecting too much. Belle couldn't be mad at him like Ivy was. She understood that it was a bad day for everyone and Ray could hardly be blamed for being unable to hide whatever it was that bothered him. If she thought it wouldn't be invasive, she would have asked what was wrong. Instead, she simply prayed for him and hustled to evade any confrontation with him.

She spotted a short line and was about to swerve for it when she saw something out of the corner of her eye. Someone was coming toward her rather quickly. All she could tell from her brief glance was that he was a mountain of a man in a tight, black, short sleeved shirt and pair of faded jeans. Whenever she was in a public place, she avoided eye contact to dodge the awkwardness of having to smile or talk to anyone. If she acted busy, they left her alone. Belle had enough of handing out fake smiles like they were candies at a kid's carnival.

Belle moved quickly into the checkout line, so the man wouldn't crash into her. But when he spoke, she realized that he didn't intend to pass by.

He stopped just behind her and spoke her name in a deep, husky tone. A coldness raked up her spine when she heard the voice she could never forget. His light Scottish burr rolled off his tongue and sensually licked her ears, making her breathless again, like she had been the night they met.

Belle whipped around, her ponytail smacking against her neck. Her defenses buckled when she saw Leo staring with those striking blue, almost gray eyes that beamed at her from under the shadow of his ballcap visor. His lips were pulled up in an eager grin, while her own soft smile almost failed as her hands began to shake.

No, she couldn't break in public like this. What if someone was watching? What if one of the cashiers or shoppers recognized her and saw her lose it? Instead of demanding to know why he wasn't far away from Levi, she forced the corners of her lips higher until her teeth showed in a grin not unlike his own, and let her face express pleasant surprise rather than the terror that rattled her insides.

"Leo! It's so good to see you again! How are you?"

Instead of returning her greeting as most people did, Leo's mouth turned down a bit and he took a half step back. Even though he looked unsure, Belle held her smile, feeling like a fool. Then it occurred to her that she must have shocked him somehow. The girl he had met and the girl that stood in front of him now wasn't the same person. Not by a long shot.

The last time they met, Belle had let her guard down and showed a side of her that no one else had ever seen. Leo must have expected a blunt, abrasive, slightly sassy country bumpkin, the same one who threatened him with a crowbar. *Tough luck, buddy,* she thought. *This is what you get, because you caught me in a bad place.*

Leo opened his perfect mouth and stuttered for a second before saying, "I'm doing fine. I just..."

Belle tilted her head cutely. "What's wrong?"

He pinched the bridge of his nose and squeezed his eyes shut. "Umm... It is Belle, right?" he asked as he gestured toward her.

"Yep, that's me. We met last week." She moved her cart forward a bit and began to unload her groceries onto the conveyor belt. "Did the shelter treat you well?"

Leo seemed to recover and sighed. "Well, they turned out to be closed by the time you dropped me off."

Belle grimaced. "Oh, I'm so sorry." The tone might have suggested that she meant it. "What did you do?"

She watched Leo glance from her to the cashier who scanned her items one by one, and pretended not to listen.

"Can we go somewhere to talk?" he asked. "If you haven't had dinner already, there's a diner just around the corner. But I'm sure you know that, since you live here."

Belle paused and felt a bit of herself crack, utterly confused. It was then that she realized how odd it was that a homeless man was in a grocery store, but had no basket or purchase with him. He also wore a different outfit than she had last seen him in. And that ball cap was new too. Was he ever really homeless to begin with? Or had his luck turned for the better somehow?

The prospect of going to eat with Leo was tempting, mostly because she wanted a chance to ask him all the questions that had rotted in her brain over the last week. The checkout line at a grocery store was not the place for a long conversation – despite what some grandmothers would think. A diner might have been as good a place as any to talk. Yet, Belle couldn't help but hesitate.

She had just been thinking about how badly she wanted to go home and be alone, away from people to convalesce her strained nerves. A diner was still a pretty jam-packed place, especially around dinner time, but she couldn't very well invite Leo back to her farm instead. Though he had permeated her thoughts and daydreams for days after they parted, he was still a stranger and she was unsure of him now.

Who was he, really? And why was he back in Levi? The shelter was at least a half a day's walk away from here, but why would he have come back?

Some time had passed, and Belle realized that she had been holding the same bag of frozen peas while she thought of her answer. When her hand was about to lose feeling from the damp cold, Belle turned back to Leo and nodded with a fresh smile.

"Sure, that sounds great. Just give me some time to go home and put all of this away and I'll meet you there in about an hour?"

A corner of Leo's mouth tilted up. "Well, I could pick you up if that'll be easier? It'll save you some petrol."

Belle squinted at him, her smile suddenly failing. "Pick me up?" she asked in a tone that wasn't nearly as gentle as she intended.

Leo must have seen her walls come down and he grinned. How could he be pleased with how she answered him? Anyone else might have started at the way she turned so quickly. "Aye. I have a motor-cycle now."

Her jaw dropped as she mechanically pulled out her wallet and was about to pay for her groceries. She didn't even hear the total the cashier had read back to her.

"Oh, no," he said quickly, waving away her wallet. "Allow me."

He surprised her one more time when he pulled out a hundred-dollar bill and handed it to the cashier. Belle placed her hand at the base of her neck, feeling her racing thoughts begin to press down on her like a heavy blanket. Was this the same man? What was he trying to do in buying her groceries?

She examined his face one more time. Yes, it was the Leo she remembered, only cleaned up and if it were possible, more handsome in the daylight. His beard wasn't so scraggly now, but well-trimmed. She could also see that he had cut his hair short to the point that only a tiny bit peaked out from the bottom of his cap in the back.

"Ok, I guess you'll pick me up in an hour then?" she clarified as she loaded her purchase into her buggy.

"It's a date," he declared as he began to help her.

Belle lost it there. "Wait, what?" she snapped. And she thought she had recovered her mask after letting it momentarily slip from her face.

Leo paid the cashier and regarded her with utter satisfaction. "I'm sorry. Is that not what a date is? Two people meeting over a meal to chat."

"No, it's just two people meeting over a meal to catch up. It's not a date." But the more Belle thought about it, she had to admit it kind of was. And in that moment, she wished the earth could have swallowed her whole.

Did she want to go on a date with Leo? Was it safe? Where would this lead? What happened if they went on another date, and then another? Visions of the potential future flashed in her mind and Belle didn't know how to handle it. She had rehearsed for plenty of social interactions, but nothing like this.

"If you don't want it to be a date, then it's not. It doesn't have to be."

Belle let out an audible sigh of relief as they left the supermarket together. It gave her the chance to build her walls back into place from the pile of rubble. All thanks to Leo. Before she could speak again, she had to mentally scramble to mend the damage.

"Great, so you'll pick me up in an hour. Do you remember where the farm is?"

The smile he gave her would have buckled her knees if she hadn't been trying so hard to stay strong. "How could I forget?"

Belle wasn't sure whether to be comforted by that or disturbed.

She turned to him, squinting in the evening sun and stared at the way his eyes sparkled in the bright light. How could one man be so enchanting and not be from a fairytale?

"Can I help you with your groceries?"

Snapping out of it, she shook her head. "No, thank you. I can manage." She returned his smile and hurried across the packed parking lot. "I'll see you later," she called back over her shoulder.

Once in her truck, she began to hyperventilate, much against her own will. Belle felt as if a scream would burst from her mouth at any moment while her heart pounded in her throat. This was too much. She had just settled with the reality that Leo wouldn't step foot in this town again, and now they were going to meet for dinner. She should have told him no. She should have made some excuse to turn him down. Why would he even make such an invitation? Why did she feel so inclined to accept?

Recalling that night, Belle couldn't think of what she had done to encourage him. Maybe it was giving out her phone number. He hadn't called her once, but she hadn't really expected him to. It was part formality, and partly blind faith that he wouldn't call or show up again. He hadn't given her any indication that he felt anything but indifferent to her.

This dinner, the way he said it could have been a date, proved her wrong. There must have been something there, and that thought made her reassess everything. This wasn't the same kind of crippling panic attack she had been used to. This was something different and that difference lay in the way her lips curled into a huge grin.

She was actually excited to go into a restaurant, full of people who would be watching her and making their own conjectures of why she was out with a handsome stranger. Excited to be around people? Had she finally snapped? Or did this have to do with Leo?

Belle's hands were still trembling when she and Leo stepped into the diner. She wasn't sure what was more agonizing, the seemingly endless period of time it took for him to come pick her up or the way she was forced to hold onto him while speeding down the road on his motorcycle. She could still feel the tingling sensation in her rear from the vibrating seat and the warmth of his body against her chest.

Either he hadn't noticed the awkward way she dismounted, light-headed from the ride, or he wasn't mentioning it for her sake. In fact, he hadn't said much at all since he picked her up.

The distraction of recovering from her first motorcycle ride faded as she realized exactly where he had taken her.

Stacy's Diner was one of the few ideal restaurant hangouts in town. There were plenty of fast food joints, but this diner had a real hometown feel that made it popular with both the locals and the people that passed through Levi on their way to the big city.

Both the interior and exterior were reminiscent of the old fifties diner, decked out in checkered tile flooring, candy apple red vinyl booth coverings, chrome accents on everything, a counter that almost stretched the length of the dining hall with swivel barstools, and a lit up jukebox at the far end of the room playing nothing but jazz, blues, and early rock n' roll hits.

Waitresses were clad in pink poodle skirts and sweaters, bustling around taking orders to pass on to the cooks through the window behind the counter. Belle had many fond memories of coming here with her dad on Saturday afternoons to share one of their famous milkshakes. Her father would amaze her by taking the cherry stem and tying it in a knot with his tongue. To this day, she couldn't figure out how to do it.

She couldn't revel in those memories just yet. When they walked in, Belle noticed that even on a weeknight, the place was bursting. Families with young children crowded into booths while young couples sat at the counter, slurping on milkshakes. Some older customers were taking their time and sipping coffee while they read the paper.

Regardless of who they were, Belle felt their eyes turn and fixate on her and Leo. Some faces she recognized, and she knew they would recognize her too. This might be the beginning of a terrible rumor. She froze, feeling as if her feet were glued to the floor. They didn't have to wait to be seated, but Belle couldn't bring herself to follow Leo for the first few steps.

And she thought she would be fine. How stupid could she possibly be?

The mask she had been wearing all day was taking its time to come back into place after the brief interlude of time spent at home. Her nerves felt like the stuttering gears on a roller coaster as the car made its slow ascent up an incline. It sometimes only took her moments to get back into the swing of being in front of people, other times it seemed impossible.

It took a minute for Belle to get a grip on herself, but before she could, Leo noticed.

He turned back to her as he tried to lead the way to an open booth. "Are you okay?" he asked, his accent strangely slowing her mask's progress to being fully restored.

Belle's eyes shifted between the faces of the people who were watching her with mild interest and she could feel the sweat droplets form on the back of her neck even though the air conditioner was blowing at full force.

"Belle?" Leo spoke as he stepped into her line of sight.

She lifted her gaze and met his worried look. All at once, she felt the mask tumble from her hands and there might have been no hope of raising it now. He made her this way. Helpless, unguarded, unprotected. She couldn't take it.

"I think I better go," she said softly with a strained apologetic smile before turning toward the door.

A truck driver was coming through just at that moment and blocked her path, startling her further. Belle stumbled to get out of the way and whispered another apology to the older man that reeked of chewing tobacco. Her eyes never left her feet.

Leo was by her side before she had a chance to make her exit again. "What's wrong?" he asked, his voice low in discretion.

Belle wouldn't look at him again, but stared out the glass door at the packed parking lot and his bike that was propped up on its kickstand. How could she form the words to explain that she was terrified out of her mind? There were too many people and she shouldn't have agreed to this meeting at all. The day had been long and tedious, filled with times when she either wanted to break down and cry or scream. Up until now, she had been able to keep a cool, level head on her shoulders. He had ruined it all with those eyes and the way he charmed the socks off her.

Now, all she wanted to do was go home and forget that she was embarrassing herself in front of Leo and all these people that would never understand. She wanted to curl up on the couch with a hot cup of tea, light one of her scented candles, and unravel like she did almost every evening.

But beneath the edginess, she felt something else. The only way she could describe it was a gentle pull on her heart. It continued to tug with growing strength until she felt provoked to look up. It was like a string had been tied between her chin and his, tightening until it was taunt. Deep down, she really didn't want to leave the diner, because it meant leaving Leo.

Afraid she would come even more undone, Belle took a deep breath and let it out slowly, waiting for the fallout from her breakdown. But it didn't come. The longer she watched his face soften from confusion into encouragement, she felt the uneasiness slip like a weight falling from her shoulders. It fell to the floor and seeped between the black and white checkered tiles until she felt she could breathe again.

How could this man make her feel so distressed one minute, but then perfectly at home the next? The rest of the diner faded, the sizzling of burger patties and clattering of dinner plates were muffled, and her ears tuned to Leo's soft voice.

"Are you going to be okay?"

Belle had asked herself that for years every time she freaked out and had to take a step back from society. Each time, she didn't have an answer. But now, she felt she did.

"Yeah, I think so."

Chapter 4

Leo led Belle to a booth, his hand gently pressed into the small of her back to prevent escape. She didn't ask for his touch, but somehow, he sensed that she needed it. Belle needed a grounding force.

Leo would have never expected this behavior out of her. It made absolutely no sense. Before him was a woman with too many faces, too many masks and he had no idea which was the real Belle.

When they first met, she seemed strong and defiant, ready to bash his skull in if he got too close. Her act of charity showed the cool side of that burning log that he thought was too hot to touch. But this... he never expected this doused, smoking pile of ash, harmless and almost boring.

In the grocery store, she was overly friendly and downright cheerful to the point that he wanted to withdraw altogether. Now, she was a timid mouse ready to run and cower in a corner in front of all these people.

In this moment, she reminded him of a once meek and passive young man who couldn't stand up to his own fears. He wasn't that skinny runt anymore and never would be if he could help it. As long as there was breath in his lungs, he was determined to not let Belle suffer the same way. No matter where this dramatic shift in personalities came from, Leo would help her in whatever way he could.

The reasonable solution would have been to take her home like she wanted. That would solve nothing. She would have to work through her anxiety and she'd become stronger for it. That was how he healed, and he hadn't been ready for the rude awakening life had given him when it happened. He had no one, not a friend in the world to guide him, but he could be there for her.

As soon as he showed that he was willing to brave this, Belle seemed to do better. She wasn't shaking and as they slid into a booth, he saw the ghost of a smile on her lips, the one he had been hoping for. One that was real, candid. One he put there.

"This may be a silly question, but have you eaten here before?" he asked, hoping to lance out any residual tension.

Belle took a little while to respond before she nodded. "Yeah, a lot of times. My dad used to bring me here when I was little."

It had been a long time since he had become comfortable with people enough to let them reveal bits of their past that might have not mattered to him at all. In Belle's case, he hungered for more. He wanted to know everything if it would help him unravel this mystery that she personified.

"I've been eating here almost daily," he said as he flipped open the menu card that was worn and littered with grease spots. "They might as well put me on the payroll."

Belle's lips tightened at his quip as if she were trying to hold in a laugh. Didn't she know he wanted to hear that laugh?

It didn't take long for the young blonde waitress to start walking their way.

Leo glanced up and inwardly groaned as he realized he had made a grave error in picking where to sit. Their waitress's name tag read "Ivy", and she had been the proverbial thorn in his side. She bombarded him with flirtatious comments every time he walked through the door and after a while, he had made a point of sitting as far from her section as possible. That kind of attention was the last thing he wanted. Leo hoped that this kittenish tart would have enough respect to leave him alone while he was obviously in the company of another woman.

He looked across the table at Belle and saw her staring in utter mortification at their waitress. But as soon as Ivy met her stare, Belle seemed to come to attention and give her a wide grin, similar to the one he had received just a little over an hour ago in the grocery store. If this was any indication of how spending time with her would be, Leo was certain she'd get whiplash.

"Belle!" Ivy exclaimed with sudden zeal. "I haven't seen you come in here in a long time!"

Belle laid her hand flat on the table and leaned over as if she were interested in what Ivy had to say. "I completely forgot that you were working today. I'm just here grabbing a bite with my friend."

Leo wasn't sure how to read her response. Had Belle wanted to avoid Ivy and only came into the restaurant on her days off? And why would Belle so readily proclaim that she and Leo were friends? They were hardly acquainted with each other enough for the title, though he wanted to remedy that.

Then Ivy turned and regarded Leo with the same coquettish, laughing eyes. "Hey, Leo. How's it going?"

Out of the corner of his eye, Leo saw the pained look flash over Belle's face. "You two know each other?" she asked.

He wished he could have screamed that he wanted nothing to do with her. It was the truth, and Leo needed to make sure that Belle knew he was not interested. Just why, he didn't know. The impulse fought against the tiny voice that persisted in the back of his mind telling him not to even bother getting involved. It'd only end in disaster.

"Oh, absolutely!" Ivy replied with a flip of her hand. "He comes in here all the time. We talk a lot. Don't we, Leo?"

He shot Ivy an unguarded, reproving look and turned back to look over the menu he had practically memorized by now. "Whatever you say," he grumbled.

Ivy swished her hips a bit, making her fluffed up skirt sway with her. "He's told me all about Ireland and did you know he works with Travis' lumber crew outside of town? He hauls logs around all day."

Leo pinched the bridge of his nose and gritted his teeth. He had mentioned his home country a grand total of two times, and only because she asked about his accent. If he had to correct one more person about the difference between Ireland and Scotland, he would throw himself in the deepest loch with cement shoes.

"Um," Belle said, "he's actually from Scotland."

Ivy wasn't daunted by her mistake. "Scotland, Ireland, Australia, they're all the same."

Leo swallowed his impatience and looked up to the blonde with a smile that struggled between condescending and menacing. "I'd like water to drink, please?"

Ivy caught on and nodded in acknowledgement. "Water. Right. And a Coke for you, Belle?"

"You got it."

As Ivy sashayed away to pour their drinks, he looked to Belle, feeling somehow exhausted already and the sun hadn't even gone down. "You know that tart?"

Belle opened her mouth, but paused. "Tart?"

Leo had to laugh at himself. He had been in the states for years, but frequently forgot that Americans didn't use the same verbiage that he grew up with. It took conscious effort to adapt their slang and forget his own. "I meant, you know that girl?" That might not have been the direct translation of "tart", but he didn't want to knowingly insult Ivy if she and Belle were good friends.

She nodded. "Yeah, she works with me. She took this job about a month ago on the side and works here in the evenings after her shift at the bookstore is done."

Leo folded his arms over the edge of the table and leaned in, his head angled forward so he could hear her better. "Bookstore?"

Belle dropped her gaze to the menu and nodded. "Yep. She works at a bookstore. Has been for... almost a year, I think," she replied with a shrug.

He hoped that his show of interest wouldn't be mistaken. He wanted to know why Belle worked at the bookstore, not Ivy. Although, it was surprising to think a girl like their waitress spent all that time around books and didn't know the difference between Ireland and Australia.

One corner of his mouth tilted up in a smirk. "And how long have you been there?"

Belle glanced up, brows a little arched at his question. "About six, I think. I lost track. Time flies pretty quickly in a small town."

"But you have that farm? Doesn't that bring in some income?"

She looked back to the menu, but he caught the hint of dismay in her eyes. "It does a little, but not enough to pay the bills." Belle folded a flap of her menu, but kept it between her fingers like she was going to open it again soon.

Wishing to probe deeper, Leo was ready to ask her just what kind of work went into a farm like hers, but Ivy came back with their drinks. The waitress then stepped away to give them another minute, even though they both seemed to know exactly what they wanted.

Belle took a deep swig of her fizzy drink and squared her shoulders. "So, I believe you owe me some explanations."

Leo gave her a toothy grin. There was that fire again. Though he wished the conversation would stay out of his court, he would gladly answer anything she wanted to know if she'd stay this confident. Well, anything within reason.

He took his time to explain how the shelter had been closed, he'd won the motorcycle in a round of cards at the bar, and that he had been working at the lumber yard for a week. But, that was as far as he got before Ivy came busting in asking for their orders.

"I'll have the BLT and a side of chips," he told her in a not-so-patient tone. He wanted her to go away, purely because she made Belle uncomfortable.

Ivy rolled her eyes. "When will you just say french fries instead of chips?"

Belle took the focus away from him for the moment and ordered. "I'll have the cheesesteak sandwich with fries."

As Ivy walked away, he gave her an approving nod. "Thank you for not ordering something like a salad."

Belle clamped her lips together again for a split second and then asked, "Why?" Even in her question, he could hear the beginnings of a giggle.

"I like a lass who has a good appetite. There are too many around here who don't have enough room in them for rheumatic pain." Leo didn't intend for his Scottish jargon to come out so strongly in that last sentence, but it was just enough to finally winkle that laugh out of Belle.

She let out a string of giggles and covered her mouth as if she were embarrassed by it. Leo thought it was a cute laugh, high and hearty, but not annoying in the least. He could listen to it for ages.

"I've never heard that phrase before," she remarked after recovering from her laughing fit, her cheeks flushed, becoming a shade of pink.

Leo shrugged. "My mother said it all the time when we were growing up."

He shocked himself with that stab of honesty. So much that his jaw went slack and he grew silent, staring at the sweat beading on the outside of his cold glass of water. He hadn't spoken of his mother to anyone in ages, not since leaving Scotland. Maybe it was the laugh that made his defenses weaken. So, it was Belle that had broken down his walls after all. It wasn't a coincidence, or some effect of the rain that night. It must have been her. But what exactly?

"So, you won the motorcycle and then what?" Belle asked, holding her chin in her palm, eager to hear the rest.

Leo lifted his gaze and swept the old memories under the rug. He didn't want to remember the past right now, and he was a little thankful that Belle hadn't pried. All he wanted to do was revel in this moment with her, no matter how long it would last.

He told her about searching for a place to stay when he found Blanche's quilt and fabric shop just a couple of blocks over.

"I know Blanche," Belle remarked. "She's a very nice woman. She goes to my church."

Leo felt the searing nails of darkness slash at his soul at the mention of church. He could only hope that Belle didn't see the wince that contorted his face for a quick second. He carried on as if she hadn't said a word about it and went into detail about his job. It took more courage than she could possibly imagine for Leo to disclose so much information after knowing her for just a short time. If he was going to get to know her at all, Leo understood that he would have to give a little first.

When he finished his speech, Leo realized how closely Belle was paying attention, leaning forward over her folded arm on the edge of the table and hanging onto every word he said. Maybe this wasn't all one-sided after all. Could this actually be the start of something good in his life for once, or would it go up in flames like everything else?

"Wow," she finally said. "And here I thought you might have just been a helpless homeless person looking for handouts." Belle's face opened into a look of surprise. "I'm sorry, I really didn't mean for it to come out that way."

Leo smiled, feeling like the air had finally been let into the room. "No, don't worry about it. I'm sure a lot of folks think that way about me."

Belle sat back just as Ivy approached with their orders. Leo could smell the savory bacon come his way. He had tried many dishes from the menu, but their BLT was by far the best he had ever tasted out of all the other roadside diners in the country. It made him wonder if the bacon was fresh from a farm nearby and the produce locally bought as well.

His eyes caught the glint of metal as Ivy set down their silverware. The fork wasn't necessary, but what truly troubled him was the steak knife with its serrated edge and sharp point. Why would Ivy bring that to the table?

Leo's stare cracked into a fierce glare. Was this done out of sheer habit or was something more devious involved? He looked to Ivy and examined her face for any sign of the darkness in her, but found none. It must have just been a mistake. A jarring mistake, but a mistake nonetheless. He tried not to take it personally.

"Ivy, please take the knife off the table." Leo tried to keep his voice steady, but the mingling of fear and anger in his gut wouldn't allow it.

A brief silence insentiently lulled through the restaurant as everyone else seemed to pick up on the tension that pulsed from Leo so strongly. He had been strong enough to resist the temptations for months, the longest he had ever gone, but Leo would take no chances, especially in front of Belle. One loud crash or irate customer could send him downhill and the knife was the last thing that needed to be within his reach.

Ivy gave him a confused look, but quickly picked up the knife and hurried back to the kitchen.

Leo let the air slowly slip from his lungs and turned back to Belle, taking in the way her eyes begged for answers.

"I'm sorry," was all he said before reaching down to pick up a chip. They were still a little too warm and the hot grease stung his fingertips. He let out a hushed curse when he dropped it and heard the tight intake of breath from across the table.

He looked up quickly, thinking that something might have been wrong, but saw her wild, shifting eyes. "What's wrong?"

Belle looked to him with vehement disapproval. "There are children here, Leo. You can't just drop that kind of word around like it's nothing."

Leo hadn't thought about where he was, but when he glanced past their booth, he did see a couple of families with small children sitting not too far away. The kids were still stuffing their innocent faces with chips and mac n' cheese, and hardly seemed to hear what he said.

He should have been ashamed of his slip. Too much time spent in bars and around blue-collar workers had rubbed off on him over the years. Being raised a teenager in a household that didn't care about what obscenities were whispered - or shouted - didn't help him either.

"They would have learned the word sooner or later. I'll not curb my tongue around bairns if I don't see a reason."

Right then, Leo knew that he had lost some favor in Belle's eyes. Her eyebrows drew together and her lips pulled as if he had insulted her directly somehow. "People around here don't appreciate their kids growing up knowing adult things before they have to."

"Why? They probably already know plenty from watching the telly or listening to their parents behind closed doors. I'll apologize for offending you, but there's no point in protecting innocent ears from what they'll need to know later."

"No one needs to talk that way, if you ask me."

Leo loved her bold opinions. He didn't mind when she insulted his appearance, his previous homeless condition, or his manners. What he did mind was the direction that this conversation was going. He loved an argument as much as the next man, but this was not the place for it, nor the time. It was too soon and he didn't want to lose what ground he had gained so far.

He swallowed his pride and nodded in submission. "I'll do my best not to misspeak in your presence, then."

With that, they resumed their meal in awkward silence. Leo wasn't sure what to say and Belle didn't seem eager to continue.

All at once, he thought his attempt at a date was over before it could really begin, and Leo had no one to blame but himself. Maybe an apology came too late.

While he frantically tried to think of a way to spark her interest again, he heard her voice break through his concentration.

"I'm an only child," she said without emotion or emphasis, as if it were a proven scientific fact that needed no reinforcement, but felt like she needed to speak it anyway.

It took a moment for him to realize that Belle was trying to make more than just a statement. She wanted Leo to reveal something about his family in return. The mention of siblings certainly would have brought about a topic that he could say plenty about. Too bad he wasn't interested in sharing that much. It was too soon for that.

"Is that so?" he probed.

She nodded, not looking up from the pile of chips still on her plate. "Yep. Just me and my dad."

Leo watched her, one hand holding the last half of his uneaten sandwich. "No mum?"

She gave an awkward, crooked smile that he wasn't sure how to interpret. "My parents got divorced when I was little. She had partial custody and she still visits, but she was never really a major part of my life."

He narrowed his eyes on her, sensing that what she said wasn't the whole truth. The way she avoided eye contact and mindlessly rotated her drink in small circles on the slick tabletop told him that she wasn't disclosing everything. Then again, neither was he and he considered them to be even.

"I'm sorry you had to go through that."

Belle shrugged and lifted her chin proudly. "There are a lot of broken families in the world, but not many in Levi. My dad said that I still turned out good, not because of what I went through, but in spite of it."

Leo let that seep into his mind, so he could fully comprehend its meaning. So, instead of being a miserable wreck, angry at the world and her parents for separating and denying her a normal childhood, she was the wonderful person that sat in front of him today. She didn't let her past dictate who she was. But if that were true, then why the sudden shift between hot and cold? Friendly and timid? Bold and meek?

Leo hadn't realized he was staring until he noticed the color rise in her cheeks.

"People say I look a lot like Audrey Hepburn," she said, as if she were trying to account for his gazing.

Leo blinked. "Who?"

This time, she let a tiny, diffusing laugh leak out. "You've never heard of Audrey Hepburn? She's the actress from Breakfast at Tiffany's. You know, the girl with the pearls and holding the cigarette?"

He shook his head. "Nope. I don't have a clue who you're talking about. I was just thinking about how your da was pretty wise."

Belle beamed and nodded. "Yes, he was." Then Leo saw the glistening of an unshed tear in her eye and the smile was swept clean from his mouth.

"What's wrong?"

Belle shook her head, her ponytail whipping behind her, and wiped at the corner of her watery eye. "I'm sorry. It's nothing. My dad passed away five years ago, and I don't mean to get sentimental in public." Then, she glanced around to see if anyone else had noticed.

Leo straightened up and dropped his food back to his plate. "I'm sorry," he whispered, finally realizing why she spoke about him so much. If he had known, he wouldn't have brought Belle to this place that reminded her of him. Even if he passed five years ago, the pain must have been fresh to elicit a tear. He understood how powerful memories could be, and how the death of a loved one could shatter someone's world beyond full repair.

Belle gave a strained smile, one similar to what she handed out so freely to everyone around them, but it was tainted by the deep sadness he had unwittingly uncovered. "It's all right, really. He's in a better place, that's for sure."

Leo wasn't entirely sure what she meant by that, but he could hear the conviction in her voice and let it go. This dinner felt like a game of Battleship. Both of them blindly reached for one another in the dark with topics both easy and difficult, gauging their soft spots and avoiding the pitfalls. Family, morals, knives, all of it was off limits unless instigated by the other. Some of that suited him just fine, but it wouldn't get him any closer to figuring her out.

A few beats passed before she spoke again. "So, in the grocery store, you said this could be a date?"

Leo felt his heart squeeze in his chest, but he tried not to let it show. "Aye, I did. But I understood that you didn't want it to be, so I wasn't going to push my luck."

He wasn't sure if that was the proper wording, but it made Belle's eyes twinkle a bit.

She wrestled with the words at first, but finally said, "This can be a date, but I may be totally ruining it for you."

"No, you're not ruining it at all."

"You must have dated a ton of women before and I know I'm not exactly making a good impression."

That tightness melted into some emotion that made his hands shake. "If only you knew how wrong that was."

Belle raised an eyebrow. "You can't sit there and tell me that this is actually going well."

"This is going extremely well compared to others I've had."

He sensed the tinge of nervousness in her and wished that he could take it away, but once more she had taken aim at a sore spot. "What exactly am I being compared to?"

"You're the first American woman I've ever been on a date with, so your nationality is a start."

Belle wagged her finger at him. "See, there's the loophole. You dated a lot in Scotland?"

Leo quirked his lips to the side as if in thought. "Well, I was maybe thirteen and she wasn't all that pretty."

"It counts, though," she said playfully and stuffed another french fry into her mouth as if to keep herself from saying any more.

Leo lifted his hands as if he were giving in. "Okay, so you're not my first date, but you are the first American I've had a meal with, so that's something, right?"

The sound that came out of Belle's mouth shocked him. It sounded like a mix between a puppy's yip and a chicken cluck. She covered her mouth and looked to him, cheeks a deep red and green eyes wide.

Leo let out his first true laugh in months, a deep rumbling sound that came from his belly and rose through his chest and throat. It felt good to laugh and the darkness cowered at the joy that spilled out. He wasn't laughing at her or even the sound that she made, it was the expression of total humiliation following the hiccup that amused him.

Even Belle couldn't resist a few breathless giggles and apologized. They must have had the attention of everyone in the diner, but to him, no one else was there. Just him and Belle.

"Don't be. That was cute," he said.

"I hate my hiccups," she said before accidentally letting another pop off just like the first. This time, Leo let himself laugh at the sound.

With each bout of laughter, Leo felt himself grow younger and carefree. They were like wee children, laughing at nothing until tears slid down their cheeks and they forgot what they were laughing about to begin with.

It was then that Leo realized this is what he wanted all along. This, the dinner, the company, the laughter, it felt right and it felt good.

But the moment of bliss was brief. Leo heard the diner door open and watched as Belle's eyes fell to something behind him.

Her expression turned sour and her eyes no longer sparkled like the emeralds he had compared them to. No more hiccups came. Whatever she saw scared them right out of her chest. It was as if her whole essence had been sapped out of her.

Leo glanced over his shoulder and beheld the man who ambled toward their booth.

He was fairly large, built like an athlete, with rumpled black hair and dark eyes. He was better looking than most of the men he had encountered in town, but there was something in the way he walked and the way he eyed Belle that made his fingers curl into tight fists under the table.

He looked like bad news and he slid into the booth right next to Belle without invitation.

"Hey, Belle!" he greeted. His thick country accent made his words sound sweet, but Leo didn't like how he hung his arm around Belle's shoulders.

The darkness blasted through the airy veil of happiness and he could feel his whole body turn hard as stone at the sight. What was going on?

She squirmed and freed herself. "Hey, Drake," she replied flatly.

"Who's your friend?" Leo asked, his voice dropping an octave as he tried to understand exactly what he witnessed.

Drake looked to Leo and acted like he hadn't seen him there at all. He offered out his hand to shake. "My name's Drake. I'm Belle's boyfriend. And you are?"

Leo paused, his gaze sliding from Belle to Drake. Boyfriend? He might have not known much about Belle, but Leo did know that Drake was not her type. Or, at least, he liked to think that he wasn't.

Even if he had a relationship with Belle, inviting himself to sit down and embrace her when she was clearly upset was not the way to go about it. From just half a minute, Leo deducted that this man was not a gentleman. Then again, neither was he.

Leo reached out and firmly shook the man's hand with the brutal strength he had built up over the years to fight men like Drake.

"This is Leo. We were having dinner, so if you don't mind -"

"Dinner?" Drake interjected.

"Well, we're not swapping stamps," Leo quipped, unafraid to be rude or biting to this man whom he already didn't like.

Belle didn't look at Drake, but kept her eyes fixed on Leo as if his presence was giving her the power to speak and not slip from the booth seat like a spineless worm. "Yes. I ran into Leo at the grocery store and we decided to catch up over a meal."

Drake looked back to Leo, sizing him up. "You two old friends?"

"Something like that," Leo replied, knowing that the less Drake was aware of, the better.

He gave a huff of disbelief. "Well, I don't suppose you'd mind if I joined you. There's a lot we need to catch up on too, Belle."

Leo watched as Belle's jaw stiffened in frustration. "No, Drake. We don't. We talked enough and I think you need to leave."

Drake wrapped his arm around her shoulders again and pulled her close until she was forced to face him. "I'm not going anywhere," Drake muttered viciously.

Belle pushed against Drake's thick chest, but she was trapped. Leo didn't need to see any more.

He jumped from his seat, grabbed Drake by the collar of his leather jacket and threw him out of the booth. The plates and glasses clattered against the table. Belle managed to wriggle her way free, but by the time she implored Leo to wait, he was already out the door, dragging the cad out of the diner.

Many had risen to their feet to see what was going on, but Leo wasn't about to stop and answer questions. Once they were out in the parking lot, the sunset sky painted in a deep orange, Leo tossed Drake to the pavement like the bag of trash he was.

He wondered if this was why Belle had been nervous all along. She didn't want anyone to see her with Leo when she was in some kind of relationship with Drake. She had been embarrassed for her infidelity, but then why had she tried to push her boyfriend away? And why did Drake force himself on her when she clearly didn't want him around?

Either way, Leo couldn't let him get away with it. Belle was too valuable, too good to be treated that way.

"What's your problem, man?" Drake shouted, dusting off the seat of his pants.

Leo charged at him and swung a right hook, making contact with Drake's jaw. He fell to the ground hard, but Leo wouldn't give him a chance to rise. He kicked Drake in the ribs, sending him rolling across the hot blacktop.

By now, a small crowd had gathered just outside the doors of the diner, but no one seemed willing to step in and defend Drake. Perhaps they knew what Leo saw in him and thought he deserved the beating.

He knew what men like Drake were capable of. Leo had an unnaturally and rather annoying gift to see pieces of the darkness in others, mimics of the same darkness that lived inside of him. And in this moment, he saw that same evil in Drake.

And for Belle's sake, Leo wasn't about to allow him to hurt anyone. Not today.

Leo crouched down, grabbed Drake by the collar again and threw punch after punch into the man's face. Drake's nose bled and eyes swelled, but Leo didn't stop.

Kill him! Kill him! The voices shrieked in delight, echoing in his skull.

That was his cue and Leo gave Drake a harsh shake.

"Can you hear me?" he demanded.

Drake groaned.

"If I catch you anywhere near Belle again, I swear I'll kill you. Do you understand?"

Drake had the sense to nod and Leo dropped him to the ground. When he rose up, his chest heaving with rage, he noticed how his hands had become stained with Drake's blood.

"Leo!" Belle cried out from the edge of the crowd. He looked up and saw her face twisted in fear and disgust. Once again, he had soiled her once good opinion of him. She hadn't asked for this violence, hadn't asked for her help in dealing with Drake. He stepped in where he might have not been wanted. But it needed to be done.

"I want to go home," she said, her voice straining for calm when he knew that she must have been anything but calm.

He wiped the back of his hands against his jeans before he led her to his motorcycle. He saw Ivy in the crowd of spectators, handed her a large bill for the meal, and told her to keep the change. The wary waitress took it, but said nothing.

The ride back to Belle's farm was silent and not even her arms encasing his waist could erase the nauseous feeling in the pit of his stomach. In an effort to defend her, Leo just might have ruined any hopes he had with Belle. That moment they shared in the diner, laughing and talking like friends, would be nothing but a fouled memory now. He might never get a moment like that again. And judging by the tautness of Belle's arm muscles, he knew that as soon as the engine stopped and they were alone, he would get a taste of the true fury that she could release.

Chapter 5

When Belle dismounted from Leo's bike, she didn't know where to start. The cursing, the weird knife thing, all of that could have been overlooked. But this altercation with Drake?

He had an air of danger about him that thrilled her, a past and mind that intrigued her. Belle thought this could have been a beautiful beginning, especially when she hiccupped and he called her cute instead of silly or ridiculous. She could already see the day when she'd look back on that first date and smile, knowing it was the start of something wonderful.

But then, Drake came and shattered her hopes. He couldn't have picked a worse time to drop in and bother her. He and Belle had no history, no relationship, and everyone in the town knew that. She thought Drake understood that too, but apparently not.

They had attended the same Bible study as kids, sat in the same classrooms through school, and practically grew up together. But something went wrong in his teenage years and Drake was never the same. He went to parties and started drinking. He slept around and dated more than one girl at a time, all before graduating. Belle wasn't one to judge, but the moment he took that detour in life, she knew he would never have a chance with her.

After school, Drake didn't grow up and move on like the rest of his classmates. He only got into more trouble and those girls who had crushes on him went on to start their own families. Drake never did. He lived for his glory days as a sports star. Few people in town admired him for the football quarterback that he once was. He could have had a future, gone to college, and settled down. Instead, he moved away from Levi for a few years and returned recently, bumming off of his widowed mother's love while he claimed to be looking for a job. That's when he started making passes at her. At first, she had kindly turned him down, but she had to become more adamant in her refusals when he didn't take the hint. He hadn't been deterred in the least.

It might have been high time that someone taught him a lesson about common courtesy, but at the same time, Leo didn't have to turn violent.

She could still see Drake's face, bloody and puffy from the beating Leo had inflicted upon him. Never had she seen such raw brutality in a person, especially not in Levi.

Leo's words continued to reverberate in her mind, his threat upon Drake's life if he got close to her again. He had the courage to do what Belle wanted to do from the very beginning, but now that she had her revenge, she wasn't sure anymore. She needed Drake to leave her alone, not end up in intensive care.

Pacing across the dirt drive, with the porchlight to illuminate both of them, Belle shook her head and thought hard for the words she wanted to say, cramming them through her filter, so they wouldn't come out so biting and demonstrative. The filter was broken around Leo and she didn't know why she bothered trying. Nothing this evening had gone according to plan, so why should it now?

"What were you thinking?" she demanded, turning to Leo who was waiting patiently for her to begin.

He peered at her in the dim twilight, his intense blue eyes mere slits. "Forgive the cliché, but I believe I was defending you."

"You had no right to do what you did!" she shrieked, stamping her foot childishly into the dust. She was confident that none of her neighbors would hear their argument. One glorious thing about living in the country meant utter privacy to scream or cry all she wanted.

"What was I supposed to do? Just let him push you around?" Leo's voice rose in defense, just as hers rose to attack his poor judgement.

"I had it handled."

He blew out a huff of air. "You were handling it just about as well as a turtle trying to turn itself over! Why was it so bad of me to beat his arrogant arse into the pavement?"

"Those people that watched you beat him up will talk and -"

"To hell with the town and their talk!" he shouted, inspiring a shiver to travel down her spine.

"Stop talking like that!" Belle screamed, fed up with his foul language. "You can't be so careless. Drake could charge you with assault and battery."

Leo threw up his hands and wiggled them in mock horror. "Oh, I'm so scared of a lad that's all bum and parsley and can't fight back like a real man."

Belle wasn't sure she understood what exactly Leo was calling Drake, but she surely understood his tone.

"What's wrong with you? Did you do this stuff in Scotland?" She gestured wildly. "You can't do that here."

"What's wrong with me?" Leo flattened his hand against his chest and glared at her. "What's wrong with you? I imagined you would be grateful for my help."

"You can't just go around beating up whoever you want. Our society doesn't work that way."

Leo stalked a few paces closer, startling her enough to make her skip backwards as she had done in the barn the first night they met. "But it allows men to push women around? I'm sorry, but where I come from, that's not right at all, lass."

Belle took a breath to calm herself. "I'm just grateful no one called the cops on you. They wanted to see Drake beat up just as much as you did."

Leo opened his mouth to respond, but the words fell dead on his lips. "Wait... So they didn't have a problem with what I did, but you do?" He looked at her in utter confusion. "Do you like this guy?"

If the situation allowed it, she would have laughed. Instead, she screamed, "No, I don't like him at all."

"Then why defend him?" Leo asked. "Why are you getting your knickers in a wad when he's the one that stepped out of line?"

Bell understood exactly why. No conflict was ever truly solved by violence. It only produced more violence, leading to broken bones or broken hearts. Not only that, but he must have not understood what Belle meant when she said that people would talk.

They would become curious about Leo and talk about who he might be or how he got so good at fighting. They would speculate her relationship with him and why she was out to dinner. Those who witnessed them laughing and talking might say that they were a couple and that Drake was creating a love triangle. Then, they may think that Drake had some relationship with Belle in the past and that would only create more gossip and slander against her name.

She worked hard to maintain her reputation as kind and gentle. They all had an image in their mind of how Chad Clearwater's daughter should act, and this was not it. Who would have known that her date with Leo would have the potential to ruin it all? How could she have known that Leo was such a brash person, cursing without remorse and willing to beat a man to a pulp over practically nothing? This wasn't the man she thought she had met. Perhaps she had been right to judge a book by its cover, but wrong to ever assume there was something deeper to this puzzle.

"It's complicated," she said, her tone softening in an attempt to bring the argument to a decisive end.

Leo came closer and it was then that she realized he was within arm's reach. "No, it's not. Nothing is that complicated."

Belle gazed up into his eyes that reflected the glow from the porch light behind her. Despite the fierce power in his voice, his stare was calm and focused with an emotion that she couldn't describe.

Belle began to slowly lose her resolve to fight him.

She didn't want that and folded her arms before turning away. "You couldn't understand," she said, willing her voice not to crack like her crumbling defenses.

"I understand plenty," Leo replied. The serenity in his eyes leaked out into his voice. A warmth spread over Belle as he spoke, compromising all hostility against him. "I understand that you care what they think of you. You put on a show for everyone. You might not have always been like that, but your mask has been there long enough that you put it up even around the people you know so well. But when you're alone, you're anything but scared. You're strong. And at the risk of sounding poetic, it's that strength that your beauty comes from."

Belle felt her eyes grow misty. Leo had her perfectly right. After only an hour of talking over dinner, he had her pegged down too well. With just a few words, he stripped her naked in front of her own house, on her own farm, leaving her bare.

He knew too much, saw too much. But there was one thing he had slightly wrong. Not only was she strong-willed when she was alone, away from the critical eyes of the public, but she felt free when she was with him and him alone. She couldn't admit that.

Leo had become something of a doorstopper. When she wanted to close the door on him, to shut him out, he wouldn't let her. He had infiltrated her mind and her heart. But right now, she didn't feel bold or strong. Belle was scared half out of her mind, knowing that someone knew the truth about her and what kind of a person she really was. He saw through her. No one had ever done that.

If pride would let her, she would have turned around and cried into his shoulder until he embraced her and chased the dark emotions away. All the fear, the uncertainty, the helplessness. Belle refused to show her tears. A piece of her mask, or maybe a different version of it, latched into place, almost without even thinking about it. She'd push him away. She'd push them all away. She wouldn't have a single soul pity her for being less of a person because of her anxiety.

Belle spun around to face him, her face tight with rage. "Shut up! You don't know anything about me! I can fight my own battles and I'm not scared to. I don't need you, Drake, or anyone else!"

Leo must have hoped that his soft words would have been the last blow to make her defenses crumble, to calm her and sooth her with that sly compliment about her beauty. But she saw through that lie as easily as he could see through hers. Once he saw that it had just the opposite effect, he seemed stunned. His charms hadn't worked and he was out of ammunition, up against an opponent that he hadn't faced before.

A long, intense moment passed. Belle's face ached as she held onto that black look, as if her peace of mind depended on it. To her, it did. Warding him off meant the difference between living in fear and the wrong person knowing her secret.

Finally, Leo broke and threw his hands up. "You don't need me?" he asked, his tone laced with fresh frustration. "Fine. I'm gone."

With that, he turned and stalked back to his motorcycle. When his gaze tore away from her, Belle felt her chest constrict with a new reason to cry. She might not have needed him, but she wanted him so badly that it burned in her very soul. But she was far too gone to admit it, even to herself.

The motorcycle rumbled to life and sped back down the driveway, leaving a cloud of dust in his wake. Watching him leave might have been the hardest thing she'd had to do in months, in years. Harder than living a lie every day.

Knowing he was gone, with nothing but the crickets to hear her, Belle let out the tears that had been collecting in the corners of her eyes. Why exactly she was crying was unclear. All she knew was that a piece of her heart had been broken off and carried away.

But her pain was her own fault. Self-inflicted. Belle should have known better than to let him get so close, but her raw emotions and kneejerk reactions made her reckless.

She rubbed at her moist cheeks with her sleeve and shuffled up the porch. All she knew was that she had ruined her chances with Leo and a man like him only came around once in a lifetime. He was kind, considerate, perceptive, and not afraid to do what he believed to be right. He could have been the one to free her from her own twisted mind, and she rejected him for that very reason.

She also knew that it would take time for her to rebuild her defenses and reconstruct the mask that Leo had shattered to pieces. Hopefully, Ray was in a better mood and wouldn't throw a fit when she called out sick for the first time in months. It would take an entire day of prayers, bubble baths, tea drinking, and candle burning to center herself again. But nothing would make her forget this night.

Leo slammed the door to his flat and began pacing the length of the room like a caged lion, seething over the evening that had ended in epic failure. He had hoped the ride home would have pacified him somehow, but it only gave him more time to mull over everything Belle had said and all that he had done.

She probably thought he was nothing but a barbarian who preferred to talk with his fists or out of his arse. Why had he let slip that comment about her beauty? It might as well have been like a band aide over a gushing wound. Did he actually think it would help? Did he think it would change her mind and convince her not to hate him for what he had done to Drake?

But he saw the tears in her eyes and the way she put on a brave face for his sake. No, she couldn't have hated him. Just like Leo said, she was scared. But of what? If anything, she should have been relieved that he understood her better than anyone else.

Leo knew fear all too well. It had become his constant companion for years and he could sense its presence in others just as vividly as he could sense it in his own self.

She's afraid of you. She's afraid of your power, your strength. She's afraid you'll kill her.

Leo pressed his palms against his temples to shut the darkness out. He couldn't afford its intrusion. Not now while he was on the brink of losing control. His eyes searched for something he could break, but there was nothing that belonged solely to him. Every piece of furniture belonged to Blanche and he wouldn't risk eviction just because he lost his temper.

Standing in the middle of the room, he took a deep breath and dropped his fists to his sides, struggling to gain his center.

Just as he was ready to take hold of it, he felt the room's temperature drop by several degrees. The single dome light above him flickered. Shadows seemed to preternaturally lengthen and grow black as a starless night. The hairs on the back of Leo's neck quivered and stood on end. A feeling of dread settled over the room, seeping into his skin like a suffocating smog.

Leo's lips tightened together and he closed his eyes, knowing what was coming... What had arrived.

"You've been a naughty boy lately, Leo," the voice said, taunting with a thread of wicked intent.

Leo slowly turned and looked up to the thing that spoke. He looked like a man and spoke like a man, even wore a dark suit like one, but Leo had learned long ago that he was anything but human. Two eyes, completely black as lumps of coal stared back at him, his mouth twisted into a nefarious smile. His hair was slicked back, each lock frozen in place.

For twelve years this demon, the darkness, haunted his every step. It was his claws that dug into his flesh and made him succumb to unimaginable levels of despair and anguish. It was the darkness that infiltrated his mind every waking hour and whispered devious things in his ear late at night. It was the darkness that tormented his sleep and gave him never-ending nightmares that seemed so real that he'd wake up screaming in a cold sweat.

"You haven't been listening. Whatever happened to the days when you played along and did what we asked?" The darkness gave him a toothy, dingy yellow grin. "We had a lot of fun back then."

Leo knew exactly what fun he meant. Fighting, drinking, drugs, women, taking risks, and running for his life. Too much of his adult life had been wasted on doing what the darkness wanted him to do.

"I got smart," Leo replied, never taking his eyes off the darkness as it began to circle the room like a hungry beast waiting to pounce upon its prey. All the while, it kept that villainous smile plastered across his face to remind Leo exactly what he was capable of.

"No. You got boring," it whined, sounding genuinely upset.

"I'm not here for your entertainment," Leo growled.

"Then what are you here for?" His tone became as dark as the shadows that stretched along the floor and walls. "What's your purpose? All you do is cause pain and suffering everywhere you go. You should have learned that by now."

Leo refused to acknowledge his questions with any form of answer. This game was getting old and Leo had learned the rules long ago. He knew how to evade the mind traps that the darkness set before him. It wasn't him that caused the trouble. Not really.

The darkness stopped his circling and chuckled, a sound that might have been pleasing coming from any other mouth but his.

"Come on, Leo. Don't give me the silent treatment. We haven't talked in weeks. There's so much to catch up on." The darkness ventured a step closer to his prey. "Who's this new tart you have?"

The darkness was not Scottish and any kind of slang he spoke was just a trick to lure Leo into a false sense of security. It sounded so wrong coming from him.

"She's not a tart," the true Scotsman replied.

"Oh, sure she is!" the darkness exclaimed. "At least, she will be when you're done with her."

Leo scowled at what he was implying. "I'm already done with her." He leaned in. "And you are too."

The smile faltered, but only in enough time to say, "And who are you to be giving me orders? Besides, she's pretty. I can just imagine her lying in bed and..."

Leo tuned him out and pretended like he was looking for a weapon with which to hit the darkness. But he knew it was no use. The darkness was like mist, untouchable and immune to his worldly influence. The way he began to describe Belle in such lustful detail made him sick to his stomach.

"Stop talking about her like that!" he shouted, turning back, his body tense and more than willing to fight something that might have only existed in his own mind. Anything to get him to shut up.

He looked to him with grotesque satisfaction. Leo let him win this time, getting his goat on something that shouldn't have mattered at all to him. But it did. Belle mattered to him more than anything right now. He couldn't explain why, but she was the key to some lock he hadn't figured out yet.

"I thought you said you were done with her?"

"I am." Leo turned away, but kept the darkness within his peripheral vision.

The demon came closer, almost close enough that he could reach out and stroke Leo with his gnarled claws that masqueraded as fingertips. "But you know what? I think she might look prettier with her throat sliced open and bleeding. I always preferred the sound of the last choking breaths of human life, rather than the moans of pleasure."

Leo lashed out at the darkness and screamed. "Enough!"

But his fist passed through the darkness as if he were nothing but an illusion. The demonic spirit chuckled at his feeble attempt at retaliation.

"Don't you dare touch her," Leo bellowed, his glare like a roaring fire. If only the darkness could have burned from such a look.

"So, you're not done with her, then?" it questioned, his voice upturned with intrigue.

"She doesn't want me," Leo admitted. "This thing between us doesn't involve her."

The darkness stepped up closer, his footsteps soundless on the floor. "Just like it didn't involve that girl in Jonesboro?"

Leo felt unbridled fury swell in his chest, fused with the pang of regret for the mistakes he had made.

The demon sensed that and continued, "Don't get too close, Leo. We may have to deal with her, so you'll learn your lesson about getting too attached. You've already spent too much time in this town as it is."

Leo was tempted to accept defeat against the darkness, but he followed Belle's example and refused to show the weakness that he felt deep inside. His poor choices weighed heavily on his soul. Until this demon came and reminded him, Leo had done a fine job of forgetting what he had done in Jonesboro.

"You won't have to worry about me getting close. It was over before it had a chance to start. Just leave her alone."

The demon gave him an eager look. "Will you leave this town?"

"I will stay where I wish," he spat.

The demon sighed as if he were exasperated by Leo's stubbornness. "You're putting them all under the guillotine if you stay."

Leo wasn't fooled by his artificial show of concern. The demon really wanted him to stay, to have a chance to destroy the town and everyone in it. It would feed on that suffering he brought to Levi. But Leo was smarter than that and knew how to play this game. He'd been an unwilling player for most of his life. "I will stay where I wish and associate with whoever I want." It took little effort to lace his words with the same kind of venom that the demon dished out. "I will not let you dictate what I can and can't do."

This was only a half truth. The demon always had the upper hand, no matter how hard Leo struggled to take control of his life.

It laughed. "But you'll let this girl shoo you away?"

"I respect her," he said, jutting out his chin defiantly. "I do not respect you."

The darkness hissed and adjusted his tie as if he were uncomfortable. But it was all a show. "My feelings are hurt, Leo. Really hurt. After all we've been through together. Twelve years, isn't it?"

Leo narrowed his eyes upon the demon. He was completely right. How could he forget that it had been twelve years since they were first tethered together? They had become unwilling life partners since that terrible day in Brooklyn.

"Get close to Belle and she will pay the price, just like your family did. You can't say I didn't warn you."

Toxic hatred pulsated through his body at the mention of his family. How dare this demon, this thing made of pure evil, desecrate their names by letting them roll off his forked tongue? It was this hatred that fueled his drive to escape the evil that caused him so much misery. He didn't know how or when, but Leo would exact his revenge one day.

"Leave," Leo growled, deep and threatening.

The demon smiled and wagged his head as if Leo had just told the funniest joke. "There you go giving orders again. I won't leave that easy. You know what I need."

Leo could feel the edges of his nails indent into his palms as he squeezed his fists tighter. "Not this time. I'm done with that. You'll leave without blood payment."

The demon rubbed his fingers together, giving the universal sign for money. "But you know that I need some payment for the trouble of making this visit. It's our deal."

Leo wished he had never made that deal years ago. He was young and stupid, desperate to make the demon leave, at least for a little while. He fed off the pain and suffering of humans and Leo had been a willing donor. In those days, he had given up on life anyway, thinking his sins were too great and life too tainted by his mistakes.

There was no way he could go back on his deal without sacrificing his sanity. Leo looked around and saw a lone tack pressed into the wall by his bed. It might have held up a picture at some point, but now served no purpose at all.

He went, plucked it from the wall and pricked the tip of his thumb until a tiny droplet of red blood surfaced. "This is all you'll get from me." The pinhole wasn't much compared to what he used to do, but it caused enough discomfort that the demon could feed from it.

The demon stepped closer and put his hand over Leo's, sucking the pain from him like a vampire might leech away blood from its victim. The only way that Leo knew it was working, was by the way the wound tingled and seemed to sting more intensely. It was a vicious cycle that the demon created. He fed on the pain, causing more pain until Leo could have been screaming in agony on the floor from a single puncture wound.

"I suppose that's enough," the demon said as he dropped his hand. "You know, just between us guys, I think I enjoy your suffering so much more than anyone else's. Because, I know it will never end."

"Get out!" Leo barked.

The demon began to fade, his image warbling like a mirage until he completely disappeared into a puff of black smoke that left behind a potent sulfur stench. The deep shadows followed him close behind, leaving the room exactly as it was before the darkness consumed it.

However, Leo wasn't the same. More emotions closed up his throat and he wasn't sure what to do.

Belle had rejected him, pushed him away when all he wanted to do was help her.

The darkness had followed him to Levi and still had a tight grip on his life, coming to this place with threats of death and destruction by Leo's own hand.

Memories of a past that he couldn't outrun clouded his mind, bringing on a sadness he hadn't felt in many months.

The worst of his life was certainly not over. There was more to come, especially if he stayed in Levi. How could he even begin to think that things would be better here? Yet, Leo's strong will could not be denied. Running would only prove that the darkness was right and still had dominion.

He would stay for as long as possible until the risks became too great for him to ignore. Approaching Belle was out of the question. Any interaction with her would be seen by the demon and her safety couldn't be guaranteed. Even a phone call was impossible.

Leo went to his nightstand where he kept the little note with her number written on it. He picked it up and prepared to tear it, but hesitated. Ripping up her number would have been the nail in the coffin for them both. He would not visit her at her work or home, now that he knew the exact places to avoid. Even if a chance meeting happened again, he would have to turn and walk away from the woman who had enchanted him. Getting rid of her number would ensure that he didn't contact her at all. He would purge the temptation from his path before it could destroy them both.

He closed his eyes and listened to the paper shred in his hands.

He expected to feel something, anything, when he did that. But he could still sense their bond within him. Destroying this tiny link did nothing to abate the pain of this ending.

The longer he thought about it, the more he realized that nothing would truly bring him closure but time and distance. Leo would wait, but he wondered how long it would take for him to let go of Belle and her brilliant green eyes that reminded him of the home he lost.

Chapter 6

It'd been nearly a month since Belle watched Leo speed away from her home, leaving her to cope with the brokenness he had left behind.

Each passing day, it got a little easier to get up in the morning and go on as if Leo had never waltzed back into her life. Yet, every time she passed by the diner where they had dinner, when she went to the grocery store, when she walked up the porch steps at the end of the day, even when she prayed, Leo crashed through her mind like a wrecking ball and reminded Belle that she had left things in a mess.

Belle had thought it over so many times and came to the conclusion that she had overreacted. Drake deserved the thrashing he got, and Belle should have been grateful. Replaying the events that followed the fight, Belle realized she hadn't thanked Leo at all. That left her ashamed with a permanent knot in her stomach.

The first week after the fight, Belle struggled to rebuild her walls. Even a whole day off from work spent in prayer and relaxation did little to ease her rampant anxiety. She tried everything from her usual lavender candles to her chamomile bath salts, but it had done little good.

One blessing remained. She hadn't run into Leo again and for a moment, she feared that she never would.

Either Leo had left Levi, or he was doing a good job of evading her. Living in such a small town, Belle imagined they would bump into each other at some point. As the weeks dragged on, she began to succumb to a whole new world of feeling.

Her mind went to work, coming up with all the reasons why she should feel the way that she did. In the same train of thought, she could curse him and want him back at the same time. Though she might never forgive him for what he did to Drake, she was thankful for it in the end. Leo had violated her carefully ordered world with his honesty. He pierced through her defenses with those silvery blue eyes that could steal the breath from her lungs and made her want to give him everything she had. No one else had ever done that and she wondered if anyone else ever could.

In the short time that they had been together, Leo had become much more to her than an acquaintance. Despite his brash character and rough edges, he brought a certain kind of violent harmony that refused to be denied. Her mind stopped racing, the knots in her stomach untangled, and she could take a full, unguarded breath. It set her whole being into a whirlwind, but she stood in the eye of the storm, untouched and protected in his chaos. And now, with him gone, she finally understood what he did to her. And she hated herself for feeling that way, hated herself for destroying the one good thing she could have had.

Belle and Ivy worked at sorting through a section of the store, grabbing books from the mobile cart and arranging them in alphabetical order according to author names on the shelves. It was a task that didn't require too much thought on Belle's part. Having done this job for years, alphabetizing anything became like second nature. This kind of task didn't help when she needed a serious distraction.

"Belle?" Ivy asked. "Didn't you just do the Rs?"

Belle glanced up from the small stack of books in her hands. "Yeah. Why?"

"You put Ramsey after Reynolds."

She sighed and quickly adjusted the section of shelving she had completely botched up, but Belle could feel Ivy's eyes on her.

"Is something wrong? You've been acting funny lately."

She shook her head. "Nothing wrong."

"Horse sh-... dung," she corrected herself. "You've been out of it all week. What's going on?"

Belle pressed her hand to her forehead and smoothed back the flyaway hairs in her ponytail. Had it been that obvious to everyone? Her defenses must have been weaker than she thought.

Belle longed for someone to confide in, but could she step out and be personal with her coworker again? God was an excellent listener, but Belle rarely ever heard that still, small voice that Pastor Kendall always spoke of. The storm of her anxiety seemed too great and she couldn't hear His voice through the wind and rain.

"Does this have to do with Leo?" Ivy asked, almost in a whisper.

Belle simply nodded, not trusting her own voice to speak the words.

"Did you two break up?"

"We were never together."

"That's not how it looked to me. You two couldn't stop laughing that day at the diner. I'm surprised you haven't said anything else about him since then."

Belle turned to her colleague and braced herself against the cart between them, ready to do what Leo had done and tear down the walls herself. "We got into a fight when he took me home."

Ivy cocked her head. "About what? How he beat up Drake?"

"I'm sure everyone in town knows about it."

Ivy snorted. "Yeah, everyone knows what Drake's been spreading around, which is that Leo just came out of nowhere and started swinging like a maniac." She leaned in, mirroring Belle. "You know what else he's saying? That Leo got off worse than he did."

Belle wasn't necessarily surprised. Drake had an egomaniac streak in him that wouldn't be put down just from one fight. "Did someone call the cops on Leo? I haven't seen him in a month."

A crease formed between Ivy's brows. "You haven't seen him in a month? He's still been coming to the diner pretty often."

Belle felt her legs grow weak. So, he hadn't left town. "He didn't get arrested or anything?"

Ivy laughed. "No! You think Drake would press charges against the guy who beat him up? There's over a dozen witnesses saying that he got his butt whooped. And no one who saw what really happened has any sympathy for Drake, you know that."

"Has anyone been talking about why it started?"

Ivy shrugged. "I don't even know why it started to be honest. I thought maybe Drake popped off some comment like he normally does and Leo took it the wrong way. No one could blame him for that. I'm sure everyone's wanted to get a good swing at Drake lately."

Belle went silent, processing. Ivy had a valid point and now her previous arguments to Leo were invalid. Drake didn't press charges, and no one seemed to care about the fight at all, let alone her involvement in it. If Ivy, who worked at the diner and served them, didn't even notice what Drake had been doing seconds before Leo grabbed him, then it was likely that no one else did either. And If Ivy hadn't heard other rumors through the grapevine, it was a safe fact that no one knew that Belle was the catalyst for the fight.

"What did you two argue about?" Ivy asked again.

"I got upset with Leo because I felt like the whole thing could have been resolved without violence. He seemed to think otherwise." Belle was careful to avoid mentioning anything that would change what Ivy believed she already knew.

"I agree that fights can get kind of scary, but you know Drake. Nothing's going to get through his thick skull unless you drill it in with a sledgehammer."

Belle cracked a smile. "I know, but I guess I was just too upset about it all and I said something that I shouldn't have."

"Why not go and apologize?"

Belle blinked and fell dumbstruck for a few seconds before stammering, "I didn't know if he was still in town or if he would even want to see me... I said some really nasty things to him, Ivy."

Her friend looked nonplussed for a moment, then said, "I can't imagine anything nasty coming out of your mouth. Maybe you're just overthinking it."

Belle could tell this conversation wasn't going where she wanted it to. If she told Ivy exactly what she had said, it would be as good as throwing their friendship down the drain. If Leo could be scared away so easily, then Ivy certainly could. And if Ivy probed deeper into exactly why Belle had been mean, apart from the Drake situation, then they'd never be able to look at each other the same way again. Ivy couldn't know about her anxiety or the mask.

"I think you're right. I should apologize." Belle's stomach leapt and clenched as she thought of facing Leo again, looking into his beautiful blue eyes and saying that she was sorry for something that should have never happened to begin with. They should have never gone out to dinner, never explored the possibilities of a relationship.

"He's still working at the lumber yard, I think. You could try and run by there on your lunch break."

Belle stood up and looked back to the books, biting her lips together thoughtfully. More than anything, she waited for that inner prodding, telling her to go for a second chance at making things work between them.

Leo knew the truth about her now, more than he had known before. He knew she was a fake, a fraud, someone who lashed out when they were told some hard truths. Who would want to spend time with a person like that? Why would anyone be interested in her in the first place?

Almost more importantly, was she brave enough to continue a connection with someone who knew her deepest fears and understood the innerworkings of her heart?

The last month had been a living hell for Leo. The demon had seen through Leo's lies and his usual nightmares had changed. Seductive visions of Belle played on loop, arousing him to no end. The dreams made him want her, crave her both physically and spiritually. Each morning he awoke, he wanted to go see her and beg for forgiveness for his actions, even if he didn't mean it. Only pride and common sense kept him from finding her. That's what the darkness wanted.

He learned long ago that the demon couldn't read his mind, only his actions. And if Leo sought after Belle, the demon would strike and there was no telling what would happen.

After a week of these provocative dreams, they began to take on a more ominous theme. When he closed his eyes, Belle came to him as before, wearing barely anything and beckoning him to follow her into the abyss of sin, only to bring him more torment when her effigy became drenched in blood and supple flesh was slashed to pieces by monsters from the shadows. Instead of driving him with sex, they tormented him with fear.

After only a few nights, Leo knew he couldn't continue this way. He evaded sleep as much as possible, traveling to other towns and staying all night in the bars. When he grew bored of the lack of skill among the poker players, he resolved to stay home and drank pots upon pots of coffee to keep his eyes open. Occasionally, he would spike it with a measure of whiskey just to ease his nervousness.

That day, Leo was alone, delimbing trees that had been cut down hours before. It was late in the afternoon and he could hear men working some distance away. Within the same clearing stood a forwarder and pile of ten-foot logs ready for transport to the main road when the carrier came to take them away.

His supervisor might have wanted him to use the chainsaw like the other men, but Leo preferred the old fashion way and hacked the limbs off with an axe. It helped to release some of the pent-up energy that had been building up over the last few weeks.

With his shirt tossed to the side, his bare chest glistened with sweat rolling over his dirty skin. Besides the distant sound of his colleagues laughing and joking in the distance, Leo concentrated on the steady rhythm of steel thudding into wood. That was all he could do nowadays. Focus on work, on staying awake, on anything but the unrequited longing and regret for the mistakes he had made. Those thoughts were like a thick, miasmic fog that he could have been lost in for hours or days. He couldn't allow himself to slip again. *Just keep moving.*

If it weren't for the sharp snap of twigs and rustling of ferns from behind him, he might have never known he was no longer alone. The intruder didn't make himself known, but who else would have been this far out in the middle of the woods besides one of his coworkers?

The movement stopped, but Leo didn't pause in his work.

"If you're just going to fecking stand there, you might as well grab that saw and help me out," Leo said, none too gently.

When he heard no smart answer from whoever had entered the clearing, Leo propped his axe head against the fallen tree and turned.

Standing there was Belle, looking out of place amongst the trees and wilderness. Not even the seductress in his dreams could compare to the woman who stood before him, hands twisting together in front of her nervously as the afternoon sun filtered through the canopy above them. She wore the sunlight as if it were tailormade to her, magnifying her beauty so much that he thought he might never breathe again.

Despite her twitching hands, she appeared calm and Leo wondered if this was the mask she donned so much or if Belle decided to be open with him.

"You look terrible," she said, her face warped in a grimace, borne from genuine concern.

Certainly, she saw the dark circles under his eyes and the obvious signs of sleep deprivation. Leo didn't even think anything of the fact that after a month of silence, the first words she spoke to him decided to be a near insult. He didn't need a "hello" or typical greeting. They were beyond such formalities and she must have known that he didn't need them either. Anything more formal would have been a lie.

"You shouldn't be here," he stated, easing his tone down from the frustrated state it had been in.

Belle gestured behind her. "Your boss said it was ok if I came out here for a minute to talk."

Leo hadn't considered that this area was restricted to civilians. He thought only of her safety from the darkness that had threatened to kill her. To be cruel to her would have been like swimming against a great river, but he had to do it. If she perceived that he didn't care for her, then perhaps the separation would be easier for both of them. Then again, maybe she needed closure as badly as he did.

He pulled back his shoulders, stretching his chest muscles in an attempt to intimidate her. "You have a minute."

Belle's eyes dropped to his naked torso and he could see the way her eyes dilated. She took a deep breath and nodded.

"I came to apologize for what I said that night," she began. "I should have been thanking you for what you did, and I took it the wrong way. I was afraid people would talk and it turned out that nobody talked about it at all." She shrugged. "Well, they weren't talking like I thought they were going to. Drake's blabbing around that he beat you up instead and no one believes him so no one seems to care. I thought they would. So, I'm sorry for getting so crazy about it."

Leo watched her in silence for a few long beats before nodding. "Apology accepted." He knew all along that people wouldn't talk about what had happened, but he wasn't about to argue with her that night about it. This might have been a small town, but from what he had witnessed at the diner, they would have all agreed that Drake needed a good thrashing.

"But," he continued, "I won't be apologizing for what I did."

Belle shook her head quickly and took a few steps toward him. "I wouldn't expect you to. You did what you thought was right and I really am thankful." She swallowed hard. "I know I didn't say it that night, but I'm saying it now. Thank you for defending me."

Leo didn't want to gaze into her eyes and feel the ice around his heart thaw, so he cast his attention to the tree trunk he had been cutting. "You're welcome," he muttered.

Belle drew closer and he could feel her stare hot upon him, making his flesh crawl in a pleasing way. It took a real effort to remember that this woman was not the same one in his dreams. This woman was real, alive, close enough to truly touch. Her soul was more attractive than any part of her body and that's what called out to him now. He ground his teeth and fought the urge to take her into his arms right then and there.

"Can we start over? Like, go on another dinner date? We can have dinner at my place where we won't get interrupted."

If Leo didn't know her better, he would have thought her offer to mean something far more than what it really was. Belle had an innocent spirit, one untainted by the things of his recent nightmares. He knew that she couldn't imply anything beyond what her words conveyed. But that didn't even matter. For her own safety, they could never be that close, no matter how much he wanted to save her.

He looked to her and gathered every ounce of willpower he had left. "I don't think that's..."

Leo paused and listened with his head cocked to the side. The men in the distance were gone, their voices replaced with a silence that he wasn't accustomed to during the work hours. Yet, that's not what made him stop in mid-sentence. It was the popping and groaning of wood fibers grinding against each other. He knew that sound well after working this job for a month.

He turned and saw a tall pine tree start to give way in their direction.

"What's wrong?" Belle managed to say before Leo grabbed her about the waist and threw both of them a safe distance away.

She cried out and a few wide-reaching branches scraped against his back as he shielded her from the rough bark. The tree came crashing down on top of where Leo had been working in the middle of the clearing. The top half of the tree extended toward the stack of already delimbed trunks, knocking them loose from their bonds. He could hear the pop of the cords as they came undone, one by one, unleashing them in a cascade.

The logs tumbled down, spilling into the clearing like a tidal wave of wood and bark. All Leo could hear was the roar like rolling thunder, except for a soft whisper that sounded so close to his ear that he jerked at the words.

Ask for help and we shall give it.

Leo shook his head, willing the voices away. With Belle still encased in his arms, he scrambled out of the path of the logs to the edge of the clearing. He could feel her hot breath on his neck and shoulder and her rigid body melting into his.

When the din of crashing timber finally subsided, all Leo could hear in its place was his heartbeat thrumming in his own ears and Belle's ragged gasps. He looked down and saw her head tucked against his chest, eyes shut tight.

"Are you okay?" he asked, unwilling to let her go to inspect her further.

She nodded, tendrils of hair quivering from the motion. Leo pulled back as much as he was able without freeing her from his embrace and looked her over. There was no blood, no cuts, no flesh wounds that were obvious to the naked eye. Relief washed over him like a cold splash of water on flushed skin.

Instead of letting her go, he held her even tighter, being careful not to smother her. Thin and shaking hands found their way to settle on the hardened muscles below his shoulder blades. He sucked in a breath at her touch, but gritted his teeth until it hurt. That might have been the only thing to bring him back to reality.

Glancing behind him, he looked for the man responsible for cutting the tree that created such a domino effect of destruction. Not a soul was around, but he did notice something burned into the bark of the tree that had fallen.

Normally, the men would go around and mark the trees that needed felling with spray paint. But this mark glowed and penetrated the coarse bark like a brand. Leo squinted at the symbol and recognized it immediately. No mortal man cut down that tree.

He mumbled a curse under his breath, regardless if Belle could hear him or not.

This was no accident.

The hex symbol on the tree faded and vanished completely in front of his eyes, leaving no trace of the sabotage. Typical.

Belle stirred and the softest of whimpers captured his full attention. Leo pulled away, but she continued to lean into him. That was when he noticed that she favored one of her feet over the other. Without asking permission, he helped her to the ground and shoved her pant leg halfway up her calf to examine it.

With a gentle finger, he eased down the edge of her sock. Her ankle was beginning to swell, and the first signs of bruising discolored her skin. It could have been sprained, broken, or simply twisted. Anything could have happened while he was manhandling her. Yet, even a broken ankle would have been better than being crushed beneath tons of wood.

"Can you move it?" Leo asked, trying to stay in the moment rather than worry about what the darkness would do next.

Belle tried to flex her toes forward, but cried out in pain and shook her head. "Not really. But I don't think it's broken. It doesn't hurt bad enough."

"We need to get you to a hospital."

Belle reached out and grabbed his shoulder, fingertips pressing into his skin. "No, it's not necessary," she replied through a few sniffles. It was clear that she was making a real effort not to cry or seem weak in front of him. Leo could appreciate her courage, but now was not the time to be brave. She had every reason to be terrified for her life as long as she was near him.

"You need to have a doctor look at that to make sure it's not broken."

Belle shook her head even more furiously. "No, I'm sure it's not broken. I've had my ankle broken before and this is nothing."

Leo didn't have time to ask when or how it happened. What she needed now was an ice pack and the proper bandaging. His supervisor might have a first aid kit in his trailer.

"Put your arms around my neck," he ordered and then told her of his plan.

Belle didn't protest and let him lift her up into his arms. Being careful not to jar her ankle or knock it against anything, he carried her back to his supervisor's trailer nearly half a mile away. He wanted to enjoy the feel of her so close to him or to revel in the way her fingers warmed his shoulders. This was the closest they had ever been to one another, the closest they ever would be again.

Belle was helpless in his arms, and the whole scene would have looked romantic to any outsider. One swift jerk and he could pull her into a kiss if he wanted. But they wouldn't have known the true gravity of the situation. No one could. None but him. This was his fault, but the darkness was to blame as much as him.

If nothing else, this was proof that he and Belle couldn't be together. Not how he wanted. Measures would have to be taken, another deal made. Leo didn't relish the idea, but while Belle's ankle was wrapped in athletic tape, he began to form his plan. Maybe there was something he could do after all.

Chapter 7

Leaning against Leo's stable arm, Belle hobbled her way up the porch, keys in hand ready to unlock the front door. Ever since he had cradled her in his arms, and all the way to getting out of her truck just minutes ago, Belle tried to not think about how close they were and the way he touched her.

Even though there was nothing but platonic motives behind escorting her to the trailer to have her ankle wrapped and then driving her home, there was always a kind of tenderness in Leo's actions. He didn't raise his voice or berate her for coming to his job site in the first place. He didn't wash his hands of her as soon as she was ready to go home. Belle didn't want to believe it meant things were better between them, but the idea was pushing forward with each passing minute, each fleeting glance he cast her way.

They hardly exchanged any words on the way home. Belle hadn't even asked for the ride, but he insisted and she wondered how he would get back into town without his motorcycle.

Once inside, Leo helped her to the sofa and threw the thick pillows against one of the arms, so she could lounge comfortably with her leg elevated on the cushions. She watched him wordlessly walk into the kitchen and prepare a bag of ice for her ankle. Somehow, he was able to navigate the interior of her home without even asking. Part of her enjoyed seeing him rummage through the cabinets and drawers in search of a baggy for the ice cubes.

She had been in a worse state before. The mild, over the counter pain relievers that came with the first aid kit somewhat dulled the pain. She hoped that within an hour or so, it would be reduced to a mere throbbing. There pulsed another throbbing elsewhere that Belle was a little ashamed to acknowledge, but it had lessened when Leo finally put a shirt back on at the supervisor's trailer. Thankfully, his sickly look was transformed by adrenaline to make him seem more alert and less like a borderline zombie. It made her wonder if he was getting enough sleep, or if he was tossing and turning at night just as she did.

He came back into the living room and let down the chilled ice pack on her ankle. It was nearly impossible to flex the joint since it was so tightly wrapped in athletic tape and bandages. Leo's boss was obliging and trained in first aid procedures. He was the one that confirmed what Belle thought all along, that her ankle wasn't broken and only twisted. That didn't stop him from giving a thorough reprimand to Leo, but Belle assured that she wouldn't press charges at all against the company. It was an accident, but Leo didn't seem to think so.

Still, she would have to refrain from moving her ankle and probably have to call out sick to work for a day or two. Limiting her mobility would prove to be difficult with a farm to take care of. Belle knew she would have to call in a few favors and have someone come over to take care of the daily chores outside.

She wondered if Mr. Johnson would be available to help look after the animals. It wasn't lambing season, so he should have been free to leave his own spread a few miles north of her. When he wasn't occupied by his own work, he could always be relied upon to look after her flock and herds. He and her father had been close friends and his wife was the first one to suggest selling her eggs and wool at the farmer's market in town. She'd have to make a point of calling him once Leo left.

He knelt next to the sofa, his eyes fixed on her iced ankle and holding the top of the bag, as if that would make it heal any faster. She noticed how speckles of dirt still clung to his cheeks and forehead, how the hairs around his temples were dampened by sweat, and how the whites of his eyes were slightly red. This whole time, he had been solely devoted to her comfort and safety. He didn't give a moment's hesitation, jumping to action as if his whole world revolved around her and her alone.

"Thank you," she managed to finally say.

"You're going to need to stay off of this for a few days," he said softly.

"I know," she replied. "I'll be calling my work soon to let them know what happened.

Awkward silence reigned again, and Belle hardly knew what to say to make things any better. She had no idea why he was so quiet or why he was still here, holding the bag and repositioning it occasionally, so the ice was evenly distributed. After a while, she was sure she had lost all feeling in her joint and the cold sweat from the bottom of the bag seeped through her bandages, making her skin go numb.

"I'm sorry," he whispered.

Belle blinked and regarded the way every line of his body seemed to tense. "You have nothing to be sorry for. It was an accident."

She saw the muscle jump in his jaw, but Leo said nothing in response.

"You were about to say something before that tree fell," she said. "I had asked if we could start over." After a long pause, she gestured toward the kitchen. "I know I can't cook anything because of my foot, but there's this one pizza place in town that delivers out this far and - "

"No," Leo grumbled, cutting her off.

Such a simple word, and yet it felt like a sucker punch to her gut. She bit her lips together and looked away.

"I don't think it'd be such a good idea after all that's happened."

Belle turned back to him with a puzzled look and crossed her arms over her stomach, willing it to stop doing backflips. "What's happened besides the obvious? If it's me, I'd rather you just come out and tell me. I know I said a lot of things that night and I can't blame you for not wanting to start over, but at least say it to my face."

There she went being blunt again, stepping on toes and demanding explanations that she didn't deserve. But instead of getting offended, Leo cracked a mirthless smile and shook his head.

"It's not you. Not at all."

"Did you meet another girl?"

He gave a haughty huff. "No, I haven't met any other women."

If nothing had changed on his part, then surely it had something to do with Belle and he was telling a white lie. The tight ache in her core turned sour and she felt just as sick as he looked.

"Listen," she began after she took a bracing breath, "I know I'm not the sweetest lollipop in the jar. I've been kind of dishonest with you from the beginning, being two faced the way I am, but you need to know I do it for a reason."

Belle had never opened up so plainly to anyone before and Leo seemed to sense that. His gaze turned to her, giving her his full attention while she continued with the story she had kept to herself for so long. Not even her father understood how and why the mask came into existence. She chose her words carefully, no matter how long the pauses between sentences while she tried to grasp them. Maybe if he knew, he'd change his mind.

"That night when you said that I hadn't always been this way... well, you were right. I was a really happy kid. I went up to people and told them all about myself and acted as rambunctious as my dad would allow. I didn't have a filter. I said what I wanted, no matter how sassy it was. They all said it was cute, that I had a wild spirit. But when I got older, I was told that it wasn't cute at all. I was sometimes rude and unladylike.

"My mother was the one who finally broke the news to me. She never hesitated to point out my flaws, no matter how small. She got on my case about my hair, my clothes, my manners... everything. She'd ask me to comb my hair for the fifth time, ask if I brushed my teeth and then make some comment about my breath, tell me my shirt didn't go with my top. She'd correct my posture, how I spoke, what I said... The minute I hit puberty and I got my first zit, she took me to the store, and we got all this makeup. My dad didn't even want me to wear it, but she said I needed it, because I wouldn't look good anymore without it."

Belle struggled to bottle the mounting rage she felt toward her mother, knowing it wasn't right to dislike a family member so much.

"Every time I was with her, she'd correct me, even if it was in front of other people. I'd see the look on their faces, as if they agreed with what she said. It made me believe my mom was right and my dad didn't tell me any of these things, because he didn't want to hurt my feelings or something. It made me wonder what the people at church said behind my back, if they really thought I was cute or if I was being obnoxious instead. I saw the world in a whole new lens."

"And that's when you started to care about what others thought of you," Leo astutely pointed out.

Belle nodded. "I started taking my mom's advice. I watched what I said and because I was always afraid of saying the wrong thing, I'd just say nothing. But I found out that I couldn't go through life without at least interacting some..." She gave him one of her fake, toothy grins. "So, I practiced this smile and rehearsed everything I would have to say before I went somewhere. I hate it when plans are changed at the last minute, because I never go into a situation unprepared. It's the only way I feel all right about stepping outside my door. I ask people how they are and greet everyone with the same warmth and politeness, all the while my heart's pounding out of my chest, because I'm terrified. I attend church functions, go to work, and run errands when all I want to do is curl up on this couch with a cup of tea and read. Because that's safer than risking total embarrassment in the real world."

It must have been the combination of her smile and the words she spoke, because Leo let out a soft chuckle. But Belle didn't find any of it funny. It was a torturous life she lived. Walking on eggshells every minute of the day, afraid of the next looming social disaster that might have only existed inside her head.

"It's such a conflicting thing. I used to be such a social butterfly, but after everything, I couldn't stop thinking about what others thought of me. I think people can be so fascinating and I want them to like me, so I can get to know them and help them, if I can, but I'm always too scared. I can function, but sometimes I feel like I'm just barely getting by. I want to have friends, I want to have a life, but I'm so terrified of screwing everything up if they find out that I'm not the person they think I am. My mind goes into overdrive, thinking about all the ways my words and actions could negatively affect those around me and all I want to do is go in a hole and hide.

"Not a single person on earth knows who I really am because of this social anxiety. No one knows that I shout curses in my head when something goes wrong or the ongoing commentary on what I really think of things. I don't feel like I can ever really be myself around people anymore. Sometimes, I don't even know who I am. I've played the role of a phony for so long..."

"So, when you threatened me with a crowbar in your barn, was that you or the phony?"

Belle had thought about that every day since they first met, and she couldn't explain away her behavior. "All I can think is that I was unprepared. I had already dressed down for the day, and I was ready to unwind. I had retired the mask for the night. I didn't expect to find you. And even after I realized what was going on, it was too late to switch gears." She paused, debating on whether to continue. But, she had ruined everything else, so she figured she might as well go ahead and do away with the rest.

"Even when we bumped into each other again at the supermarket, I had a hard time keeping up appearances. Dinner was even harder."

Leo nodded. "I could tell you were struggling with something."

"And when you took me home that night, I'd never been so mad, so scared. The mask just couldn't stay on around you."

Leo shifted the ice pack. "And now?"

She went quiet for a few hot seconds, trying to assess exactly what it was she felt. "Now I wonder if I've just destroyed any chance I might have of a real friendship with an amazing and interesting guy."

Leo's soft smile faded, and he looked away. If that told her anything, it was that she might have been correct. Never had she felt such utter disappointment and embarrassment.

There was the possibility that one day she would understand why Leo didn't want her. Yet, those ideas disagreed with everything he had done up to this point. If he didn't truly care for her, why would he have gone through all this trouble?

And then there was what he said that night. Her beauty came from the strength and boldness she hid from the world. Yet, when she bared her dark side to him in a fit of rage and just now in her confession of her past, he shied away and wanted nothing to do with her. What had he been thinking for the last month to make him change his mind? Was her own apology too late? Or did he decide that he didn't want to deal with a girl with so much baggage? She might have been doomed from the very start.

"I suppose the horses will need feeding," Leo suddenly said.

That might as well have been the death knell, the final hammer stroke to drive the nail in her coffin. If he could give her no hope, no reassurance, then it really was over. Belle desperately tried to quell the wailing in her heart and keep the tears from pushing their way forward. Life would go on as it had before she went to the lumber yard. She had been wasting her time, but that's not what hurt the most.

"Yeah, I guess they do," she replied, leaning her forehead against her hand as she propped her elbow on the back of the couch. There was so much to do and no hands to do it.

Leo stood up and handed her the makeshift ice pack before walking around the couch and toward the back door.

"Where are you going?" she asked quickly, pushing herself up a bit as if she were ready to run after him.

"I've helped out on a farm before. I'll get the animals fed and tended to for the evening. It'll give you one less thing to worry about." Leo returned to the living room as if he forgot something and stared down at her. "Promise me you won't move?"

Belle wasn't sure how to respond. In one moment, he wouldn't crush her fears that she had lost a potential friend and the next he was lightening her load again. Did Leo think that he had to repay her for something, but was not obligated to return her plea for companionship?

"You don't have to, really. I've got a neighbor that can come by later."

Leo leaned against the back of the couch, casting a shadow over her. "Let me help you in what little way I can for now."

It wasn't a question. It was a demand and there was little Belle could do about it.

She finally nodded and said, "I won't move." She thumbed to the end table and stack of books behind her. "I've got some reading to catch up on anyway."

Leo cracked a smile and Belle listened as he exited out the back door. However, the queasiness in her gut wouldn't fade. No matter how many times she read the same passage over and over again in her book, Belle's mind refused to rest.

What did he mean when he said, "*Let me help you in what little way I can for now*"? Was it a forewarning that he wouldn't be around much longer to help her at all? Was this the last day they would ever see each other?

Last time they parted, she was sure that she had ruined her chances with him, but they were able to rekindle a little bit of something after all that happened. Maybe, even though she opened her mouth and spilled her soul to him with no reward for her bravery in return, there was something left in the ashes. There had to be a silver lining to all of this, a saving grace, a tiny ember of mutual affection that remained burning in the wreckage. Belle refused to think that it was over, no matter how hard her heart and her gut told her to leave the issue alone.

After making sure that Blanche was nowhere to be found in the sewing shop and that the doors were all securely locked, Leo paced the floor of the room he rented. If he were a cartoon, smoke would have been billowing out of his ears and fire blazing in his eyes.

He had been careful to hide his anger from Belle while he helped her home and even when he tended to her horses and livestock. It took all of his self-control to not speed home after picking up his bike from work and even the brisk walk in the dark back to the site did little to calm him down.

"I know you're there!" he shouted, speaking to the ever-present darkness. "Show yourself."

"What's all this yelling for?"

Leo spun around to see the demon perched upon the top of his dresser smoking a cigar. With the suit and slicked back hair, he fit the bill perfectly for a man ready to make a deal. And Leo was happy to oblige. That might have been the only reason he appeared on command now.

"Where's Matthew?" he asked.

The demon feigned a look of confusion. "Who?"

Leo bristled at his games. "Don't play dumb. That tree that fell had his mark on it. Where is he?"

The demon sighed and rolled his eyes as if bored. "He's not here yet... But he will be. That was just a calling card, you know that."

Leo paced a few laps again, thinking it over. So, Matthew had found him. Staying in Levi for too long must have tipped him off. Maybe the demon told Matthew where Leo was staying. He wouldn't have put it past him. They were in league together, after all, tag-teaming in this game to ruin Leo's life. If the darkness couldn't make him leave, Matthew certainly would light a fire under him.

"How much longer until he arrives?"

The demon pulled a face in thought. "A couple of days... A few months... Not sure really. I'm just the messenger, you know."

If the demon had been a physical man, Leo would have grabbed him and beaten him to a pulp by now. He had no patience for this.

"Belle came to me and I was trying to tell her to lay off. That shouldn't have triggered anything. That was what you said before. If I got close, she would get hurt."

The demon hopped off the dresser and flicked his fingers to throw away the cigar that vanished into a plume of purple smoke. "Was that exactly what I said?"

Leo paused, searching his memory. The darkness was always particular about wordings. Just one wrongly phrased deal and it could mean a lifetime of suffering.

But, it didn't matter. Belle had been injured because of this. If Matthew came, all hell would break lose and Leo had to be long gone before then. Not knowing exactly when Matthew would come made things even more difficult.

"I want you to leave Belle alone," Leo said.

The demon gave a huff of a laugh. "Why should I do that?"

"And I want you to keep Matthew off my tail."

The demon narrowed his eyes on Leo and a tense silence filled the room. "What are you thinking, Leonardo?"

To hear his full name spoken was a little disturbing. No one had called him by that name in so long.

"I made a deal with you once," he said. "I want to make an addendum to it."

The demon looked intrigued now.

"When I bleed, you feed off of my pain and go away..." Leo once again picked his words carefully to form the idea he had in his mind. "Now, when I bleed, I want you and Matthew to leave me and Belle alone."

The darkness folded his arms. "That's a tall order there, buddy. There's more involved than just the two of us. I don't know if I can accept those terms. You know there's the higher-ups to consider."

"You'll take the deal, or I won't be your feeding trough anymore. You can get pain out of me the hard way, or you can take the easy way. I'm a willing donor, as long as you agree. "

The two men stared down one another, both wills combatting in the space between them. Leo knew exactly what he was getting into. With this kind of deal, the demon could demand blood payment from him on a regular basis. Each night after he came home from spending time with Belle, he would have to bleed for the darkness. Each time Matthew came close, Leo would have to pay the demon off to send him on a rabbit trail and buy him some time.

Leo made this proposition for quite a few reasons. He was growing attached to this small town, to his job, this room, and most of all Belle. He could see the hurt in her eyes when he - in so many words and ways - rejected her and any hopes for a relationship. With this deal, Leo could stay in Levi and try his chances with Belle - if she would have him back. It was security, protection by neglect, and it was the only way to unlock the door to a facet of his meaningless, miserable life. He wanted to know true affection that could only come from a woman. It might end in disaster, but this would delay it for a time.

Finally, the demon gave him a nod. "I believe I can accept on one condition." He began to circle Leo. "To keep Matthew at bay, the payment will have to be much larger than what you've given me before."

Leo let his eyes close, knowing exactly how far he would have to go now. With greater privileges came a greater price to pay. It made sense. It might have been an unavoidable consequence.

"Is that all?"

The demon's voice turned cheery. "That's all, buttercup. Just a little more blood and both I and Matthew will leave you and Belle alone. No hexes, no manipulations, no temptations, nothing."

Leo's eyes followed the demon as he came back into view. "For how long on each stretch?"

The demon tapped his sharp chin with his finger. "I'd say that really depends on how much you are willing to give."

So, the more he bled, in addition to the increase to accommodate Matthew, the longer they would be in peace. That seemed an even trade, though he hoped he could have tricked the darkness into agreeing to some lopsided trade where Leo wouldn't have to bleed so much or so often. This was for Belle as much as it was for him. And even if it were all for Belle, he'd be willing to do more. There was so much work to be done with her, so much to heal and mend. No one else could do this but him, because no one else understood her like he did.

He nodded. "Deal."

A cold settled over his heart, an ominous sensation that he might have just gotten himself into much more than he could handle.

The demon gave him a crooked grin. "Excellent. I'll take my payment now."

Leo looked over to the pin stuck in the wall, the same one he had used last time to prick his thumb.

"And that little thing won't do the job, I can tell you that much," the demon said.

"I don't carry knives anymore."

The demon chuckled. "I know." He waved his hands in a mystical, slight-of-hand way and manifested a sinister-looking dagger. Its elaborately etched blade gleamed in the florescent light of the room and Leo didn't have to test its edge to know that it was sharp enough to split a hair at its end. The handle was fashioned from what looked like carved ivory, depicting a scene of skulls, fangs, and claws tangled together in a macabre scene of death and evil.

With a hesitant hand, Leo took the blade from the demon and used it as a mirror to glimpse his face, still hollowed with exhaustion. Looking to the inside of his left arm, he saw the faded scars from years ago when he'd made his last cut. Back then, he didn't care about the demon's influence on his soul and it showed. Those were tumultuous times when he stepped out of the darkness and into a life on the run.

All those years, running from Matthew and the demon had come to this and it almost seemed counter intuitive. Here he was, regressing to his old ways and taking a stand against the curse, just so he could live a normal life somehow in the midst of it all. How did he know that this wouldn't bring about something even worse than what he had?

However, unable to go back on his deal now, he braced himself and tightened his left hand into a fist, so the veins would pop beneath his tanned skin. The demon waited with bated breath.

The first cut went quickly, the pain slick and smarting. He didn't quite feel it at first, but when the warm blood came into contact with the cool air of the room, he began to realize what he had done, and his nerves reacted in kind.

Afraid that he would drip on the floor, Leo moved into the cramped bathroom and held his arm over the sink.

This isn't worth it. She isn't worth it.

He blinked and snapped his head away, letting the pain intensify. The demon was beside him, floating in a dark mist, his true form, feeding on the cut.

She'll just reject you. She doesn't want you.

Leo felt an ache in his chest at their words, but tried not to hear.

Matthew will still find you and kill her. You know it's true and yet you make these deals that are worth nothing.

"Go away already!" he growled at the darkness that tried to invade his mind.

"*It's not enough. I need more.*"

Leo didn't hesitate to cut again, creating a slice just below the first one. Anything to get this ordeal over with.

Why would she want you? You're nothing but a liar and murderer. She hates you, that's why she acts so cruel to you and so nice to others. She's been lying to you this whole time. She thinks you're worthless too, just like your father thought.

Leo ground his teeth and squeezed his eyes shut. He leaned heavily on the sink and bowed his head. The skin on his arm seared as if it were engulfed in fire. He heard the soft plopping sound of the blood dripping onto the porcelain. He tried to tell himself the voices were lying. It was the darkness making him weaker, wearing him down. He couldn't give in. Not now.

You're nothing but trouble. It's your fault she got hurt today. It's your fault Drake tried to hurt her.

He had to be strong. He had to hold on and reject everything they said, but he could see some of the truth in it all. If he hadn't come back to Levi, Belle would have never been injured. She wouldn't have been at the diner where Drake found her. She would be happy, if he hadn't come into her life at all.

It's your fault your family suffered, and you'll be the reason Belle suffers too. She doesn't deserve you.

Their faces flashed through his mind. His parents, his brother, his little sister. He saw them, smiling and happy in their family photos. A life that was nothing but ashes now. All because of him.

With the dagger still clutched in his hand, Leo cut again, this time across the two he had made before. Blood coated the bottom of the sink and spilled into the drain. His arm and the knife were covered in the deep crimson liquid. His legs began to buckle, and a tear slipped down his cheek as the pain became too much. Three slices of a knife shouldn't have been this agonizing, but the demon's devouring powers made it even worse.

He managed to stumble to the bathtub, dripping as he went, and collapsed to his knees. Letting his arm hang over the edge, he cut for the fourth time. The voices melded together in a cacophony of despondent thoughts and threats. It was all he could hear.

The storm inside him grew into something he couldn't distinguish anymore. There was anger, despair, and hopelessness, then a numbness in his soul that couldn't be willed away. He cut again just so he could feel something.

But there was nothing.

He groaned at his stupidity and the demons cackled and thickened around him like a fog.

Leo didn't know how much time had passed and it hardly seemed to matter anymore. He no longer cared about anything and fatigue made him begin to believe the voices. If he didn't have Belle and that hope of a future, then what was the point?

Killing himself would have been both a blessing and a one-finger-salute to Matthew. His big brother couldn't torture him anymore if he was dead. Yet, Leo wasn't thinking about that. He wasn't thinking about anything but the pain and the grogginess that suffocated his mind.

When he lifted his right hand, he realized that the blade was gone and there was no more damage to be done. Before his consciousness slipped away, Leo looked at his mutilated arm, caked with both fresh and old blood, still pouring out the last bits of his essence.

Leo's head throbbed and all he wanted to do was sleep. So, he closed his eyes and let the void consume him.

But just before he could feel the cold claws of death take hold of his spirit, he heard another voice in the abyss that he didn't recognize. It wasn't hateful and menacing as the others were. Instead, Leo likened it to the trickling of a fountain, a waterfall, or the sweet trill of bells.

You are not finished. There is more here for you.

When Leo opened his eyes, his entire body ached with stiffness, as his chest and arms hung over the edge of the bathtub. From the beams of natural light that streamed into the bedroom behind him, he judged that it must have been morning now.

His vision blurred for a moment and he blinked away the cloudy patches that impaired him. When things became clear again, he realized what had just happened. A dark brown layer of dried blood coated the bottom of the tub.

With some difficulty, he sat up and turned on the faucet to clean up the remnants of his horrible mistake. He might have thought it all a dream if it weren't for that evidence that washed down the drain now.

It had been ages since he let the darkness toy with him so easily. He barely put up a fight, which was unlike him. There was a time when he needed little encouragement to contemplate suicide, but he had thought Belle was worth living for. Evidently, she was worth dying for as well.

When he effectively scrubbed away the dried blood, Leo saw no fresh cuts at all. Only faded scars littered his arm and he realized he had cut more times than he originally recalled. These scars, however, looked like they had been healed over for months. They were still a pretty gnarly sight, but nothing as bad as it would have been if they were only hours old.

He stared at his arm, examining it carefully, and then looked at himself in the mirror. Was he dreaming? There was no logical explanation for this. In all reality, he should have been dead. How was he still breathing? How could the cuts have healed like this?

Along with this miraculous healing, came the feeling of being refreshed, as if he had slept for days.

Leo looked around the bathroom, then briefly inspected the bedroom. He found no one. No demons, no darkness.

He pinched the bridge of his nose and tried to recall what had happened. Leo was sure that death had been about to take him. Then, there was that voice that seemed to pull him back from the threat of perdition. It was a beautiful voice and he remembered feeling something akin to peace when he heard it, if only for a brief second before he woke. All depression and sadness that assaulted him the night before was a distant memory.

It couldn't have been the darkness at work. Why would it nearly destroy him and then go back and heal the damage he had caused? Or was this some sick joke to keep him alive? If he were dead, he'd be useless. No more pain, no more payment. It would have been the best revenge, but there was something else at work here. Maybe it was true what the voice said. There was more for him here. But more what?

Chapter 8

"**A**nd then he just left," Belle said, completing her account to Ivy of what happened between her and Leo three days ago.

"And he didn't say a word?" Ivy asked as she slapped another barcode sticker on the back of a new book they were cataloguing for the store.

Belle took the book from her and wrote down the number on the inventory spreadsheet. "Not a thing."

After Leo had left Belle to convalesce on the couch, the hours ambled by in a blur until the sky darkened with the approaching evening. Leo never came back inside to tell Belle that he was done or to announce that he was leaving. He simply vanished, leaving her with her overacting thoughts and stomach full of butterflies.

In the days that followed, Belle iced her ankle and babied her injury until she felt well enough to return to work. Mr. Johnson came to take care of the animals in that time, and even brought casseroles baked by his wife, who had heard about the accident and thought she'd need the donation. Ray, needless to say, wasn't happy about losing an employee for so long, but he didn't give her a hard time about it.

The isolation gave Belle more precious time to think and recover from the devastating blow of truly losing Leo. Part of her had hoped that coming to the lumber yard and apologizing would heal every unintentional wound she had made. Even more, she thought that opening up like a stubborn spring flower would make him see that her outburst had a reason. But like everything else, Belle felt as if she were beating her head against a brick wall. Nothing she could do would bring him back now. His disappearing act was proof of that.

The world hadn't ended just because she told someone about her flaws, but it sure felt like it. So, she did the only thing she knew to do. She prayed. Prayed for herself, for Leo, for the guilt and heartache to go away, and all the thousands of other things on her long list. After she opened her eyes and unlaced her fingers, she felt a little better, but a niggling voice in the back of her mind kept telling her that nothing would feel right again unless Leo came back.

That, however, she was sure wouldn't happen. It was something she'd have to accept, as much as she didn't want to. Because, accepting that it was over and moving on would be the only way to heal and learn.

Ivy was a good listener though, and Belle found it easier to trust her colleague, since she was the only one privy to this drama involving Leo. Part of her hoped that Ivy would give some tried and proven advice to ease her bruised spirit. Ivy had far more experience with the male sex than she did.

"Well, I don't think you've seen the last of him," Ivy remarked confidently as she peeled off another barcode sticker.

A breath caught in her throat. "Why's that?"

"Because he was in here just the other day."

Belle thought her heart would stop beating. With wide eyes she regarded her friend with skepticism. "What are you talking about?"

Ivy thumbed toward the front of the store. "I saw Leo come in on Saturday asking about you."

It was too good to be true and as much as Belle believed in the power of faith, she couldn't believe that Leo still cared.

"I'm sure he had a good reason... Maybe he wanted help with a book or something."

"No, he was asking if you were here, because he wanted to talk to you."

Belle froze, her pencil in mid-stroke and gaze unwavering. "You're kidding."

Ivy shook her head, blonde hair swaying. "Nope. I overheard the conversation myself. I wanted to talk to Leo, but he slipped out before I could even get out a hello." She resumed her sticker stamping. "If you ask me, he's kind of rude. I mean, I try to be nice to him at the diner, but he's all standoffish. It's like he doesn't like people or something. Who doesn't like people?"

Belle bit her lips together to keep her mouth from blurting out anything that might incriminate her. She also wanted to let Ivy know that not every straight man on earth lusted after her. But, that wasn't a conversation to start today. Not any day.

"He's just shy, I guess."

Ivy flipped her hair over her shoulder and sighed. "Well, maybe. But he hasn't been shy with you."

Belle shrugged. "I don't know, then. Maybe we'll never know."

"You mean, you're not going to try and see him again? What if he comes by?"

Her stomach turned at the thought of Leo walking into the bookstore again. She hadn't anticipated him trying to find her at all. If he really wanted to see her, why didn't he go directly to her house? It wasn't like she could go anywhere.

"If he comes by, I'll talk to him, but I'm not going to go seeking him out like some stalker."

The tiny bell over the front door tinkled to signal that a customer had come in.

"Finally," Ivy grumbled. "Someone to shake things up."

Traffic had been uncommonly slow for a Monday morning, which freed up their time to get this monotonous work finished, but Ivy was never content in the silence.

A few long minutes passed and she heard Ivy mutter one of the only acceptable curses Ray allowed to be spoken in the store. Belle finished writing the barcode skew and looked up.

Leo walked toward them down the aisle of bookcases. He no longer looked like he would pass out from fatigue and his gait had a self-possessed swagger to it. Everything from the bright look in his eye to his upright posture showed that he must have been happy. This was a completely different man than the one she had last seen.

He smiled to them and Belle felt as if the tightly knit string of sanity within her would come undone and fray to pieces. She had no time to prepare, no time to strengthen her defenses against him or practice what she'd say. She never thought this would happen. It was like that day in the grocery store all over again and she forgot how to breathe.

"Hey, Leo," Ivy greeted cheerily.

"Hey," he replied. "Can I talk to Belle alone?"

Ivy seemed a little taken aback by the request, but he sounded so confoundedly polite and civil about it that she couldn't do much except nod. She walked into the back room, no doubt to browse through social media on her phone.

This left Belle totally exposed and she didn't want to stand to greet him for fear that her legs would give out.

"How's your ankle?" he asked, saving her from having to initiate contact. Maybe he knew how nervous she was. He knew her all too well by now.

Belle spoke slowly so her words wouldn't get tangled coming out of her mouth. "Better. I still have some athletic tape around it, but it doesn't hurt anymore unless I turn it a certain way."

Leo nodded and sat down where Ivy had been. "That's good to hear."

"Why did you just up and leave that night without saying good-bye?" Belle felt like slapping herself for diving right into a conversation that could start an argument. But, Leo had that effect on her. No filter, no control. Reckless and blunt.

He sighed and dropped his gaze, shame written on his face. "I'm sorry about that. I've been going through a lot and I should have been more open with you about it. I was... I didn't know what to say at the time. I guess I needed to take some time and think."

Belle blinked and felt terrible for bringing it up so soon. "I thought it had something to do with me."

He shook his head and gave a humorless laugh. "No, it's not you at all... Though, I didn't want it to affect you."

Belle crossed her arms, something she had always tried not to do. She had read somewhere that it gave the impression of being closed off. Right now, maybe she was. Whatever had driven Leo away, whether it was truly her or this mysterious personal dilemma, she hoped it was over. The tiny flame of hope would have been coaxed back to life if she didn't keep a damper on herself. "You look better than you did."

The smile returned. "I'm sleeping better."

"It shows." Belle could have kicked herself for repeating a point she had already made. She took a deep breath and held it to fight off the jitters.

"Hey, you're okay," he assured, leaning forward over the cart and folding his arms on the books they had been working on. "Well, besides the fact that you look tired."

Belle paused and felt her mouth go dry. Why did he say that? She was tired, but why would he try to assure her that she was okay? She hadn't heard those words in years. Most of the time, it was her own voice inside her head, repeating it like a mantra until she could believe it.

Leo had obviously read something in her speech or mannerisms that told him she wasn't comfortable. No one had been so perceptive, but then again, no one had ever extracted her true self through the barriers she had built. The heaviness of anxiety lifted from her chest for just a moment and if Belle didn't keep a tighter hold of herself, she might have been tempted to get a little misty. It was such a liberating feeling, but she couldn't trust it.

Don't get attached again. Don't let him hurt you.

Belle's eyes dropped just in case tears did come, and she noticed something peculiar. From her vantage point, all she could see were the pointed edges of dark scars. Lots of them.

Without asking permission or explanation, Belle grabbed Leo's wrist and turned his arm over so she could see the mangled mess of nearly a dozen scars. They all intersected in random patterns across the sensitive canvas of his skin.

A pulsating chill swept through her. "What's this?" she asked, her voice barely above a whisper.

Leo didn't withdraw his arm as she expected he would. "It's been there."

She shook her head. He might have tugged on a sleeved shirt after the accident at the lumber yard, but when he was shirtless, she would have noticed something this obvious. "No, it hasn't."

"They were there." The firmness in his voice warned her not to press further, but Belle didn't take the hint.

"Why did you do this?" she asked fiercely before she glanced up to see if either Ivy or Ray were watching.

"I didn't..." She gave him a hard look that demanded the truth from him. "That has to do with what I was going through. It's not a problem."

Not a problem? How could this not be a problem?

Belle met his gaze and saw the pain behind his eyes for the first time, the look that begged her not to pry, but there was no way she was going to listen. She cared for him too deeply to let this slide. "But why?"

He swallowed, his Adams apple bobbing with the effort. Belle didn't want to be the one to ruin it all again, but she needed answers. And if her boldness was truly something that he admired or thought beautiful, Leo shouldn't turn her away.

"I was just having a hard time coping with something. But, it's over now and things are better."

Belle didn't want to accept that brushoff.

When she first began to understand herself and her social anxiety, Belle searched all over the internet and educated herself about mental illnesses. Depression and self-harm went almost hand-in-hand with anxiety disorders. She knew this wasn't just "nothing" and unless Leo had truly resolved everything with his demons, scars like this would continue to appear.

But the best thing she could do was simply show that she was there for him and try to support in whatever way he'd allow. So pushing the issue wouldn't help in the end, even if everything in her soul told her to mend the unknown hurt.

She let go of his wrist, letting her fingertips trail across his skin as they dropped to the table top.

"You didn't answer me," he said. "Why are you tired?"

Belle rubbed at the corner of her eye, careful not to smear her mascara. She had hoped that no one would notice how distraught she was over Leo, but instead everyone seemed to notice the slight redness in her eyes. Earlier, she had yawned and popped her jaw so hard it hurt. "I might have a coyote problem," she said with a sigh. "I heard it howling last night and spent an hour putting my animals away. I usually let them graze in the pasture unless it's raining, so I had to go out and corral them all back into the barn. I wasn't so worried about the horses, but I've lost a couple of sheep and plenty of chickens in the past to coyotes."

"Aren't those what fences are for?"

She shrugged her brows. "Yes, but I have a broken part of my fence out in the fields somewhere. It's pretty far back and I don't think any of my animals know it's there, but I'm afraid the coyote might. I'm usually so wore out from work that I don't have enough spoons to fix it."

Belle could tell that Leo had no idea what she meant about spoons, so she smiled at his bemused expression. "It's a saying. It's like I don't have enough mental or emotional energy to do something. I saw it online once and kind of adopted the saying for myself."

Leo seemed to have forgotten how she had tried to pry back the steel layers of his private life, and wholly gave himself to hers. "I'll stop by and fix the fence. The lumber yard's been cutting my hours, so I don't have to work today."

Belle waved him off. "No, you don't have to. I'll go fix it myself. I need to. I won't learn otherwise."

Leo leveled a look at her. "The sooner it gets fixed, the better. I know a thing or two about coyotes and if they really want to get in, they'll find that hole."

As much as she wanted to be grateful, Belle kept herself guarded again. Distancing herself might have been the best remedy at a time like this, but something inside kept pressing her forward. That something urged her to accept him and his help no matter the consequences. "I don't think I could pay you right away," she said hesitantly.

"Consider this as payback for running out on you the other night. Believe it or not, I do have manners. I just didn't show them the way I should have."

Belle didn't want compensation for his behavior. She wanted explanations. But, maybe if she played her cards right, she could get the answers out of him. "All right. I've got some fencing materials in the shed behind the barn and you should have all the tools in there that you need." She smiled. "I guess I don't have to give you directions either."

Leo grinned and nodded. "I'll get right on that," he said just before he checked the clock on the wall behind her. "But, before I do that, we're going to lunch."

Her eyes were fully round now. "Lunch?"

"Aye. You know, that meal you eat in the middle of the day between breakfast and supper?"

A giggle fought its way to the surface, and for once, she allowed it. He knew how to make her forget her fears. He brought out the playful side that she kept buried with everything else she didn't think anyone wanted to see. "I brought my lunch, thank you."

"Save it for tomorrow. I want to treat you."

This couldn't be the same Leo that practically snubbed her, nor was he the man who had taken refuge in her barn. If anything, he was a little closer to that guy she ate with at the diner. He was a man of many faces and just as many secrets.

"I can't leave for very long," she said. "I only get a half hour lunch. That's hardly enough time to go somewhere, order something, and eat it."

"Why are you making silly excuses?" he asked, leaning in and whispering as if they were discussing surreptitious plans, his eyes dancing with unfounded excitement.

Belle mirrored him, ignoring all caution. "Because you told me yourself that you weren't interested in a second try."

A corner of Leo's mouth curled up. "You remember a lot, don't you?"

"More than I'd like," she sighed. "I don't appreciate being played, Leo."

"I'm not playing you," he replied with complete sincerity. "But I'm not asking for a second chance either. I don't want to start over, but continue where we left off. I'm asking to treat you to lunch, fix your fence, get to know you more, and we'll see where it goes."

Belle wanted to believe him so badly. "I think you know quite a bit about me, but I know hardly anything about you at all."

Leo nodded, as if he understood exactly where she was coming from. "You're thinking it would be fair if I gave a wee bit, then?"

"It'd be more than fair."

He sat there, staring and looking at her for what seemed like a century and as far as Belle was concerned, he could stay there even longer if he liked.

"You have a deal. In fact, let's do this. I'll let you get away with lunch plans, but I'll go mend your fence and do some work around the property. We'll have dinner together when you get home and I'll answer your questions."

"All of them?" she asked, hope laced in her words.

He chuckled. "Maybe not all of them, but most."

Belle drove up to the house and saw Leo's motorcycle parked near the porch steps. The way her insides felt, she was ready to turn the truck back around and go anywhere other than home. But she forced herself to see this through, even if it wouldn't last.

All day, it took every ounce of her self-control not to wonder about this change of heart and those scars on his arm. Leo wasn't telling the whole truth and Belle had a feeling that she wasn't going to learn what she truly wanted to know. So far, Leo had shown himself to be like a clam. He'd open a little and then snap shut when she least expected it.

She'd never admit how scared she was to let him in again. To let him charm her with those blue eyes and convince her that they could really move on and be friends – or more. But something she had read once about anxiety echoed in her mind. The same biological sensations of nervousness were nearly the same as excitement.

But excitement meant hope, and hope meant hurt in the end. It always did. Belle didn't know how to hope like this. If everything went well, this could really be something good, but how could she let go?

She grabbed the two large pizzas from the passenger seat and brought them inside. Unsure of how long it would take him to fix the fence, she changed into her farm boots and went outside to feed the animals before it became too late.

The three horses trotted up to her, expecting a meal and a rub-down. The sheep began their usual loud, obnoxious chorus of bleats and groans. The chickens, who were by far the most skittish of her livestock, fled from Belle as she entered the barn.

While she shoveled fresh hay into the wheelbarrow and brought it out to the feeding troughs, Belle watched for Leo on the horizon. The cleared acres of rolling hills, broken up by patches of trees here and there, stretched on far out of sight. If the gap in the fence was far toward the back of the lot, she'd never see him. That didn't keep her from trying.

After dumping out a hefty portion of feed for the sheep and tossing a few handfuls of corn into the chicken run, Belle went to look again. Upon seeing no speck of motion on the horizon, she made up her mind to be brave. It was her property after all, and she deserved to know exactly where the breach in the fence had been.

Before she could change her mind, Belle quickly saddled Chestnut, her brown and white mare, and rode her way along the fence line to find him.

Mindful of her sore ankle, Belle rode her horse for the first time in what seemed like ages. Between work and taking care of her farm, she hardly found any time to enjoy the spread of land her father had left her.

The sensation of the cool breeze playing in her ponytail and the exhilarating sense of freedom made her grin and spur her horse faster up and over the hills. Only the sound of Chestnut's panting, her hooves thumping against the ground, and the whipping of wind against her ears grounded her to the earth. If it weren't for the destination, Belle would have been tempted to feel liberated by this ride.

Then, she saw Leo working on the piece of broken fence in the distance. She raced toward him until he became more than just a colorful dot in the landscape. Beside him was the small tractor towing a flatbed trailer filled with posts and rolls of fence wire.

He was in the process of reconnecting a section to the post when she rode up and swiftly dismounted. He turned to her, his face dotted with sweat and a bit of dirt on his nose where he might have rubbed his hand earlier.

"You shouldn't be riding with that twisted ankle," he scolded, trying to put on an apathetic air when she could hear the worry in his voice.

"I've been riding since I was old enough to walk," she said. "I know what I'm doing."

He shot her a look that made her giggle and she came up beside him. He had certainly been working hard, and it showed in the mantle of dark, water-logged fabric around his collar. Belle inwardly remarked that he didn't stink of rancid body odor. In fact, his masculine scent seemed to be magnified.

"Do you need a hand?" she asked, eager to explain away why she had come out to check on him.

Leo hammered a nail with surprising precision. "I think I've got it."

Belle brushed her foot against a tall weed beside her like a bored child as she caught her breath. "You said you used to do farm work?"

"Aye. I've done a lot of different jobs over the years," he said as he pulled out another long nail from the box at his feet.

"Like what?" she asked, remembering the deal they had struck before he left the bookstore.

His powerful shoulders shrugged. "A lot of things."

Her silence induced him to turn and he chuckled at the perturbed look on her face. "I promised you the truth, didn't I?"

"Yes, you did," she purred playfully before sitting herself on the flatbed. "Let's start with your first job. Was it here or in Scotland?"

Leo turned back to his work, but she could tell that he struggled with his answer. Was it really that hard to talk about himself? "I left Scotland when I was fourteen. My first job was with my great-uncle in Brooklyn. He owned a hardware store and I started working there after school when I was sixteen. He didn't pay me, of course. Why should he?"

Belle listened through the noise of the hammer driving in the nails, totally hinged on every word. For a girl who had never traveled outside of Arkansas, Brooklyn and Scotland might as well have been on the other side of the world.

"When I was eighteen, the bank finally gave me the money that my parents had left me, and I headed west. I've moved around from place to place. Boston, Richmond, Charleston... It was easier to find work in the bigger cities, but over the years, I found out that I prefer the smaller towns. I've done everything from framing, construction work, flooring installation, warehouse foreman, ferryboat operator... I worked in a harbor once, and that was fun. I like the ocean."

Belle grinned and crossed her fingers that he'd keep talking. His deep voice chased away every bit of fluttering in her stomach, leaving her feeling like herself for the first time in so long. Why, of all people, did he have this effect on her? Why not Ivy, Pastor Kendall, or even Mrs. Johnson. They were all nice, polite, and showed that they cared. Yet, she gravitated toward this nomad. Why? What was it about him that made her so undone?

She wanted to know more. Why did he leave Scotland? Did it have something to do with his parents? He mentioned that he had gone to live with another relative and money that was willed to him. Where was the rewind button when she needed it?

"Cutting lumber is pretty new to me, but I've enjoyed it. I'm only pissed that they're not giving me as much work. They didn't tell me that the job wasn't permanent. Things may pick up in a few months, but after this week, I'll be out of work again."

Her heart sank into her shoes. "What will you do, then?"

Leo drove the last nail into the post and stretched out more of the fencing to the next, the box of nails pinched between his fingers.

"Don't know. Blanche told me I could stay for free for a month or so until I could find more work, but I don't want to bum off her charity for too long. It wouldn't be fair."

Belle hopped down from the flatbed and followed him. Unsure of what possessed her to do it, she hastily began with, "You could work here."

Leo froze and stared with a completely blank expression.

"I mean, I can't pay you a lot," she quickly continued. "But there's so much to do and it'd help me out a lot. You said you worked on a farm before, so you're definitely qualified. I'd just have to – "

"Stop."

She did, standing perfectly still as if one move would put the whole world off kilter. She'd said too much – again. It was too forward of an offer. He must have seen how thoughtless it had been. Belle knew she couldn't pay him much. Mr. Johnson helped her for practically nothing and her job at the bookstore was just enough to pay the utilities. The animals paid for themselves, so where could she possibly get the money to support Leo, when she could barely support herself?

Oh, God, please don't let him clam up again. I just want to help. That's all.

But her silent prayer wasn't needed. Leo's eyes were no longer focused on her, but to the patch of ground between them. She followed his eyes and saw something curled in the grass. The orange and brown diamond designs along its scaly body gave it away.

She had seen copperheads before on her property. Although they never came close to the house, she recalled a calf had once strayed too far from the herd and was bitten on the leg. Her father had to call for the local vet to take care of the wound.

Belle shivered and held her breath, as if that would help. The snake's body slowly unfurled from its coil and she could see its unblinking, beady eyes staring at her. Its forked tongue flitted, tasting the air.

Leo slowly let go of the fencing and turned with his hammer raised. Before Belle could say anything, he had the serpent pegged to the ground with the edge of the wooden handle. The tail writhed and rolled, still very much alive.

Taking the chance, Belle skittered backward and out of its striking range. "Are you going to kill it?"

Leo stooped down to grab it. "Nah. I'll just toss it beyond the fence." With his thumb pressed just behind its skull, he dropped his tools and let the harmless end of the snake wrap around his forearm.

"You act like you've done this before."

A grim smile touched his lips. "A few times. Come look. I've got it, so it won't bite."

He took a few steps toward her and Belle resisted the urge to jump back. She'd never seen a copperhead up close before, and honestly never thought she'd get the chance. Its tongue continued to test the air and the slant of its brows made it look angry. It was no wonder the serpent had always been associated with the devil, even though there was nothing in Genesis to suggest the association.

With a shaking hand, Belle reached out and touched the slick skin of the reptile.

"See? Not so bad."

She met Leo's gaze and felt a burst of heat radiate through her core and course further south. The shadows cast by the nearby forest gave his face just the right tint that made the gray of his eyes pop in the light. He was far too handsome to be real, but here he was standing in front of her, so close, and yet she felt worlds away from him. Those eyes, the sweat, the allure of everything he was and everything they couldn't be, was too much.

Belle took a step away and broke free of the spell he had unwittingly cast over her. "Only because you're holding it."

With a thoughtful slowness, Leo moved toward the fence and she heard a sudden rustling in the woods beyond when he tossed the snake away. "There are some things that don't look so horrible once you see them close up."

There was so much truth in what he said. Getting close to Leo meant also putting herself at risk, just like getting close to the copperhead. But, what was holding Leo at bay? Was anything? Could she risk slipping into that dangerous false sense of security?

She hadn't known the full extent of her feelings until just now, but she couldn't bring herself to take back her offer. How could she explain such a revocation? Or would he save them both and turn her down?

"You're braver than you think you are," he said as he picked up the fencing and supplies again. "You didn't even scream."

Belle bit at her lips and forced herself to watch him, as if to prove him right. "I'm not a screamer." As soon as the words came out, she wrinkled her nose. "Oh, I didn't mean it that way."

A deep, rumbling chuckle came from Leo and she felt her stomach tingle again. "It's all right. I know what you meant... As for the pay, I wouldn't need much. My rent is pretty reasonable. I wouldn't need more than a hundred a week."

Belle winced. "A hundred?... What if I fed you? You wouldn't have to eat at the diner every day."

Leo pinched a nail against the post and made a face as if that deal sounded more than agreeable. "That'd be a nice change. It's nice food, don't get me wrong. But, a man can only eat so many BLTs."

A smile graced her mouth. "I'm not that great of a cook."

"Neither am I," he replied and passed her a warm smile. "Do we have a deal?"

Belle let her mouth hang open for a moment, a secret battle raging between a timid yes and a resounding no. To agree meant more days like this. More days of watching him work and finding another piece to the jigsaw puzzle. To say no was to stay safe. Safe from those eyes, that body, the fatal attraction she felt for him, and everything in between. Saying no meant she'd never know what could have happened if she said yes.

So, as fear stole her voice, she only nodded.

Chapter 9

Leo let the cold water from the bathroom faucet wash away the specks of dirt from his arms, lathering the soap with a concentration he normally wouldn't have used for so simple a task. But he had to. If he didn't, his mind would wander and tell him to go downstairs and take back the agreement to work on Belle's farm. It wasn't safe, not by a long shot. So much could go wrong, and this one act of kindness had catapulted them forward once again. It was all too fast.

It had only been a few days since he made the deal with the darkness. The protection over both of them was still in effect. The demons and Michael couldn't hurt them as long as his blood payment held out. But who was to say if getting closer would drain its efficacy? Could a few weeks, or even a day, use it all up?

He splashed his face and rubbed until the skin became tinged with red. Only then would he look at himself in the mirror and take a deep breath to expel the worry. If becoming Belle's employee, temporary or not, would bring the darkness closer, Leo would just make another payment. It was worth it to see her again, to feel her skin touching his, and have those green eyes watch his every move.

It'll be okay, he told himself. *I won't let them hurt her.*

One benefit of working so closely with Belle lay in the fact that now he could get to know her in ways that he never could from a distance. If this social anxiety was truly crippling, Leo wanted to help her walk again without it. He wanted to heal her, to understand. He wanted to study every aspect of this mental illness and free her of its chains somehow. Having been a captive of his own problems for so long, he needed to free someone else in turn.

His gaze wandered through the bathroom, taking in the articles that spoke volumes about her private life. Tiny brown bottles of essential oils wrapped in colorful labels, sat upon the sink vanity with a half-used lavender-scented candle beside it. The gallon of chamomile bubble bath soap next to the clawfoot tub was nearly empty. A radio sat next to it, and as he predicted, the music CD inside played soft, relaxing jazz and piano compilations. The disc looked as if it had seen better days. The overflowing hamper indicated that she hadn't gotten around to doing the wash in quite a while, but one set of clothes lay folded on the toilet seat. He recognized it as the pair of pajama pants and Longhorn shirt he had seen her in the first night they met. Makeup, perfume bottles, deodorant sticks, body spray, and other feminine beauty products littered the other half of the countertop, which told him how much effort she poured into looking her best every day.

However, the bathroom itself was less than tidy, with mats of hair gathering around the base of the cabinet and a thin layer of dust in those neglected corners. Leo remembered what she had said earlier that day about not having enough spoons to take care of those chores and responsibilities. Cleaning must have been one of them.

It all proclaimed one truth. Belle spent so much time taking care of herself that everything else fell to pieces. One thing he hadn't seen, which both puzzled and encouraged him, was the absence of any pill bottles. Either Belle kept medications stored somewhere else or she had avoided using them altogether. While some could cope with life without the help of medicine, others could not. Leo didn't know whether to be glad that she hadn't resorted to pills, or to be worried that she really did need them, and her pride convinced her not to take that controversial step toward recovery. While he could appreciate her efforts to hold it together, Leo knew she couldn't live like this forever.

He dried off and stepped into the upstairs hall. All three doors to the other bedrooms remained closed, barring his nosiness, but the walls yielded far more for his curiosity. Pictures, old and fairly new, hung in a collage, all in an assortment of different frames. Grayscale photographs of the farm, of family reunions, newspaper clippings from the Levi Gazette, pencil sketches of old men in vintage duds, and color Kodak moments from Belle's childhood were all there, a feast of history and heritage.

His attention focused on the pictures with Belle in particular. One showed her as a child, smiling and splashing in a kiddy pool. Another during a birthday party, her little cheeks puffed out as she blew out the candles on the cake. Others featured her with a man, whom he presumed to be her father, and only one where she stood beside a woman who also bore the same emerald eyes. The one thread that linked them all was that smile. The genuine, heartfelt smile of a child who knew nothing of fear or anxiety.

Leo wanted to see that girl again.

The creak of the stair treads alerted him to Belle's approach, but he didn't care if she caught him staring at the picture of her playing in the mud with a potbellied pig.

"Oh, please don't look at those," she laughed. "Some of them are kind of embarrassing."

Leo only smiled and shook his head. "No, they're great. This is your da?" He pointed to the man with the dark beard and striped tie, standing on the front steps of a white church.

She nodded as she came close. "Yep, that's my dad. And my mom." Then she gestured to the one photo near the bottom of the collage he had noticed before.

"She's a little misplaced, don't you think?" he wondered aloud, peering at the woman who passed on much of her beauty to Belle.

"Not really."

The curtness in her tone said enough. Belle didn't value her mother as much as she did her father. After the speech she had given the other day, he couldn't blame her.

"If you don't mind me asking, why would you live with your da if your mum was still around? Don't the courts usually give full custody to the mother?"

And just like that, Leo had stepped into a minefield. He looked to Belle and saw the tightness in her face, the way her enticing lips dipped into a frown. Instead of blasting him with honesty or some remark about prying, she lifted her chin and cut her eyes at him. "If you don't mind me saying, I think you're trying to throw the scales out of whack."

"Scales?" he questioned, slipping his thumbs into his pockets.

"You haven't told me enough about you. You have to tell me a few things before I tell you anything else."

Leo chuckled and looked heavenward. "You're going to hold me to that, aren't you, lass?"

"Absolutely." That frisky smile returned, and Leo was almost compelled to tell her anything as long as she kept it. Of course, the more he told her, the less likely that was to happen. His story wasn't exactly a pleasant one.

"Well, I'll start by saying that if that were a picture of my mum, and if this was my wall of photos, it'd be right in the center." Leo tapped a blank space between two central photographs to make his point.

"You and your mom were close?"

Fighting the tightness in his throat, he nodded. "A lot closer than I was to my da."

There were days when he could still hear her buoyant laughter or smell the ghostly scent of her discontinued perfume. He remembered how she would bake cakes when she was happy and how, in that last year, she had stopped baking altogether. No one could read a bedtime story like she could, and no one sang more beautifully than she did. If anyone could personify an angel, it was his mother.

"Why is that?" Belle asked, pulling him away from those haunting memories.

Nostalgia gave way to bitterness when Leo remembered his other parent, the one who was never around and drank away his problems. Of course, it only passed them on to everyone else in the house when the fallout came. It was his father's voice, yelling in the family room, that kept him awake on school nights. The particular stench of his pipe smoke still turned Leo's stomach to this day. There might have been good days, but they were few and far between. When everything went to hell, there was nothing good in his home.

Leo found it harder to maintain his smile, even for Belle's sake. "He wasn't a nice man. That's all."

"I'm sorry to hear that... I told you before that my mom wasn't very encouraging, but I saw that it wasn't just me. She was just as condemning of everyone else. A real judgmental type. I didn't want it to rub off on me, ya know?"

Yes, Leo knew about that all too well. "Aye, I understand... It was the same with me and my da. I didn't want to be like him, so I tried to avoid him while growing up."

What he wouldn't have told her was how he saw a piece of his father rear its ugly head every so often. When he faced the darkness, when he beat up Drake, when the man at the bar attacked him, all of it harkened back to those early years in Scotland. The broken glass, the bruises, the excuses...

"You had sort of alluded to your parents... that they aren't around anymore."

There wasn't exactly a question in there, but Leo heard it anyway. He had thought talking about his late great-uncle in Brooklyn and his inheritance would be relatively harmless. It was a lot easier than explaining what happened in Scotland and why he could never go back.

"They're gone," he said, forcing his voice to stay even and empty of emotion. "That's why I went to live in Brooklyn."

"I'm sorry to hear that too..."

He could handle his own sorrow, but he couldn't bear to hear it from anyone else, especially her. Leo looked to her and met that tragic, sympathetic stare. For her, he would forget about the past. Just for a while.

"Did you pick out a movie?" he asked, steering the conversation to the present.

As if forgetting where she was, Belle's lashes fluttered and she flicked her hand toward the stairs. "Yeah, it took me a while, but I found an old VHS of a movie I think you might like... I hope you'll like it, anyway."

He followed her to the living room, and he saw the thin, cardstock casing on the coffee table. On the cover was a threesome, a young woman in the middle escorted by two men with the title of "*Sabrina*" written in careful cursive above their heads.

"You said you didn't know who Audrey Hepburn is, so I thought I'd make you watch one of my favorite movies of hers. And I just got a meat-lovers and plain pepperoni pizza. I wasn't sure which you'd like."

Beside the empty VHS case were the two pizza boxes. "You thought this through, didn't you?" he asked, the restrained smile ringing clear in his question.

"It's what I do. I overthink." The laugh she gave was at her own expense as she made her way into the kitchen. "I know you ordered water at the diner, but do you like coke? The water from the sink isn't that great."

Leo stood near the sofa, hands still slung in his pockets. "Whatever sort of bevvy you have will be fine."

"Bevvy?"

He let out a huff of amusement. "Sorry. A coke is fine."

"Oh, well, it's actually Dr. Pepper. Coke is kind of a blanket word for soft drinks, I guess."

If traveling across the states had taught him anything, it was that Americans could be so picky about their verbiage. "Dr. Pepper is fine. Bevvy is my blanket word too."

Belle busied herself with pouring them both a glass, grabbed paper plates from the cabinet, and returned to the living room. "You can sit down. It's not a terribly long movie, but I think your legs would get tired after a while."

He could have laughed at himself. "Right. It's just been so long since I've been welcome in someone else's home. Forgot how to act."

"You made yourself pretty comfortable the other day when you made up that ice pack for my ankle."

Leo didn't want to think about that day or the night that followed, but she had a point. "I think I was too in the moment to care if I was overstepping."

Belle smiled as she pushed buttons on the clicker to get the movie to play. "I know what you mean. It takes me so long to get comfortable in someone else's house. I never know what's okay to touch or not to touch."

And there appeared another facet to her condition. However, could Leo even consider that anxiety? What stranger wouldn't feel awkward in another person's home? He took a seat at one end of the sofa and helped himself to the pizza, while Belle kept herself distant on the other side. Though he could have breached the few feet of space between, he stayed where he was, respecting her limits. If she wanted to sit any closer, then she would have.

"So, what's this movie about?" he asked as he looked to the case on the table. He could see the resemblance Belle had mentioned in the diner. The shape of their heads, the slant of her eyes, the high cheekbones, and her slender nose all matched the short-haired actress. If Belle's lips were painted red and her dark brows grew in a little thicker, they might have been taken for sisters.

"It's about a girl who's not too pretty, but has a crush on her father's employer's son. She goes away and comes back a woman and both her old crush and his brother fall for her. The whole movie's about the two brothers basically trying to win her for different reasons."

Leo smirked. "And this is your favorite movie?"

Belle giggled. "Okay, not my all-time favorite in the world, but just my favorite with Audrey Hepburn."

"Then what's your favorite movie?" he asked as the black and white credits began their classic fade-in-fade-out routine to waltz music.

Belle's expression twisted as if she were thinking hard on the answer. "It's hard to say... My dad raised me on the classics. Movies with Fred Astaire, Cary Grant, Grace Kelly, Clark Gable, Carol Lombard, Maureen O'Hara... Elizabeth Taylor was great."

"Those sound like actors, but what movie?"

She let out a groan and looked to the ceiling. "I don't know if I can pick... Okay, I really love *His Girl Friday*. The banter in that movie is terrific."

"And what's that about?"

Belle motioned to the television. "One movie at a time, buddy."

He laughed and took a bite of his pizza. "It hasn't even started yet."

"Fine," she huffed. "It's about this former news reporter who's about to get married, but her ex-husband – played by Cary Grant – tries to lure her back into the business with a murder case. I like it because the girl's pretty confident and back then, it was a big deal for a woman to be a reporter. A high stress, intense kind of job like that wasn't really a woman's field back then and she loved it."

Leo angled himself, so he'd be facing her more than the telly. "Do you like it because you want to be like her? Confident and daring?"

Belle's smile failed her a bit. "Maybe. But, like I said, I enjoyed the banter. Cary Grant's a brilliant actor... Oh, it's starting."

The credits disappeared, displaced by the portrait of a vast estate. Leo listened to the tender, husky feminine voice that set the scene of the Larrabee family and the heroine whose name lent to the title of the movie. But, his attention wasn't focused upon the story of the two brothers and the chauffeur's daughter. His eyes and ears were riveted upon Belle alone, watching her from the peripheral as the movie went on. She never noticed how attentively he studied her. He saw her slip off her shoes and curl her legs up on the sofa cushion, how she delicately bit into the pepperoni pizza and managed to stuff four slices into that small stomach of hers.

Even in the silence between them, he could feel a bit of that ease return. His tired muscles relaxed and once he ate his fill, he sank lower into the sofa. It had been so long since he had taken the time to just breathe and enjoy something without the fear that it would be ruined. The room wouldn't be swept up in a chill, the shadows would stay where they were, and the sharp claws of despair couldn't reach for him here. If only it would last forever.

When it came to the scene where Sabrina snuck into the garage with the intent to kill herself with the carbon monoxide poisoning, Leo sighed. "There are easier ways, but I guess she wouldn't have known better."

Belle's eyes snapped to him, but said nothing. No doubt her mind went straight to the scars on his arm. If he could have predicted her reaction, he would have worn a long-sleeve shirt or concealed them some other way. Anything to keep her from worrying or asking questions that he couldn't answer.

"I'm hoping it gets better, but why exactly do you fancy this again?"

Though it was far from diffusing, Belle was distracted from his previous comment. "It's just a sweet romance. It does get better, I promise. That guy," she said as she pointed to the older brother, "is really the better man for her, but she doesn't see it right away."

As he watched Humphrey Bogart's character carry Sabrina up the spiral staircase to the apartments above the garage, Leo realized that already. "He's certainly giving her the time of day, unlike the other brother."

Belle nodded. "He does. He... Well, you'll just have to keep watching."

Leo passed her a soft smile and did as she asked. But the longer he watched, the less he understood. Yes, it was a romance, and he supposed all women liked romances to some degree, but why this one? What was it about Sabrina that made Belle favor it?

Did she see some of herself in Sabrina? The only daughter to a single father, a less than talented cook, a woman in the steel jaws of unrequited love... He thought of Drake and how she had declared that she didn't like him at all. Had that always been the case? Or, like Sabrina, had she fallen for the wrong man?

He looked to Belle, who was completely engrossed in the movie. There must have been a reason she liked this sappy but tragic love triangle.

The answer came when Sabrina wrote a letter to her father.

"I have learned how to live. How to be in the world and of the world. And not just to stand aside and watch. And I will never ever again run away from life, or from love either."

And that was it. Belle wanted to be Sabrina, but not the timid little nobody they met at the beginning of the film. She wanted to be the grown up, sophisticated Sabrina who returned to Long Island with a little dog and trunks full of fashionable clothes. More than that, she wanted to be that confident and poised.

If only Belle knew that she didn't need to take two years off in Paris to become that girl. She was already that charming, sweet lady in black and white with the glittering smile.

Time passed, the movie played on, and the pizza disappeared between the two of them. The outside world became dark as the sun sank from the sky, leaving the room in shadows.

When Sabrina and Linus were on the sailboat, he heard the faint nasally snore coming from beside him. Belle's head leaned against the back of the couch, her eyes closed and totally asleep. Pale light from the television danced across her serene face. She had said earlier that day that she hadn't gotten much sleep the night before. And now, as the late evening turned into nighttime, she probably couldn't keep her eyes open much longer, movie or not.

Leo smiled, picked up the empty paper plate near her knees, and stacked it with his own. He wondered how easy it was for her to doze off on any other day. Did she stay awake for hours before finally succumbing to sleep, or did she use those essential oils to calm her heart and mind for just a few moments? What did she dream about? Did she have nightmares like him? Or was it all black and void?

In the movie, Sabrina had said, "*I always thought you walked alone.*"

Linus replied with, "*A man never walks alone from choice.*"

Wasn't that the truth? Leo closed the lids to the pizza boxes, being ever careful not to make too much noise. The last thing he wanted to do was wake her. Let her dream of the Paris the actors talked about in the movie. Let her dream of a place she might have the courage to visit one day.

He slid the throw blanket from the sofa and draped it across her. Belle stirred for only a moment to snuggle deeper under its warmth, interrupting the series of light, feminine snores. Leo watched her for a little longer, listening to the movie, but not paying much mind to it.

A piece of him, the piece that had no respect for Belle – and it was an incredibly tiny piece – wanted to stay beside her. He wanted to watch her sleep, even if it meant depriving himself of the same rest. He wanted to carry her up to bed and lay her down on the mattress, so he could take his place next to her.

But another part of him, the one he trusted far more, told him to leave while he still had the will to step out the front door. He had done his job for the day. The animals were ready for the night ahead and the fence had been mended, so no coyote could trespass. And

Leo would do his part and lock the door on his way out. No coyotes or bad decisions would ruin Belle's sleep tonight.

Belle jolted at the sound of Rocky crowing from the chicken coop. Her alarm clock would have been an easier wakeup call, and through the dizziness, she wondered how early it was. He normally didn't start belting out his morning screams until seven or eight. It was then she realized that she wasn't laying in her own bed.

She cracked open her eyes and looked around the living room, her vision a little fuzzy at first until she could adjust. Bright sunshine slanted through the gauzy curtains, giving the house a cozy, warm glow. The rough throw blanket had slipped down to her waist and sometime in the night, she had stretched out to her full length across the sofa.

Her heart skipped when she scrambled for her phone and realized she had awoken an hour late. The pizza boxes were gone from the coffee table, as were the glasses. The only remnant from the night before was the empty VHS case for the movie. The TV had turned off by itself long ago.

Belle pushed herself up and stretched out her aching back muscles before typing out a quick text to Ray to explain her tardiness. Although she wasn't completely certain that she would be late, she wanted to have the text ready in case she was.

Her head pounded as her blood pressure slowly caught up with her. With it came the memory of the night before. Had she passed out during the movie? Did Leo put the food and glasses away? Glancing into the kitchen, she saw the empty cups by the sink and the pizza boxes sitting on top of the trash can.

God only knew what Leo must have thought of her now. She didn't see him out, didn't bid him a goodbye or anything. Had he been the one to put the blanket over her, or did she do that unconsciously?

Belle tried to comb out the tangles in her hair when she heard the soft rumble of an engine. For a moment, she was sure that it came from the main road and didn't pay it much mind. Old trucks and tractors putted along the country road all the time. It was only when the roar became louder that she realized it was coming up to the house.

Throwing the blanket aside, she bolted from the couch and peaked out the window beside the front door. Leo rode up her dirt drive, his motorcycle kicking up dust behind it. She gasped and quickly jumped away. She must have looked like a mess with her slept-in makeup and dark brown mop for hair. It had been ages since she slept in her day-clothes and didn't shower. She'd be out of commission for at least an hour, trying to get herself presentable.

The engine stopped and she could faintly hear the scraping of boots as he dismounted. Belle covered her face with her hands, trying to think through her grogginess. Then came the thud of those same boots on the porch steps.

She started when he knocked on the door and she went completely still. What could she say? Could he even wait an hour for her? Should she ask? He had fed the animals in the evening, but never in the morning. There was so much more to do and she would have to explain it all, but could she talk to him from behind the door?

"Belle?" he called.

She grimaced and suddenly wanted to cry from embarrassment. She paused and knew she had little choice.

"Hey," she replied rather feebly. "I... I fell asleep on the couch."

Even through the door, she caught a bit of his chuckle. "I know. You were tired. It's understandable."

She hugged her middle and tried to breathe as she let herself be totally honest. "It was rude, I'm sorry."

"It's not a problem... Are you going to open the door?"

"Uh... No. I look like a mess. I've got to get ready for work, but I know I need to show you around the barn... Can you give me just a few minutes?"

The pause coming from the porch made her cringe and squirm, but Leo finally said, "Aye, I can wait. I don't need to be at the lumber yard for a few more hours."

Belle released the breath she had been holding. "Thank you! I'll be as quick as I can."

Not wasting another moment, she darted toward the stairs and hurried to the bathroom. There was no time for a shower, but she at least had to change.

After dousing herself in the most fragrant of perfumes, she hoped she didn't smell like a girl who hadn't showered in over twenty-four hours. She tugged her brush through the tangles until her scalp hurt and whipped it all up into her usual tight ponytail after applying some dry shampoo. Washing her old makeup off and applying fresh mascara and powder foundation took the longest, eating up another ten or so minutes.

Once she put on a clean pair of pants and new blouse, she rushed downstairs and skipped across the kitchen floor as she put on her boots. Leo was already waiting by the barn, a few hens clucking and pecking at the bugs in the yard around him.

He smiled to her, and the world finally began to slow down. Belle's steps slowed and as hurried as she felt, as bad as she believed she looked in that moment, none of it seemed to matter. She let out a long breath and suddenly the morning didn't seem so bad, despite its rough start.

"Sorry about that," she said as she approached, the chickens scattering away from her in a flurry of flapping wings.

"It's all right. Did you sleep well?"

The question had been posed to her many times by almost everyone she knew, but something in the way Leo said it made her believe he actually cared.

"It's been a long time since I camped out in the living room, and I think I understand why now." Belle rubbed at her back for a little emphasis that made him laugh.

Together, they walked to the barn and she unlatched the newly installed lock. "So, every morning, you'll need to let the horses and the sheep out of their pens." To her immediate left were the four horse stalls, only three of which were occupied. "This is Snow, Maggie, and Chestnut." She pointed to the white Andalusian, the brown quarter horse, and the black and white Shire horse, respectively. "I normally just give them a bunch of hay from that stack over there into the trough outside. They typically graze during the day, so I'm not too picky about their food, but I do give them some pellet treats in the evening. They're in a bag at the end of the stalls. Their stalls need to be mucked out every morning and the water trough filled too."

Belle opened Snow's stall and began to lead her out while Leo took Chestnut.

"Do you have a favorite?" he asked. She noticed that his gaze had swivel back around to the old beat-up Volkswagen toward the back of the barn. The canvas tarp covered everything but the tip of the iconic Beetle nose and fogged, round headlights. Would he ask about that too?

"What is it with you and my favorite things?" she asked with a giggle.

"To know a person's favorite things is to better know them as a whole, I think."

Belle opened the gate that led to the separated horse pasture and let Snow loose. The mare tossed her head and pranced across the field to stretch her legs, while Chestnut casually ambled a few paces and waited by the empty feeding bin.

"Well, if I had to pick one, I guess Snow is my favorite. My dad gave her to me when I was eighteen as a graduation present."

She looked to see Leo admiring the spirited Andalusian.

"Chestnut's the eldest and pretty mild. If any of the kids in town want to learn how to ride, they usually come here and ride her. Snow's fun, but only for experienced riders."

Belle turned and went back into the barn to retrieve Maggie, the largest and stockiest of the horses she owned.

"And this one?" Leo asked when she came back to the pasture.

"Maggie was my dad's horse. She's a little too tall for me to mount, but he let me name her. I thought she looked like a magpie bird with her white boots and the stripe down her forehead." Belle reached up and ran her hand down the marking. "She's good for riding, but I think my dad wanted to use her for plowing one day, if we ever started growing stuff commercially."

She let the Shire horse into the pasture, and like Chestnut, she waited for her breakfast. Snow, too, finally made her way back to the bin and nudged Belle's shoulder with her gray nose. She ruffled the horse's silvery hair before gesturing toward the wheelbarrow sitting near the barn doors. "You can use that to bring the hay bale over."

Leo nodded in understanding. "I used it the other day to feed them."

Belle smiled. "Right. I forgot you've done this before."

"It's all right. Anything special I need to do with the sheep?"

"Their pasture is fenced off right behind the barn and they've got their own feed, but they're pretty content with the grass." She followed Leo as he made his way to the holding pen toward the backside of the barn. The ewes made their usual ruckus upon seeing them. "The only special thing you'd need to do is give them some supplement feed and I keep that over there." She gestured to the fifty-pound bag of nutritional pellets.

"And do they have names?" he asked, leaning over the pen wall made of pallet wood.

Belle grinned. "It's a little more complicated than the horse names." She unlatched the gate and the walking masses of wool scuttled out to follow their shepherd through the back doors of the barn. "My dad used to name all the sheep after flowers or plants. So, there's Sunflower, Lily, Daffy – short for Daffodil, Tulip, Iris, Daisy, Marigold, Jasmine, Azzy – short for Azalea, Heather, and Chrysa. The one ram we named Butch."

Leo laughed as she named them off, pointing to each of the Finns and Suffolks. "Butch doesn't sound like a flower."

"It's not, but he certainly acts like a Butch." She opened the gate and they all filed through as if they instinctively knew what was expected of them. "Don't turn your back on him for a minute. He's known to ram legs."

"How the he-... How can you tell them apart? They all look the same."

Belle and Leo leaned against the railing of the fence. "The Suffolks, the ones with the black heads and legs, all look pretty much the same, so I put color markings on their ear tags to tell them apart. The Finns all have different colorations. I don't expect you to learn their names. They don't really respond to them. The names are more for my sake than theirs."

"Which one's the ram again? None of them have horns."

"The Finn rams don't." Belle pointed to one particularly large Finn with a brown mask and slightly lighter wool coat. "That's Butch. He's a little bigger than the rest, but just because he doesn't have horns doesn't mean he's harmless. They can mind themselves pretty well, but if any of the twelve are missing, you'll need to check the fencing. They manage to get their heads stuck a lot if they're trying to reach for some grass on the other side. Oh, and all the Finns are pregnant, so you'll need to keep an eye on them. They're not due for another month or so, but if you notice they're acting weird and a little more cuddly than usual, let me know. There'll be a lot of little lambs running around, just in time for the holidays."

Leo nodded. "Duly noted. And the chickens?"

Belle looked to the coop built on the junction between the two fenced-off pastures. "You can just throw some feed in the run and in the yard, and they'll be fine. For a treat, you can give them some of the corn from the barn, but make sure it's out of reach when you're done with it. They'll peck straight through the plastic if they want to."

"And the eggs?"

"No one should give you any trouble except maybe Rocky. He's the striped rooster. He might try to chase you out, but he's all... what's the term you used... bum and parsley?"

Leo laughed once again, sending a wave of warmth through her, despite the chilly autumn wind.

"They lay pretty much anywhere, so you'll have to watch your step when you get in the run."

"Anything else I should know?"

Belle could think of a thousand things she wanted him to know, both about the animals and about her, but time would stop for no one. "All the tools and stuff are in the shed, as you saw yesterday. You can help yourself to whatever's in the house. I don't drink coffee, but there's plenty of tea. If you need to wash your clothes at all, the washer and dryer are in the kitchen. The dryer can be temperamental, so it may take a few rounds to get your clothes completely dry.

The stove's a little touchy too, because I need to replace the ignition for the range, but it works fine otherwise."

Leo turned to gaze up at the two-story, blue farm house and massive barn. "This place is just full of character, isn't it?"

"My great-great grandfather built the house and the barn, and it might be due for a remodel, but I don't have the heart to change anything." She turned to admire her home as well, her hands still gripping the fence rail behind her. "It's been passed down to all the men in my family ever since. I'm the first girl to inherit it."

There wasn't a chance she would admit that she worried for its future. She still had plenty of years left to find a man, marry him, and have a son of her own that would look after the farm. Considering what a wreck she'd be in the dating world, she doubted it would ever happen. Leo might have been the first and only man she had ever opened up to, but she refused to hold onto the hope that he could help her continue that legacy. There was still time to botch the whole thing up, after all.

"When I was out mending the fence," Leo said, "I couldn't help but notice that you have so much land, but not a lot of animals. There's so much more you could capitalize on."

"There is," she replied with a sigh. "Problem is that I'm only one girl and I may be able to pay you some to help do the chores, but taking care of a big operation like I'd want would require me to stay home. I can't do that. I could probably live off of soup and Ramen, but not forever."

"What would you need to make it happen?"

Belle met his squinting gaze and felt her mind go blank for a few beats before she could list off her plan. "Well, I'd probably need to get more Finns, for a start. They lamb almost twice a year if I have enough rams, but with that many sheep, I'd need a bigger barn and a sheep dog, and I can't even begin to think about how much that would cost. I'd also love to get a stud in here to maybe breed horses, but I'd need more stalls. There's a neighbor up the road who makes good money at boarding horses, but again, I'd need a bigger barn or a stable just for that. It's a lot and I know it won't happen in my lifetime."

"It could happen if you made your mind up to do it." Something in Leo's voice made her stiffen and pay attention.

Over the years, before her father passed away, she had occasionally sat down to make some sort of comprehensive plan to make that dream a reality. This farm, as small as it was, might have been one of the best things she had. The record of her family history was written in every piece of wood, upon every patch of grass and dirt across these acres. To help it flourish to its full potential, as it had been in her father's childhood, had been a goal since she began to see its true value as a young woman.

But then real life got in the way. The economy wasn't as it used to be, her father's medical bills piled up on the kitchen counter, and the only way to pay them was to sell what stock they had and scrounge on what little they could afford.

Belle had given up on a lot of it in favor of the safe and secure. But she saw that hope again in Leo's eyes. Maybe, just maybe, if she was brave enough, she could make it happen.

She gave him a weak smile and shrugged. "One day."

Chapter 10

The dent in Leo's savings would be well worth it when he saw Belle's eyes light up. A morning and afternoon spent tinkering with the old Volkswagen Beetle in the barn cost him precious hours he could have wasted sawing logs at the lumber yard. This was a full job and Leo already called out from work to devote all his time to it. His supervisor made it clear that if he wanted the extra pay, it was his, even though he was only scheduled for half a day. He could make up the time he asked off, but it'd take weeks to earn back what he dropped at the car shop in town.

His curiosity had gotten the better of him just before locking up the barn for the day, and after finding the keys already in the ignition, he had given the Bug a start. Little happened, but from what little that was, he could come up with a few theories of why it had been abandoned in the barn for so long. After replacing the fuel lines, changing the fluids, charging a new battery, checking and patching all the leaks, and installing a new belt over the engine, he was going to put in a starter relay kit under the back seat. If this didn't work, he didn't know what would. He'd have to bite the bullet and buy a new starter motor.

All for that smile, that light that shone behind her eyes whenever she talked about the old farmhouse, the barn, or the animals. If he could help Belle in any material way, it was this.

And as he thought through all the roadblocks to her happiness, he lost track of time.

"Leo?"

He stood up and knocked the back of his head against the door frame, forgetting that he had taken the Bug off the jack that he also had to buy. He hissed at the pain and held in the obscenity on the tip of his tongue. Plenty had come barreling out of his mouth over the last few hours as he continued to adjust and tweak lines, hoses, and wires. But for Belle's sake, he would say none in her presence.

Rubbing at the back of his head, he turned around and saw her staring with wide eyes and parted lips. She would have seen a man covered in car oil and dirt, probably a straw of hay or two sticking out of his hair, and the back seat to the Volkswagen propped up against the sheep pen. No doubt she had questions.

"I'm just making some modifications to the starter," he said after clearing his throat. "You see, the battery sits under the back seat in this model and the juice has a long way to travel before it gets to the motor. I'm putting in a few wires that'll shorten its path. I'm hoping that'll help it start up a wee easier. It's usually fine when it's all brand new, but she's over forty years old and a connection like that will – "

"Have you been doing this all day?" she asked in disbelief as her eyes wandered about his workspace. Empty oil containers, tools, and torn open packages littered the hay-covered ground.

"All except for when I went into town for the parts. I got a bite to eat and came back."

Belle stepped closer and he could see that bit of excitement sparkle in her expression once the shock wore off. "The last time that thing started was... I think I was four or five at the time... You think you've fixed it?"

With a sigh, Leo went into the long list of everything that was wrong with the engine and connections when he first took a look at it. Whether or not she understood any of it, he wasn't sure, but it must have helped to explain himself, just to prove that he knew what he was doing.

"I was a mechanic in Alabama for a stretch and I used to listen to the old men talk outside my great-uncle's hardware store. I learned a few things."

She smiled. "Obviously... So, can it start?"

Leo leaned over and finished up what he had been doing with the relay system, then slid into the front seat. "Let's see. You have to hold your tongue just right."

He turned the ignition and the engine rolled over for a couple of seconds before finally cranking to life. It was loud, but he expected that. But, oh, to see Belle jump on the balls of her feet and clap her hands in childlike glee was far more satisfying than anything he had ever known.

He leaned his arms on his knees outside the car. "Now, I still want to troubleshoot a few things and it needs new tires, but I think it'll be a keen cruiser when I'm done with it."

Belle hurried over and invited herself into the passenger seat. She closed her eyes and must have been enjoying the purr of the engine, because for the longest time, she didn't even move.

"This is probably the best thing that's happened to me for weeks," she said over the roar. "You just don't even know..."

Leo watched her and was sure he could say the same. But her weeks were equivalent to his years. "I'm glad I could help. I know you didn't ask, and don't even think about paying me back for the parts. This was something I wanted to do."

Dazzling green eyes fell on him and he wished he could have captured that look of total gratitude and... would he dare think it was something more?

"Thank you, Leo. I really appreciate it. After the day I've had, this was nice to come home to." She sank a little in the seat, the cracked and torn leather creaking beneath her.

"Bad day?" he asked as he cut off the engine, so she wouldn't have to yell. After the day he had too, he was ready to just sit and listen to her, no matter what she talked about.

She sighed and smoothed back the flyaway hairs on her head. "Not any more than usual. My boss was being particularly testy today and some kid came in and tore down almost the entire self-help section while his mom was looking for a book, so I had to clean it up. On top of that, I forgot to pack my lunch this morning, so I had to run across the street to get some food, but the line was long and I didn't have enough time to wait, so I'm starving."

He dimly heard the rumble of her stomach in the silence and had to smile at the timing.

"And on top of all of that, Ivy asked me to go to the movies with her tonight."

Leo spun the keyring on his oil-smudged finger as a confused frown crinkled his brows. "You don't want to go?"

Belle shook her head and the only thing that could have made her look any more pathetic would be an exaggerated pout. If she wasn't in such anguish, he might have laughed.

"Then, don't go," he stated as if it should have been the obvious solution.

She snorted. "I can't just not go. I told her I would."

"Why would you agree to going if you didn't want to?"

"Because it's the polite thing to do."

He stopped spinning the keys and held them in his fist, pretending to think over what she said. "I think the polite thing would have been to turn her down with an honest explanation – that you had a bad day – and then stay home to take one of your lavender bubble baths."

"It's chamomile bubble bath."

Leo couldn't help but smile. "Okay, a chamomile bubble bath, then... You've never told someone 'no', have you?"

Belle's lips curled inward as if she were clamping them between her teeth. That was answer enough for him.

"All right," he continued. "So, what you do is send Ivy a text and bail."

"I can't bail!" she exclaimed. "She'll think I'm a flake."

"You're not a flake. You're taking care of yourself." Leo pulled out the dirty rag from his jeans pocket and made some attempt to wipe off the dirt and oil from his hands. "Give me your phone."

"What? No!" she cried. "I can't bail on Ivy. I'll just... I don't know. I just have to go."

"You don't have to do anything, Belle." He noticed her visibly shake and he wasn't sure if it was because of the stressful situation she had gotten herself into, or maybe the way he had said her name. "Why does it matter if she thinks you're a flake?"

Belle shrugged and looked down to the fidgeting fingers in her lap. "You may think she's a tart, but I want her to like me."

"Will one canceled plan ruin your friendship with her?" he asked, stuffing the rag and keys away. Belle didn't answer him. "Real people don't get that mad over something like this. She sprung it on you today, didn't she?" After receiving her meek nod, he continued, "So, it's not like you told her weeks ago that you'd go, and this should have been written on your calendar or something. It was last minute, it fell on a bad day, and you have more important things to do."

Belle looked up, a sad softness touching her gaze. "What's more important than spending time with a friend?"

Leo leaned in and hoped that she could hear the severity in his tone. "Taking care of yourself. You'll burn out otherwise. Today, it's an impromptu movie date. Tomorrow, it's agreeing to do something else you don't want. It'll keep mounting and you won't get a chance to breathe. I've seen how much of those smelly oils you use, and it's too much."

"It's fine," she insisted. "I've been doing this for a while now."

"And that's the problem. You're too used to pouring out yourself to everyone and you're running on fumes. You're just like this car. If you go too long without maintenance, you'll stop working and break down. You need to learn how to truly recharge and not just recoup enough to make it through to the next day. It all begins with knowing when to say no for your own sake." He held out his hand. "Give me your phone."

They locked eyes for what felt like a blissful eternity, drowning in the lush greenness of her gaze. It was like getting lost in a field of tall grass with the sun warming his face. He could have stayed lost forever, but Belle finally broke down and gave him her phone.

"I'll let you approve the wording, because you'll know what sounds more like you." His fingertips left tiny impressions behind on the touchscreen, but they could be easily cleaned off.

"What would sound most like me is not sending a text like this at all... Why not a phone call?"

"Because you don't have enough spoons for a phone call, do you?"

Belle allowed the corners of her lips to turn up in a tiny smile. "I never do."

After a few thoughtful moments of constructing a short, sweet apology, he angled the phone her way for approval. She critiqued a few words and then hit the send button.

Belle let out a groan when she took back her phone. There was no turning back now, no chance to retract what Ivy would soon read, and Leo hoped that she would thank him for it... Eventually.

"What if she does get mad?" she whined, obsessively watching the phone for the reply.

"So what if she does? Does it matter that much to you?"

Belle's throat worked and he could tell that she wasn't taking this well. "I... Okay, it sounds really conceited, but I really do want people to like me. I don't want them to think I'm a snob or too good for them."

In his book, she was better than all of them. He might never meet everyone in town, but he could already tell that Belle was leagues above the rest. She had a kind heart and a pure soul, even if she didn't believe it in herself. He knew that, because if he had been caught in anyone else's barn, they would have turned him away or truly called the police for breaking and entering. Belle didn't. Despite her fears, she let him onto her porch and into her life. For that, she was a saint, if to no one else, then to him.

"I can't see how anyone would think that."

The phone vibrated twice to indicate she had received a new message. No fingers could have tapped on it quicker. He leaned over to read, "*Totes fine. Take care. SYL.*"

"What?" he questioned, his face pinched with confusion.

Belle let out a sigh and leaned her head against the seat. "It means it's totally fine and she'll see me later." Her eyes snapped in his direction. "Do you think she's just saying that to be nice?"

"No."

"Did that sound passive aggressive to you?"

Leo smiled at her. "It sounded like rubbish to me, but only because I didn't understand the lingo. It sounds like she understands, and she wants the best for you."

She took in a shuddering breath and let it out slowly, the way she had before when her nerves were fraying at the ends.

"Come on," he said. "I think there are some leftovers in the fridge, so you don't have to cook, and afterward you can unwind in that bubble bath. Sound good?"

Despite herself, a pleasant smile lit up her face. "Yes, that sounds fantastic. Tea, too?"

"Until you hurl."

At that, she laughed and took another calming breath. "Thank you."

"Anytime. I'll clean up these tools, take care of the animals and be out of your hair before the sun goes down."

Panic flashed in her eyes and she quickly looked to him. "What?"

Leo had already slid out from behind the wheel to start picking up his mess. "It won't take me long."

He could hear her struggle to get out of her seat and walk around the hood of the Bug. "You're not..."

The silence was only broken by the few bleats from the ewes outside and the rustling of the hay as he collected the tools.

"You need time alone to refresh," he finally explained. "I'm not going to stay when you obviously need me to leave."

How he wished he could have, though. He wanted to eat those leftovers with her, maybe watch *His Girl Friday* with her, and help her to unwind. Of course, his way to help her unwind might have been far different than what she had in mind.

He didn't look back at her, didn't glance up to see her expression, lest she see the twinge of pain in his own. It would be torture to drive back to town, but it had to be done... Unless she asked him to stay.

She didn't. He heard her footsteps cross the barn and stop at the doors. "Thank you again... For the car and the text and all."

He let the tools fall from his hand and into the wooden caddy he found in the shed. "Like I said, anytime."

And then she left, taking with her the oxygen he needed to breathe and the presence that made him feel more human every day.

He fixed the car. Belle sunk lower in the tub until her knees broke the surface and her chin just grazed the layer of bubbles. *I can't believe he actually fixed the car.*

The rhythmic crashing of waves set to a soft piano score echoed off the ceramic tiles. Lavender, peppermint, and chamomile suffocated the air with peace and soothing aromas. Candlelight flickered across the walls of the darkened bathroom. Even while the stiffness in her muscles ebbed away under the hot water, Belle felt a heaviness in her chest.

Why did he do that? He must have spent a lot of money on those tools and the parts, but he didn't want to be paid back. He could have been doing anything else, but he decided to spend all that time on an old Volkswagen. Her family had practically given up on it since her grandfather passed, and like everything else on the farm, it was an heirloom. It sat in the back of the barn as a reminder of better times, but now, it was well on its way to being mobile again.

Instead of rehashing every embarrassing and harrowing detail from her numerous mild panic attacks at work, Belle's mind lingered on those last few moments of the day she spent with Leo. She replayed all that he said, all that he had done for her. And when it came to the part about him leaving so she could have her alone-time, Belle felt like crying. Without him, loneliness battered her spirit until she almost couldn't breathe. Alone and lonely were two completely different things, and she knew the difference well. She knew this was loneliness, because it was what plagued her for months after her father died.

Two cups of herbal tea and all this home-spa treatment had done almost nothing for her. All she could think about was her mistake. Why hadn't she asked him to stay? She wanted him to. She might have not wanted to go to the movies, cook, go grocery shopping - which she refused to do after the events earlier that day, or be around people in general - but Leo wasn't just a person. Not anymore. He meant so much more and he didn't drain her like the others did. Even when he pushed her out of her comfort zone one more time to send that text to Ivy, she wanted him around a little longer.

Only with him could she feel like herself. She could put down the mask, because she knew that he had seen her worst and still came back. To him, she could voice her fears and her anxieties, and not feel judged. But his opinion mattered above all else, which was why his words rang the loudest in her ears now.

You're too used to pouring out yourself to everyone and you're running on fumes. You're just like this car. If you go too long without maintenance, you'll stop working and break down. You need to learn how to truly recharge and not just recoup enough to make it through to the next day. It all begins with knowing when to say no for your own sake.

She knew about self-care. Nothing he said was new or revolutionary, but the firmness in his voice and earnestness in his eyes made her listen. Maybe everything she did just masked the symptoms, but could never eradicate the cause. But what would happen if she stopped drinking her calming tea or lighting these candles every evening? What if she never had to take a bubble bath again, unless she just felt like it? How would a day without anxiety feel? How nice would it be to come home and not collapse in a heap like formless jelly?

Was it even possible?

Belle had a choice to change, but change seemed even scarier than staying stagnant. If she just took baby steps, then maybe she could build up that courage she dreamed about. She had been waiting for the moment when God or some event would just dump it all into her soul. There would be no transitioning period, no growing pains. She'd just wake up one day and not be so afraid to be herself.

Leo made her realize that wasn't going to happen. Even though God worked miracles, she would have to meet Him halfway. Starting with her choices. Letting go of her preoccupation over what people thought of her would be her first move.

With a deep breath, she resolved to put it all into motion tomorrow. Belle would turn away from the things that didn't give her peace, and start asking for the things that did. Leo, being one of them.

Chapter 11

Leo smelled the cooking bacon before he heard the sizzling drifting through the open living room windows. He stayed on his bike, the engine off, and waited for a moment, wondering if he should go in or not. He was worn-out, a little grumpy, and the only reason he didn't want to see Belle now was because he didn't want to infect her with his foul mood.

The decision was made for him when the front door opened and Belle stood in the threshold, her shirt splotched by patches of flour and one rogue dapple on her cheek. He was sure this version of her was cuter than when he saw her standing on the porch in her Longhorn shirt.

She smiled and struggled to hold in whatever excitement she felt upon seeing him. All of it was a little too much for Leo, who hadn't had a speck of coffee yet. The coffee maker in Blanche's shop had broken, and since he was making an effort to conserve money now, he didn't go to the diner. He thought he could slip onto the farm, do the chores and leave to go to the lumber yard before Belle had a chance to see his bad-tempered Scottish side.

"Good morning!" she called, her eyes bright and cheerful as they had been in the barn the previous evening when the Volkswagen came alive again.

"Mornin'," he grumbled as he kicked out the stand and leaned his bike on a solid patch of dirt.

"I was just cooking breakfast."

Leo took a deep whiff of her efforts and nodded. "I can tell." He wanted to avoid stepping onto the porch, but his stomach had other plans. "Any chance of brewing coffee with that breakfast?"

Belle's brows pinched together and that smile turned sour. "No, I'm sorry. I stopped drinking coffee a long time ago. It wasn't good for my nerves."

He should have seen that coming. She even mentioned the day before that she had no coffee in the house, but he failed to remember it. With a sigh, he closed his tired eyes, trying to order his thoughts without the aid of caffeine. His brain was masked in a thick fog of grogginess.

"Have you eaten already?" she asked, a dusting of worry piquing in her voice.

"Not yet," he replied as he rubbed at the back of his neck.

Belle waved him forward. "Maybe a little food will help wake you up."

It was worth a shot, so he followed her in and closed the door behind him. The aroma of bacon had almost masked the faint burnt stench and he wrinkled his nose. "What else are you making?"

Belle hurried into the kitchen and a groan preceded the clattering and scraping of a frying pan. A whirlwind had swept through the kitchen, leaving behind dirty pots and pans, mixing bowls, measuring cups, and splashes of white flour across almost every surface. Leo found it hard to understand why the white powder had managed to stain the dark wood cabinets.

"Well, I was trying to make pancakes, but they just aren't turning out right."

Leo watched her take the pan from the stove and slip a burnt flapjack into the trash to join several others. She still had half a bowl of batter to go through. Taking a quick look at the consistency of the slop and the high blue flames on the propane range, he understood.

"You've got the heat too high. They're burning on the outside, but I'll bet they're still soupy on the inside." To make his point, he reached into the trash, bypassing the broken eggshells to pinch one of the discarded pancakes. It broke open and a bit of the batter oozed out over his fingers.

Belle looked to the pancake and then to her stove in amazement. "I've never really cooked on any other heat than that."

"Maybe that's why you're not so bully of a cook. It's not you, it's the stove." He reached over and turned down the dial. "Let the pan cool a bit..." He picked it up and moved it to an unused eye. "... and we'll give it another go." Then, he looked to the frying bacon. The strips popped and sizzled as they should, but they too would be burned crispy if she didn't flip them soon.

Practically pushing her away from the counter, Leo reached for the pair of unused tongs in the caddy by the stove and began turning the bacon, making the oil fizz and splatter him. He barely felt the sting on his bare arms.

"Well, look at you!" she laughed. "I thought you said you couldn't cook either."

Leo shrugged and once more turned down the heat of the eye, making the leaves of blue flame shrink. "I was a short-order cook for about three weeks in a diner in Tennessee. I wouldn't say that makes me a good cook, but I know a few things about breakfast foods."

Belle crossed her arms and smiled. "Learning a little more about you every day."

Taking the rag, he began to clean off some of the flour from the countertop. "I'm sure you'll run out of things to learn. There isn't much to me."

"I'd beg to differ," she replied, joining him in the job with her own towel. "I think you're being pretty modest. You've been solving a lot of problems around here since you came."

He wouldn't reply to that remark. He couldn't. Not without confessing or alluding to the truth. She might not have seen it, but trouble followed everywhere he went. He might have worked in a mechanic shop and a diner, but he didn't tell her about how those businesses almost failed because of him and the darkness. The influx of customer complaints that didn't have anything to do with him, money vanishing from the boss's office, employees suddenly quitting or acting out on the job. He was cursed and almost everything he touched became infected in the same way.

Now was different. Now, he had the extra deal with the darkness, and they were safe for the time being. He suspected that the demon would show up in another week demanding payment. Leo only wondered if this next installment would finally kill him.

"Something wrong?" she asked, leaning to meet his drooping eyes. "Or are you just tired?"

Leo blinked hard and shook his head to clear it. "Just a wee stroppy, that's all... I mean tired. Sorry."

"I think I've got some caffeinated green tea if you'd like to try it." Belle dropped the rag and went to rummaging through the drawer where she kept all of her herbal tea bags and packages. "It'll have some caffeine. Maybe not enough as coffee, but it might help."

She had already pulled out a mug and snatched up the empty kettle to fill in the sink before he could answer her.

"I'm going to guess you got some much-needed rest last night," he said, flicking the flour off his rag and into the trash.

"I did," she answered over the running water as she filled the kettle. "I took that bath you recommended and totally burned down one of my candles while I slept."

"You shouldn't have a candle going while you sleep," he lightly reproached.

She tossed a pretty smile over her shoulder. "It's not like the flame's going anywhere. It's one of those big ones in the – "

"You can't take any chances." Leo didn't mean for it to come out so biting, so snappy. But it did, and that's what he had been trying to avoid. He knew what candles she talked about. The flame might not have jumped off the wick, but it could crack its glass container and let the hot wax spill out onto the tabletop. It was a freak accident that could have been avoided... if he hadn't been there.

He turned to see Belle's face frozen in wonder and timidity, as if he had just screamed at her for something else more serious. He cared, and that might have added fuel to his fire, but she didn't deserve to be scolded. Not this early in the morning.

"I'm sorry," he said, making an effort to soften his tone. "I didn't mean to come across that way... Is that a trigger for you?"

Belle shut off the water and returned to the stove, her steps slower. "Maybe a little... I'm not used to people raising their voices at me, anyway. I do my best to avoid pushing that far." She turned on the gas and took his advice to heart, using only as much heat as she needed to boil the water in the kettle.

Leo forced patience upon himself and hung both the rags on the rack before facing her. "Please tell me what your triggers are – if you know them – so I won't hurt you."

His quiet plea made her go still. A touch of something akin to shock came to her eyes, but with a quivering of her lashes, it was chased away.

"I do know them. Some of them, anyway." Belle tore open the green and black package containing the tea bag. "Truly upsetting someone is a big trigger. I hate to offend, even if I'm right, which is why I stick to the golden rule."

"Always wear matching socks?"

His sly joke brought back the smile and she giggled. "No. If you don't have anything nice to say, don't say it at all... Another is being in the way. I hate being in people's way, even if I can't help it. I'd rather just completely avoid a tight spot or leave the room entirely if I know I'm going to block a path or something. I feel like a waste of space a lot of the time, so I also tend to talk a little fast, because I think that I need to get as much out as possible before someone loses interest or gets annoyed with me. That's where rehearsing comes in handy. I never want to stutter in a conversation if I can help it."

Leo leaned his hip against the counter and watched her poke and move the bacon around in the skillet. "What else?"

She thought for a moment and then pointed the tongs at him. "Interrupting."

"People interrupting you?"

"No, me interrupting others. If I need my boss's attention, but he's busy talking to someone else, or even looks remotely occupied with something, I'll stand and wait to be acknowledged. I don't want to butt in and risk getting yelled at."

"Even if it means waiting for thirty minutes?" he asked, his eyes riveted upon hers. Belle continued to push the strips of bacon around in the grease, as if that would help them cook more evenly.

"Well, thirty minutes, no. I'll probably go off and do something else and wait for a better time. I also hate feeling like I have a thousand things to do, but no time to do them in. I'll literally sit and just stare at all of it and I can't decide what to do first. So, often times none of it gets done, which isn't good either."

Seeing that her pestering the bacon was only a redirecting habit, Leo reached out and gently took the tongs from her. Their hands, for a moment, touched in more than just a grazing way. He felt the effect of it deep in his core and in the electricity that revitalized him better than any strong cup of coffee. Green eyes found his and stared before he finally broke away to give his attention to the bacon.

"Crowds and strangers, I assume, are on that list?" he questioned, reaching for the plate she had set aside before he arrived.

"Oh, yeah," she replied, recovering rather quickly. "Changed plans too. Anything that comes up unexpectedly, like when Ivy asked me to the movies. I wasn't prepared for that, and so I didn't have enough time to adjust." The kettle whistled, and she jumped to pull it off the eye, so she could prepare his tea. "Loud noises too," she continued. "A sudden banging noise, a shriek, that sort of thing."

"What about thunder?" Leo pulled the bacon from its greasy bath and slid it onto the plate.

"Actually, thunderstorms are pretty calming. I was really enjoying the night we met. I was on the couch with my book, my tea, and every time the thunder rolled, I'd stop and just take it in."

A frown formed between his brows. "I'm sorry I came and ruined it."

Belle shook her head, making her ponytail swish with the movement. "You didn't ruin it... I mean, at the time you kind of did, but... I wouldn't have..."

The tea was steeping, the grease popped in the heated pan, and he could barely hear the songbirds outside. They might as well have been the only ones in the world in that brief several seconds while they stared into one another's eyes. He wanted to memorize that look on her face, that eager and yet shy expression that told him enough.

Belle was an open book to him, so full of feeling and emotion that it couldn't help but leak out in everything she said and did. But that was only when they were alone. When they met in the grocery store, everything had been screened. It was like the bursting well had been boarded up. Leo wanted to rip those barricades down, so they could never be used again. Such passion, such feeling should never be dammed up behind civility. Let it all come tumbling out, because that was the only way she could be truly free.

The few inches he had moved downward were nearly imperceptible, and he was glad for it. Not a single rational thought existed in his mind when he wanted to kiss her.

Belle looked away and grabbed for a small plastic container near the backsplash. "Do you want sugar with your tea?"

He wanted sugar on his lips, that was for sure. But he shook his head. "I'll drink it straight."

"Careful, it's hot." She handed him the steaming mug, her hand cupping the bottom, so he could grab the handle without risking another touch of their skin.

He took the bacon and his mug to the dinner table and cleared off a spot to sit while he watched her have another go at the pancakes. They sat in silence as he sipped the tea, but he no longer felt tired. Just being with Belle had cured him.

"So, do you have any triggers?" she suddenly asked, making him speculate if silence might have been one of those things that made her come unhinged as well.

The question, though understandable, wouldn't be answered as she wanted. "Nah. I don't have issues with crowds, I can normally navigate most social encounters, I can handle loud noises, and I don't often care if I'm in anyone's way."

"What about knives?"

He went rigid, the mug halfway to his lips. "Knives?" For once, he was glad she wasn't looking at him.

"I remember what happened at the restaurant. Ivy set down a knife and you asked her to take it away. And then your arm... with all those scars." She glanced over her shoulder, but by now he had recovered and took a long sip of the hot brew. "That's one thing you'll learn, I'm hyper-observant. I remember little things like that, mostly so I can replay them later and overanalyze... Bad habit."

Leo smirked. "Clearly. Knives are... I guess they're just attached with too many bad memories and thoughts."

Belle turned, a batter-coated ladle in one hand and the other bracing the counter. "Like what?"

His lips parted, almost ready to tell her the truth before he caught himself and thought on it. If he told her, what was the likelihood that she would turn him out? What if she became afraid of what he was capable of? How would that change everything – if it changed it at all?

In a moment of either pure trust or lunacy, he replied, "Along with being a mechanic, a short-order cook, and a million other things, I did prizefighting on the side. Nothing big. Just a few engagements here and there in the larger cities like Atlanta, Montgomery, New Orleans... I could earn a whole month's wage in one night if I played it right. I was good, but the kind of lads you meet in that part of town aren't the nicest. That's actually how I came to be in your barn. I got done with a fight in a town a ways off from here and the guys thought I cheated. How can you cheat in a fight? Anyway, they mugged me, took my shirt and what I had on my back. They didn't think to check my pockets, so I still had some cash, but no way to get around otherwise. That night, it was me against eight armed lads and I didn't have a thing to protect myself. I usually keep a knife for my own protection, but I trashed it some time ago. I had to use it... more often than I wanted to."

A bit of sympathy shone in those eyes he loved so much, and he wished he hadn't told her. But the damage was done.

"That explains why you could beat up Drake so easily."

Leo let out a huff and rolled his eyes. "Aye, and why I typically try to keep a leash on my temper... One of the only gifts from my da that I can't shake. A short fuse and a talent for a square go don't make a good pair."

"Did you think something was going to trigger you into using that knife at the diner that day?"

She always knew the right questions to ask, and as long as Leo was under her gaze, he was sure that he would continue to be honest. It was the least he could do in return. "I wasn't very sure of myself that day. I didn't want to take the chance... You need to flip the pancake."

Belle quickly spun around and hastily worked at turning over the flapjack. From where he sat, they were a perfect golden brown. Even if he had only been a short-order cook for a little while, he could tell by the smell of the pancakes when they were ready.

"You seemed fine to me," she remarked, this time keeping a closer eye on the pan.

Leo smiled ruefully to himself. "Maybe I've got a mask of my own... Are you working today?" he asked, setting his mug down so he could steal a bit of bacon from the plate on the table.

"Yes, but I've got time before I have to go in. The shop doesn't open until nine."

He glanced to the clock on the wall with its spindle array of bird breeds for each hour. "And the store closes at...?"

"Five, but I'll be going straight to church after I clock out, so I won't be back until really late. I might not see you this evening before you're done."

Leo paused in mid-chew. Church? Had she mentioned that before? It was a Wednesday. Didn't only devoted worshippers go to church on a Wednesday? He should have known. Her abhorrence to cursing should have been a big clue, but he thought perhaps it was a moral thing, not a faith thing. He hadn't expected her to be a Christian, but it made sense.

He swallowed what was in his mouth, so it'd be clear for him to speak, but he had no words. What could he say? Pray for him? Have fun? Don't go? Stay with him?

The giddy wiggling of her hips drew him out of his pensiveness. Belle displayed for him a perfectly round and well-cooked pancake. Not a single burned patch or discolored air bubble. "You want this one?" she asked, all smiles and proud of her accomplishment.

With a shake of his head, he motioned to the bacon. "I'll just eat this. Thanks."

Those enticing lips curled into an impish grin. "What if I wanted some bacon?"

"You might have to fight me for it," he teased, taking up another long strip and ripping off a piece between his teeth.

Belle giggled. "I think I'd lose that fight." The next several minutes were spent making up more pancakes – the majority of which would be saved for a later morning – and finishing off the plate of bacon.

The moment her old pickup engine stopped knocking against the hood, Belle could hear the soft piano music drifting through the open doorway to the sanctuary. A warm fluorescent glow streamed through the tall windows on either side of the building and spilled out over the front white stone steps. Mingled in with the melody was the unintelligible din of conversation. The evening sky was streaked with dark clouds floating almost stagnant against the bright gradient of orange to violet.

How she would have loved to just stay in her car and watch the sunset. As ready as she had been to turn over a new leaf, Belle wasn't ready to forsake the congregation. Wednesday night services had been a tradition between her and her father as far back as she could remember. Prayer meetings weren't as routine, but Sunday and Wednesday had always been marked out on their calendar. Any and all engagements on these days were canceled in favor of fellowship with the other members of the church.

For now, Wednesday nights wouldn't change, out of respect for her father. But Belle could already feel her insides twist and knot at the thought of hugging everyone who greeted her when she walked through those doors.

Steeling herself with a few big breaths, she stepped out of the car and took the plunge up the walk to the big oak doors. The crowds on Sunday were consistently bigger, but the few dozen believers who stood around the pews were still too much for her.

She knew just about everyone she saw, or at least knew of their connections with the older members of the church.

The old men who formed the Men's Breakfast Club stayed toward the back of the sanctuary, their numbers made up of farmers, ranchers, and small shop owners in Levi. Their wives, who sewed and orchestrated every bakery, fundraiser, community event, and monthly pot luck social, occupied one corner of the pew section toward the front. Their airy, withering voices were nearly indistinguishable when spoken in the same room with their boisterous spouses laughing and grumbling about one complaint or another. Younger couples stayed close together within their own social groups, their kids chasing one another around the pulpit at the front of the hall.

The only bit of Pastor Kendall she could make out in the congregation was the top of his head peeking out from the wall of parishioners talking and asking for advice. The more visible of the spiritual duo was his wife, who sat with the other older women as if she were the matriarch to them all.

Belle gripped her Bible a little tighter and made her way to her usual spot near the center of the room, where she and her father had sat countless times. Out of respect for the late deacon, no one ever sat beside her, which allowed some kind of social buffer she could be thankful for.

Before she reached her customary place, a cry rose up from the women's circle. She turned and saw Miss Georgina wave a slim hand at her to come closer. *Here we go*, she thought as she put on her mask and smiled to the old ladies who looked her way.

Without hesitation, Belle took a place by Miss Georgina and allowed herself a hug, her arm wrapping around the bony shoulders of the woman who had organized the fall festival hay rides for the last twenty years. Belle would never forget the smell of that rosewater perfume the old lady had been using for as long as she could remember.

"I'm so glad you've come tonight," Miss Georgina said. "I have a favor to ask you."

"Oh?" Belle tried to sound eager, though she inwardly screamed. The matronly woman had a unique talent for roping anyone and everyone into doing favors for her. She wasn't sure if it had to do with the fact that Miss Georgina was a well-respected member of the congregation or because she had a special way of making one feel obligated to help, and then guilty for not helping.

Whatever would come next out of her ruby red lips, Belle would have to be strong.

"Margie's husband is sick, and she doesn't think she'll be able to teach Sunday School this week. I remember you did a fabulous job last April when Marge had to leave for the birth of her fifth grandson, so I thought maybe you'd be ready to do it again. I know it's terribly sudden, but we can always count on you to be here on Sundays."

The screaming in Belle's head rose to a fever pitch. She remembered that Sunday so vividly that she still had nightmares about it. Six and seven-year old rug rats running around, the screaming, and the incessant questions. Belle had kept up a brave face, but for the first half of the lesson, she could barely get them to behave and sit still. Of course, she wouldn't tell any of the parents that. They saw their kids as perfect angels and she wouldn't ruin that fantasy. Besides, she was too afraid that one of the mothers would scold her for either not having a firm hand with her child or for trying to deface her little sweetheart's character.

Belle would have rather given a live oral presentation to a million strangers than teach Sunday School again. But when she hesitated to give Miss Georgina an answer, a few of the other ladies close by began to do what they did best. Encourage.

"You did an amazing job last time, Annabelle."

"My granddaughter always asks if you'll be teaching her class again one day."

"Tommy just loved when you read to them. You should do that again."

"You have such a way with kids, just like Margie."

"I think you'd make an excellent Sunday School teacher one day. God's given you a gift, I'm sure of it."

Her heartbeat quickened and if this were a cartoon, Belle's head would be spinning like a top as she tried to catch up. They all believed in her, or at least it seemed that way. But they could have been saying all those things just to make her feel easy about filling in for

Miss Margie. And Miss Georgina had a point. She never missed a Sunday, not even when her ankle was sprained last weekend. She didn't have plans, didn't have a life – and they all knew it. There was no reasonable excuse, and if she came up with one, then she'd have to skip Sunday church for the first time in years.

Her only plea for not teaching Sunday School was because she flat-out didn't want to. Even if she prepared for weeks in advance, she'd never have enough spoons for that again. That first time nearly drove her to call out sick on the following Monday and her fingers were wrinkled when she soaked in the bath for over an hour.

Just then, a couple a little older than Belle came in the door with their two children in tow. Lindsey Harper was known for her way with kids and her two daughters were probably the best behaved of their age group. Her husband worked on an oil rig and if he came with her to Wednesday service, it was likely he'd be here for Sunday too, and he would be able to look after their girls while she taught.

That was the idea, anyway.

Belle tried not to appear as hopeful as she felt. "I would love to, but I think Miss Lindsey might do a better job. She told me before how she used to teach Sunday School in Bentonville before they moved here. Why not ask her?"

Miss Georgina craned her long, wrinkled neck to look in Lindsey's direction and those brightly painted lips widened into an even bigger smile. "I didn't know she used to teach Sunday School!"

She then proceeded to wave and beckon to the young mother. Belle let a slow, easy breath glide out from slightly parted lips. It was a close call. Weeks ago, she would have granted Miss Georgina this favor and hated herself for it later. That was before she met Leo, before she began to realize the price of her own sanity and emotional health. Yes, she could have done it, but it would have cost her so much happiness, so much peace. And although she felt a little guilt when

Miss Lindsey beamed at the offer, knowing it was made because Belle had bailed, she couldn't regret her decision. It wasn't a deadpan no, but it was a step in the right direction. With Leo's help, she just might have been well on her way to taking control of her life again.

Chapter 12

Leo propped his foot against the bottom rung of the fence, his arms folded over the top rail and eyes fixed on the dusky, darkening sky. The sunset blanketed his stony heart, warming it until he almost felt alive again. He saw the sun go down almost every day. Why should this one be different? Was it the way the gauzy clouds were so fixed against the fading shades of gold and indigo? There was hardly any wind, making the whole scene look like something out of a painting. But no artist could capture this. Only human eyes could look upon it and feel it.

And for once, Leo felt it. Felt its freedom, its beauty, and the stillness of the farm as the animals had their dinner.

In a few moments, he'd have to bring in the horses for the night and he had to decide whether he would wait for Belle or not. He wasn't sure how long the church service lasted, but it wasn't as if he had anywhere to go. There was nothing for him back at the loft above the sewing store except silence and solitude. Being alone was the last thing he wanted, but was it what Belle wanted? After being around a bunch of holy folks, she might want to take it easy on socializing for one day. She still had her workday to recover from, too.

The soft smile that had unconsciously curled over his lips began to fade, knowing that even if he wanted to, it was a smart idea not to stay.

Once the coolness of night began to settle in, and the sun finally gave way to the moon, Leo moved toward the horse pasture to round up the mares.

Something stopped him before he could grab the latch to the gate. A chill swept through the yard, a wintery freeze with a touch of gloom that he knew had come too early in the season to be natural. He stood still, hand outstretched to the gate and listened. No sound. Not even the bleating of the sheep in the far field. The crickets had been silenced too, and he knew what this was.

He turned back to the barn and found it nearly encased in shadow, its outline clearly defined against the night sky, but shrouded in that murky, preternatural film. He knew what was waiting inside, and if he felt no obligation to keeping this property safe, he would have tried to ignore it.

Leo strode away from the fence and toward the open barn door. Inside was nearly pitch black until he turned on the string lights. The space was lit, but the tiny bulbs didn't burn quite as brightly as they should have.

Standing in the middle of the floor, almost untouched by the feeble lights, was the darkness. In all his pinstripe-suited malevolence, he stared at Leo with a look of annoyance and discomfort. That was unusual. The darkness always bore that wicked grin that told Leo exactly what he intended. This was something else, something worse.

"I'd tell you to leave," Leo said with his arms folded, "but I have a feeling it won't be that easy."

The demon raised his hands and clapped slowly. "Bravo. After all these years, he's finally figuring it out."

"What do you want?"

He lowered his hands to the front of his jacket and seemed to fiddle with the polished black buttons. "You're getting mighty comfortable with that lass, Leo."

"That's my business."

A bit of the darkness' true form blurred his outline and black eyes blinked into a shade of scarlet. "No, it's not just your business. That girl..." The mist collected back together as his voice leveled out again. "That girl will cause trouble for you, me, and your brother. I'm telling you to leave."

Leo's brow cocked at his disturbed speech. "Is this a warning?"

"I'm doing you and your brother a favor."

He barked a laugh. "Aye, right. I'm supposed to believe that? I can't remember a single time you've ever – "

"Listen to me!" the demon thundered, causing the rafters to tremble. His whole form seemed to flicker to the immaterial, just long enough to make Leo actually pay attention. The darkness pulled himself together and lifted quivering hands as he summoned whatever calm was left in his evil spirit. "There are things you can't possibly comprehend, things I can't tell you. If you stay here, there won't be enough blood payment to protect you. You're in the middle of a warzone and Matthew won't be kept away with a few cuts and bruises. This goes beyond you. Leave her and this town. If you stay, it'll kill you and Matthew."

He studied the darkness' face, so full of anger and fear that Leo was tempted to believe him. Only tempted.

"Matthew wants to keep me alive to make my life miserable. Neither you or any of your lackeys can kill me. I understand that much. As long as you're getting your payment, why should you care? As long as I'm willing to hurt myself to feed your sick appetite, you should want me to stay right where I am."

The darkness charged forward, a once proud and composed assailant turned a sniveling mass of pathetic merger between man and evil. "No, no, no. If you stay, I have to stay. If I have to stay, I will do everything I can to make you leave, because I don't want to stay. Staying means death for all of us. Blood payments won't keep this back for long. Do you understand?"

Leo took a startled step backward, glaring at the darkness that was ready to claw at his shirt in desperation. "Yer heid's full o' mince. You're not making any sense at all. What's going to kill us if we stay?"

More than that, Leo wondered what could possibly be higher than Matthew or the darkness that wielded that kind of power to destroy everything below it? Leo at least understood that he was nothing, but if the darkness was scared, then there truly was something bigger lurking out there.

A vile hiss slipped through his sharp teeth. "Like I said, there are things you can't know about. Just know that if I have to stay too, then we'll both be tormented, and when Matthew comes – because he will – then he'll be in danger too and both of you are too important to be sacrificed in this. I'll... I may not be able to kill her, but I can make this place a living hell for both of you. Don't think I won't. I don't care who tries to stop me. If I have to stay here with you, then I'm going to make the most of it... but I don't want to... Do you understand how conflicting this is for me?"

"Do you know how much I wish you were solid so I could deck you right now?"

The darkness slunk backward, the body of a man dissolving into that dark mist that was nearly blotted out by the electric lights. "Just do us all a justice and leave. That's all I'll ever ask of you."

That was a laugh. "All you'll ever ask? You ask for everything from me. You really think I'll do anything for you if it doesn't benefit me too? I know how this works. I'm not leaving. Not yet. You'll get your payment and I'll hold up my end of the deal. You just hold up yours."

The darkness seethed. "Oh, I'll hold it up, but know that whatever payment you give won't be enough to make up for the risks."

"The payment keeps you away and you don't want to be here, so what's the problem?"

The haze collected again, but the red eyes of the demon still gleamed at him. "You know how moths are attracted to flames? Well this farm, that girl, is a white-hot flame. The payment you gave last week would have lasted much longer if you had just kept away from her."

Leo narrowed his eyes. "You're drawn to her, so my payment isn't strong enough to keep you away, but you want to stay away for some reason... You want me to leave to save your own hide, but as long as I'm here, I'll have to give more and more payment to keep up our deal."

A sneer wrinkled his face. "That's a piece of it, yes. A mere human can never understand these politics."

And he could see why. Motivation seemed to have been thrown out the window. Now it was a question of physics, which Leo had never considered before. He knew the darkness had been tethered to him for a reason, but he had never given much thought into how evil could be pulled in one direction or another. Why should it want Belle so badly? And how much more payment would he have to give to protect her from whatever was coming? Or, like the darkness said, could his payment be enough? How much grander was this scheme in the demon's world? What other factors played into this?

"I'm not leaving... I'm not ready to."

Leo could see the torn expression contorted upon the darkness' face, how much he hated and yet enjoyed the prospect of being staked down in this future warzone, as he put it.

"Fine. If you won't listen to reason, I'll take my payment and go. But don't you dare forget that I tried to warn you. I told you death would come and it will, unless you leave."

He glanced to the old rusted sickle hanging on the wall. "Duly noted." He reached out with some hesitance and plucked it from its hook. The wood of the handle was chipped and worn, its curved blade just sharp enough to do the damage he needed. At first, he looked to his arm and the array of scars, and thought better. Belle would notice anything new there, now that she was on the lookout.

He leaned down and rolled up one of his pant legs. He took the blade and positioned it over the meat of his calf. The cut wasn't overly deep, but enough to cause some pain that would linger each time he stepped. "Feed off that," Leo said as he tossed the sickle away, hoping to avoid any further temptation.

The darkness drifted toward him and the shadowy fog encircled his leg, making it burn and ache all through his limb and up into his hip. Leo clamped his teeth and suffered through it until the demon was satisfied. Then, it vanished. The string lights brightened, dazing Leo with their intensity for a brief second. Hot blood trickled from the open wound and seeped into his shoes.

He swallowed hard and grabbed for one of the rags hanging over the horse stall door. Doing what he had done countless times before, he wrapped up the wound with his makeshift bandage and tied it off. Why hadn't it healed like the cuts on his arm? Leo half expected it to, but whatever force had patched him up before was inconveniently absent this time.

As he tested the stability of his injured leg, he thought over what the demon had said. If all those cuts from last week had only bought him several days, then how much time could this afford him? What was coming that put them all in such danger? And would Belle be safe from it all? He had to do what he could to protect her, but if it was one thing he had learned in this cursed life dealing with the devil and Matthew, if the demon wanted her, there was little force on earth that could stop it. Those gnarled claws would reach for her, but Leo had to stand in the way, even if it killed him.

Belle lay in her bed, buried deep under the covers. Rocky had crowed six times already, but autumn was fast approaching, and the dropping temperatures sent her hiding beneath the plush duvet. The electric heater was across the room and her bare feet would have to touch the cold wood floor. The very thought made her curl up and grip the edge of the blanket even tighter to her chest. The nearest pair of wool socks were well out of reach. The gray September sky bathed everything in a dreary light that would have put her to sleep if her restless mind wasn't pestering her already.

She thought of all the things she would need to do that day, including clean the house and balance the accounts. Most of the time, her day off was spent mired deep into some self-care routine to recover from the work week. But on this Thursday, her motivation had spiked. Most of those things she had to do, like sweep the floors and clean off the appliances, didn't seem so taxing as they would have before. Still, she didn't want to leave her comfy bed and snuggled deeper against her mountain of feather pillows.

That was until she heard the motorcycle rumble down the driveway. She pushed herself up and leaned to get a good view out the window, though the curtains distorted much of the outside in a frosty veil.

She just barely glimpsed the bike ride up to the house and slow to a stop. The cold and promise of a restful day could keep her in bed, but not when Leo was factored into the mix.

Thinking quickly, she stripped one of her pillows of its cotton casing and laid it on the floor beside her bed. Positioning her feet carefully, she was able to shuffle across the room to her dresser to grab a pair of socks. Donning them, she grabbed a knitted shawl from her closet and threw it over her shoulders. She'd have to act quickly before Leo dove straight into work.

Running on nothing but adrenaline, she rushed down the stairs and into the kitchen. On her way home from the church, she had stopped by the grocery store and purchased some coffee grounds and a basic French press. She didn't see the point in getting a massive coffee maker when she didn't drink the stuff anyway. So, instead of offering Leo a cup of tea, she had something more substantial to give him.

As the water in the kettle boiled, she hurried to peek out the living room window. Leo sat on the edge of the porch, his arms resting over his bent knees as if he were already waiting for something. At least he hadn't gone into the barn yet. It was then she saw the cigarette dangling between his fingers.

Her first reaction was surprise, and then concern. She didn't know that Leo smoked, but given everything she knew about him, it shouldn't have been so shocking. Out of all the people she had come into contact with over the years, Leo certainly stood out. A mechanic, blue-collar worker, Scotsman, prizefighter, smoker, and as hardcore as they come. But his tender side was what she craved. That man who took the tongs from her the previous morning with such tenderness that he might has well have been taking her heart with a single touch. She wanted more real, meaningful conversations like they'd had in the Volkswagen. She longed to hear him speak and breathe life into the silence of her life.

This went beyond fascination and Belle could feel herself being wholly given to it with every talk, every look and touch. She was pretty sure she would have gone to the ends of the earth for him, and she began to believe that he might do the very same for her. But why?

The kettle screamed and she rushed to prepare their drinks. A strong cup of English black tea for her, and a mug of unsweetened coffee for him.

It took a little finagling to get the front door open, but she stepped out onto the porch without spilling a drop. It wasn't so cold that she could see her breath blooming out when she talked, but it would be in a matter of weeks. The rogue thought came to mind, and she wondered if Leo would even be around by then. Unsure why she'd think something like that, she quickly shook it off and joined him on the top step of the porch.

"Coffee?" she offered, handing him the plain white mug - her father's old mug.

Fatigue and drowsiness was written on his face, just as it had been the previous morning. As if in a daze, he looked to the mug first and then up, blue eyes arresting her once more with their clarity and striking color. One corner of his mouth quirked up and he nodded.

With his free hand, he took the mug from her. Belle encased her hands around her own, letting its warmth leach into her palms.

"I got a tin of coffee last night, because I figured you might want some this morning."

He nodded and took his first sip of the scalding brew. His brows furrowed for a second and then he nodded. "Good and strong. Just needs a touch of whiskey and it'd be perfect."

Belle's lips parted at the comment, but she said nothing. Again, it shouldn't have been surprising. He was a man of the world and drinking should have been a given. To expect a saint would have been lunacy. And she would have berated herself for being so attracted to a man like him. But she wouldn't deny what her heart felt. Not anymore. Self-care might have involved rejecting what she didn't want, but it was also about taking what she felt she needed.

And right now, she needed Leo. She needed the company of another person that didn't come with conditions or baggage.

"Oh, I'm sorry," he mumbled, looking to his half-finished cigarette and then around for some place to put it out.

"It's fine," she said with a slight laugh. "Ivy smokes all the time on her breaks, so I'm used to it."

Though Leo didn't seem convinced, he let out a sigh and took another drag before blowing the acrid smoke upwards, so she would be spared its fumes.

"I didn't know you smoked," she remarked before taking a sip of her tea.

"Not often. Only when I'm stressed."

Belle tilted her head. "You're stressed?"

Leo scratched at his eyebrow and made a face. "Just a wee bit."

"About what?" As if bracing for a blow, her shoulders scrunched inward, and she stiffened. She didn't want to be the reason he thought he needed a cigarette.

He shook his head. "It's nothing."

Her eyes fell onto his left forearm, the one marred with scars. "Just like that was nothing?"

Instantly, she knew she had pressed too hard. But somehow, she wasn't nearly as worried as she should have been. She had pushed him before and had been rewarded for it. Maybe he would give way to her one more time.

"It's not the same thing, if that's what you're thinking."

That was a relief and Belle let her muscles release. "Anything you want to talk about?"

Leo sipped his coffee as the cigarette continued to burn, a fine stream of smoke swirling up from the burning tip. "It's nothing worth mentioning, honestly... How was church last night?"

Though she wished he would have confided in her, Belle conceded and shifted her feet, so her knees would draw closer to her chest. "It was all right... You should be proud of me."

"Oh?" he mumbled with the cigarette pinched between his lips.

Belle told him all about Miss Georgina, the church, and the offer to teach Sunday school class that weekend. Closing the story with Lindsey's timely appearance, she watched Leo for any sign of approval. Though she didn't need it, she wanted to somehow impart to him that she was listening. His advice wasn't going in one ear and out the other. She did hear him, loud and clear.

Leo did nod and finished off the last of his cigarette before tossing it onto the dirt at the bottom of the stairs. "And how do you feel?"

"Honestly... I'm relieved, but I feel a little guilty for being so relieved."

"Don't be," he said before taking another draft of his coffee. "You did what was right for you and it's not like you told them to go to hell and flipped them the bird. You gave them a better alternative."

Though she could just imagine Miss Georgina's reaction to such a substitute scenario, Belle pursed her lips. "Yes, but I halfway wish I had been willing or able to do the job. Those kids, as feral as they are, need a good teacher. I do care about the church and the people, and maybe that's why I had always said yes before."

"But you have to take care of yourself too," he said slowly, giving her a severe but tender look. "You knew that you'd be a wreck afterward, which is why you didn't want to do it. The best thing you could have done for those bairns was to hand them off to someone who would enjoy the job and cared just as deeply about them as you did. That's what you did, so there's no reason to feel bad."

Belle couldn't argue with that logic. The kids were in far better hands with Lindsey, that was certain. "That's what I keep telling myself, but... I don't know. It just didn't settle right. Just like bailing on Ivy."

"You'll get over it and forget the whole thing in a few weeks."

She cut her eyes at him. "That's easy for you to say. I still lay awake in bed at night thinking about something I said to a stranger five years ago."

Leo pinned her with a stare. "Why should you care about something you did that long ago?"

Belle shrugged. "Just a part of that anxiety thing, I guess. It's not like I think about those things every night, but when it comes out of nowhere, it'll keep me up for a while. Believe me, I wish I didn't care as much as I do."

After a pause of reflective silence, Leo said, "It's not bad to care. You just have to be careful about what you care about. Pick your battles, in a way. Like with the Sunday school thing, you care about the kids, but you need to make the choice that Lindsey was the best teacher for them and not you. But, caring about something you said or did years ago is pointless. It's only hurting yourself. If you can't do anything about it, then there's no point in worrying yourself over it. Some things you just have to let go. Some people who don't give a shi-... who don't give a crap about you have to be let go or it'll just ruin your own happiness."

"It's not that easy," she said with a regretful smile.

"No one said it was easy, but it is necessary. For your own sake, you have to choose what you care about and trash the rest. It's the only way you'll have some peace. That's what it comes down to. Choice."

Just when Belle didn't think she could have admired him more, she did. "And what do you choose to care for?"

That question obliterated the line she had drawn in the sand, the one she had played hopscotch with since they met. It seemed they were constantly doomed to ask the hard questions, talking about those things that were hard to mention. To shed light on those damaged roots they tried to hide from the rest of the world. And still, she felt like she didn't have all the pieces. Not yet.

Leo downed the last drop of coffee and handed the mug to Belle. "I care about getting the animals fed this morning."

And just like that, he had evaded her once again, as coolly as he always did. She shook her head as he stood and took a few steps down from the porch.

Watching him, she noticed a slight gimp in his leg. When he came to his burned-out cigarette, he ground his toe to effectively bury it, but he still seemed to favor one foot over the other.

"Are you all right?" she asked.

"Right as rain," he replied, an audible wince in his words as he strode away. Catching a glimpse of his face, she saw the pain written there.

"Something wrong with your leg?"

He stopped. His shoulders rose and fell steadily as he heaved a big breath. "I hurt it yesterday while bringing in the horses. It's nothing."

Belle instantly set down the two mugs and rushed to his side, indifferent to dirtying the bottoms of her socks. Morning dew dampened the fabric, but she barely felt the chill. "Let me look."

There was no question, no calm or friendly request. It was a demand. For once, she was demanding something of Leo, and he wasn't going to argue. If she had no manners at all, she might have yanked up the pant leg herself instead of letting him do it.

When she saw the bloodied bandage, she sucked in a tight breath. "That looks bad."

"Not as bad as you think."

"Did you disinfect it?" she asked, bending lower to get a better look.

"I washed it off."

Belle glared at him. "That's not cleaning it. What did you cut it on?"

Leo took a little longer to reply than she would have liked. "A, uh... I just snagged it on a nail near one of the stalls."

Unconvinced, she became bold and grabbed his hand. "Come on. We're going to clean it the right way. A cut like that needs an antibiotic and proper gauze. There's a first aid kit in the bathroom."

As unwilling as he might have been, Leo's fingers tightened around her own and she helped him up the stairs. With every step, she tried not to think about the way their hands fit so perfectly. Or how the warmth of his touch sent her through a spiraling of crazy emotions and feelings that she could describe in no exact terms, except that it was like falling in reverse. Like being on the edge of insanity and only his grip held her back from disappearing. This platonic connection fed her desire to be closer and feel that heat everywhere else. That might have been easier to handle than the shots of electricity coursing through her blood.

Even while he sat on the toilet lid with his foot propped on her knee, so his injured leg was elevated enough to work on, she made a strong effort to control her thoughts and make her hands steady.

Don't look at him. Don't look in his eyes. Don't think about whose leg you're holding. Just clean the wound.

And what a wound it was.

"Are you sure a nail did this?" she questioned as she tossed aside the soiled linen.

His Scottish brogue restricted her from grounding herself in the moment. "Aye."

"This looks really deep." Much against her own will, her face screwed in sympathetic pain. "Looks more like you..." She didn't want to think about it. She didn't want to believe that Leo would do this to himself. He said the smoking had nothing to do with the issue connected with self-harm, so she had to believe him; as hard as that was. "It just looks a lot worse than you let on."

She grabbed for a fresh package of gauze from the kit and the bottle of hydrogen peroxide from under the cabinet. "This will sting a little," she warned as she popped the lid.

"I'm used to it."

How she hated to hear that. She never wanted him to be in pain, not by her hand, his own, or anyone else's. She carefully poured the liquid over the cut and watched the white bubbles fizz as it worked its magic. Leo didn't flinch or hiss in the least.

"I used to hate this stuff," she confessed. "Every time I got hurt playing in the barn, my dad would clean my cuts with this, and I'd wail like crazy."

"Did you play outside a lot?"

Belle kept her eyes on the wound to monitor the bubbles. When they died down, she'd give it another bath and then wipe what she could without making it bleed any further. "I did. I loved playing with the sheep and chasing fireflies when the sun went down. If I had my way, I would have slept in the barn with the animals. One time, I snuck out of the house with my blanket, a flashlight, and copy of *Anne of Green Gables* and stayed out all night reading in the hayloft. My dad was so mad when he found me the next morning."

The silence prompted her to do what she had determined not to do, and her eyes met his. There was a softness to them, an affection that she had only seen once before. In the diner, he had stared at her like this, so entranced and lost in everything she said.

Belle blushed and quickly looked away. "I'm sorry, I didn't even put any makeup on before coming to see you. I probably look like a mess."

"I didn't notice."

She closed her eyes and her lips tightened into a thin line to keep herself from screaming. *Don't say things like that*, she mutely begged him. *Don't make me think you care if you really don't.*

And she didn't know if he cared about anything. His blatant avoidance of her earlier question might have postponed that conversation, but Belle wanted to know. What was it that drove him? What motivated him to do the things that he did? Did it have to do with his family? His home? Did he hope to someday go back to Scotland? Did he want to stay here in Levi?

Then she remembered that uneasy feeling in the pit of her stomach when she brought him his coffee. Was there anything worth staying for in Levi? Or did his goals lie elsewhere? She still didn't know how he had come to be in her barn and where he had been before they met. His portrait was still swathed in muslin, his sketch unfinished, a painting with little color. But she wanted to see more, unveil the rest and see the soul beneath. How much longer would he keep her guessing?

Chapter 13

Leo could count the number of times he had been in a bookstore on one hand. If he ever felt the desire to read a book, there were libraries in almost every town he visited. And the same could be said of libraries as of bookstores. Reading was something he had done in school, because he needed to, not because he enjoyed it.

But as his eyes roamed over the many titles in the biography section, he couldn't find the one he needed. If he only knew this Anne girl's last name, he might have been able to narrow the search. In the silence of the bookstore, he heard Ivy approach the end of the aisle and he ground his teeth, hoping she wouldn't come his way.

His hopes were dashed.

"I never thought I'd see you in here," she whispered as she flipped her blonde hair over her shoulder.

"Just looking for a book," he mumbled, well aware that they were almost alone together. The only exception was the elderly man toward the back of the store reading a magazine and the owner sitting at the front counter. If they listened closely enough, they could hear every bit of Ivy and Leo's conversation.

"Well, obviously. What are you looking for?"

Torn between accepting her help and combing through every bookshelf in the store, Leo let out a sigh. "It's called *Anne of Green Gables*. I don't have a last name."

Ivy beamed with amusement. "Her last name is Shirley, but you won't find her book in here."

She led him to a particular section against one wall of the bookstore dedicated to the classics. Leather bound novels of all colors stretched across the shelves with gold embossed titles framed in decorative designs.

"It was written by Lucy Maud Montgomery. The only reason I can remember that was because it's my aunt's maiden name." Ivy stood on her toes and looked for the book that Leo had mistaken for nonfiction. Once she found it near the middle, she plucked it from its resting place and handed it to him.

He wondered how anyone could have missed the thick blue volume with its vibrant, flowery, and unmistakably feminine cover. Leo made a face and wished it wasn't so gaudy.

"Will you need it gift wrapped?" Ivy asked.

Leo opened the book and flipped through the pages filled with thin text. "No. This is for me."

"You like reading about little orphan girls?" she asked, her tone suggesting that she was suppressing a giggle, though his focus remained on the book.

"I didn't know what it was about," he confessed. "Just heard it was good."

"It is good, if you like that sort of thing. My mom made me read it when I was a kid, but I could never focus on stories like that. Too sweet and innocent, I guess. And Anne talks way too much."

Leo smirked and turned to look at the quote on the back cover. *"Looking forward to things is half the pleasure of them."*

It seemed profound for a little girl to say and he began to understand why Belle liked the book so much. Maybe she found a hero in
the orphan painted on the cover with her red hair.

"So, what's going on between you and Belle?"

Startled by the suddenness of the question, Leo looked up and
blinked. "Nothing. Why?"

A cunning grin split her face. "Something must be. She hasn't
been herself lately... Or maybe she's being herself now. I don't know."
She shrugged. "She's just a lot less nervous now. Much happier and
she's really been opening up. Like, she was really honest with me the
other day when I asked her to go to the movies and then texted me
to say she couldn't make it, because it had been a rough day and all.
I totally get where she was coming from, but I didn't think she had
rough days. The girl's always so perfect, ya know? Or, she acts like
it. Not in a conceited way, but just always has her life together, ya
know?"

Leo tried to listen past her grating voice to hear the words. So,
she knew somehow that Belle didn't put off her true self. How many
more did? How many more wanted to see the real her underneath
the mask?

"But it all started when she met you," Ivy continued. "She gets
these far-away looks like she's thinking about something and – I hope
you don't mind me saying this – but I think she's thinking about you.
She's just so happy now. And I saw how you two looked at each other
in the diner, so you can tell me if there's something between you two.
I won't tell."

When she was finished, she smiled and waited for some kind of
emotional outpouring that wouldn't come. Not because it wasn't
inside him, but because Leo wasn't going to tell her anything about
what had subliminally been taking place between him and Belle.

He could have talked about the way she made his heart pound nearly out of his chest at the sound of her voice. How the touch and feel of her skin was the closest thing to home he had ever known. He could go on for days about her eyes that reflected back her beautiful soul, and how he couldn't decide what he loved best about the anxious farm girl. Belle was funny, intelligent, compassionate, and didn't see her true value. But he wanted her to know it. All of it.

"We're not dating, if that's what you want to know," Leo finally said. "We're just friends."

The words were like nettles on his tongue, sharp thorns that dug into his chest. He didn't want to just be friends. He wanted so much more. He wanted to know everything about her, hence why he had embarrassed himself enough to look for this book that might have been a symbol of her childhood. He wanted to know every curve of her body and explore the dark corners of her mind until he knew her by heart.

Belle was the only thing he cared about anymore. Before he came to Levi, his own life could be forfeited, his existence snuffed out in the blink of an eye and he wouldn't have minded. Back then, it didn't matter. But Belle was worth living for.

But he wouldn't tell Ivy any of that. He'd tell no one.

"Keys... Phone... License and cards... Hair's good... Makeup's good..." Belle muttered the list under her breath, standing by the front door with her eyes and hands roaming to each article.

For once, she felt as if she wasn't leaving home in disarray. Her day off from work had been well spent. The floors were cleaned, everything dusted, and she even managed to clean the upstairs bathroom for the first time in weeks. Every room smelled of lavender cleaning solution and somehow the air just seemed lighter, fresher.

She smiled to herself in the mirror by the door and plucked at the perfect, tumbling waves of brown hair. Instead of whipping it all up into a ponytail, she decided to make herself look nice for the prayer meeting at church. She wanted to walk into the sanctuary and not look like she had just crawled out of bed or had been sniffing essential oils all day to prepare for just one hour of social interaction. This week, she wanted to look the part of a girl who could hold her own, who could look someone in the eye and not start shaking or have to rehearse a conversation. She wanted not only to look the part, but *be* the part.

Tonight, she'd be all right.

Belle securely tucked her phone into her jacket pocket, but as she reached for the handle, a car pulled onto her drive and sped toward the house. She could actually feel the air leave her chest at the sight of the red Chevy Malibu. The windows were tinted, but she didn't have to look through the windshield to know who sat behind the driver seat.

A groan came unbidden and she leaned her forehead against the door. Of all people to show up at a time like this.

No, don't lose it, she told herself. She held fast to her mental state, fortifying herself for the moment the doorbell was rung. Waiting a moment so her mother wouldn't think that she had been standing there, she took a breath and opened.

The woman standing before her was the same woman as the one in her picture upstairs, only a little older with wrinkles at the corners of her eyes. Her hair was still black, but Belle could spot a few grays on the crown of her head, ones that had been missed by the box dye. The black and burgundy paisley dress hugged the curves of her hips, the sleeves widening at her elbows to give the dress a casual, yet elegant quality. But the woman inside could not be described in the same terms.

Melinda Clearwater reached out to Belle. "Hello, sweetheart!" she greeted, the crow's feet deepening as her big smile reached her eyes.

Belle received the hug with an equally fake smile, the one she had learned from her mother so well. "This is a surprise," she said once she pulled away and moved aside to let Melinda in.

"I was in the neighborhood showing a house and I thought I'd drop by."

Belle watched her mother gaze about the living room, as if it was the first time she had stepped foot in it. What was she looking for? A book out of place? A remote not angled the right way on the coffee table? A speck of ash in the fireplace?

"You were showing a house an hour and a half away from Fayetteville?" she asked, hoping her true doubt didn't shine through in her tone too much.

"My client was looking for a rustic farmhouse, and I thought Levi was the best place for it."

She'd let it go for now and prayed that her real motive was nothing serious. "You want some tea? Or coffee maybe? I picked some up yesterday."

Melinda looked to her, one finely crafted eyebrow cocked in disbelief. "You drink coffee now?"

One good thing about Belle's anxiety, it helped her to think on her feet. "A friend of mine does and she comes over periodically, so I thought it was best to have some on hand."

The less her mother knew about Leo, the better.

"Oh," Melinda said and strutted into the kitchen, her heels clapping against the wood floor and tile. "You should have bought coffee for me a long time ago. You know I can't stand tea. You should at least keep some around for when I visit."

Belle waited until her mother had her back turned before closing her eyes to harden herself one more time. More comments would come. She had to be ready. *Let them roll off you like water off a duck's back*, her father had always said.

"Did you already eat dinner?" her mother asked after she dropped her patent leather purse onto the kitchen table.

"I did. I was actually about to leave to go to church."

Melinda's lips puckered in confusion. "It's Thursday."

"Prayer meeting."

For a minute, Belle wondered if her mother was going to wear that baffled look all night, but then she shrugged and sat in one of the chairs. "Well, I'm here now. You can go to the meeting next week, right? It's not like God's only available one night a week. I could die tomorrow, so we should make the most of the time we have."

That had been her mantra for years, ever since her grandfather passed, but Belle felt its meaning because of an entirely other person. One whom Melinda hadn't cared about or probably thought about for ages.

So Belle went to the stove to make them both something to drink. She'd need some calming chamomile for this unexpected meeting. The electric starter on the gas stove decided to glitch and Melinda heard her daughter fiddling with the controls to help the ignition.

"I thought you were going to get that fixed?"

Belle sighed. "I haven't had the money to get a repairman out here yet."

"You should. That's a safety hazard. Just charge it on a card. Don't they take credit cards out here?"

The gas finally lit and exploded over the eye for a brief second. Belle skipped backward to avoid being burned.

"See!" Melinda cried, pointing her finger accusingly at the finicky stove, her jewelry jingling with the gesture. "That's what I mean.

That's dangerous, Belle. You ought to get a new one anyway. Everything here is so old."

Belle snatched up the kettle to fill it at the sink. "A new stove is expensive, as is getting a repairman. I need to save up for that."

"Don't you have any credit cards? You can apply for one with a low interest rate and – "

"I don't want to have a credit card, mom."

It wasn't the first time Belle had snapped like that, but to Melinda, it was the first time every time.

"No need to get snippy with me," she scolded. "I was just trying to give you a lesson about being an adult. I've done so much for you and do I ever get a thank you? Nope. It all goes through one ear and out the other."

Belle clamped her teeth together, refusing to say another word unless she thought it through. However, her actions needed more deliverance than her face or her tongue. She slammed the kettle down on the hot eye, making the whole stove rattle.

"That's probably why it's broken to begin with," Melinda said. "You're not careful enough with things. These appliances worked fine for your dad, because he did regular maintenance and wasn't so rough with them."

Belle swallowed hard and calmly took two mugs from the cabinet. No, she wouldn't say a thing. She wouldn't say how her mother had only lived in this house for two years before the divorce, or how Melinda had to buy new things constantly, because she had broken it one way or another. Of course, she could afford it. She always could.

Belle tore open her tea bag packaging and set it in the mug before turning to join her mother at the table, face blank and void of any condemning emotion.

"Aren't you wearing makeup?" Melinda asked, her green eyes squinting at her daughter.

"Just mascara."

"It's a little clumpy. What kind do you use?"

It didn't matter what Belle told her, because it was never the right brand. She grabbed what she could afford from the small selection at the grocery store and made do. The same went for her lip gloss, eye shadow, concealer and foundation. But those brands weren't good enough either. Melinda went into listing all the suitable, fashionable brands and while she was at it, berated Belle for her choice of shirt and jeans to go to the meeting.

"It's church, isn't it? You're supposed to wear something nice."

"What would look better for me to wear?" Belle asked, indulging her mother rather than reproaching her.

"A dress or something feminine. You're always wearing jeans or those ugly, plain blouses. Wear something a little more girly. That's why you don't have a boyfriend. Your mascara is too clumpy, you don't wear enough makeup, and you don't dress nice... Please tell me you weren't going to wear your hair like that either. It would look so much better if it was pulled back."

Belle felt the muscle jump in her jaw, but she wouldn't waver. She couldn't let her mother see how much these comments hurt her, how much they enraged her. Even though she could feel her hold on her composure slipping with each passing second, she couldn't give in. She couldn't break. Not now. The kettle wasn't even ready yet.

When Belle called to tell him that the evening chores were taken care of, he could tell she was happy. Exactly why, he wasn't sure, but her joy was his, and he wasn't going to question it. If he hadn't been engrossed in *Anne of Green Gables*, he might have gone over to the farm anyway, just to keep an eye on things.

In all reality, he should have been sleeping to catch up on the hours of rest he didn't get the night before. The words of the darkness circled around in his brain, twisting in his guts until he was ready to vomit, constricting his heart until he almost couldn't breathe.

No matter how many times he had gone over it, he still couldn't make sense of the warning. Why would the darkness be so afraid to stay? Why was Belle like that hot flame that drew all the moths to her farm? What made her so special that the demon would be enticed by her? Her safety was his priority, but now she had become a target. That was evident from the moment he saw Matthew's hex on the tree. But that should have all been resolved with his blood payment. Now the darkness came back to tell him it might not be enough?

And how did Matthew fit into all of this? Belle was on the chopping block with him, but there was some other force playing in this wicked game. The only problem was that the rules were changing again, and Leo couldn't predict their moves anymore.

This conundrum slowed his progress through the book, though after taking a peek at the table of contents, he knew he'd be in this for the long haul. Eight short novels in a single volume wasn't going to be conquered in one night, but it could put him to sleep.

Leo felt his eyes droop as he lay in bed, the book open and propped atop his abs, when the harsh vibration of his prepaid phone in his pocket jerked him awake. There were only a few people who had his number and none of them were likely to call except one.

"Belle?" he answered.

"Hey, Leo." The subtle whine in her greeting, punctuated by a sniffle told him enough.

"What's wrong?" Leo jumped out of bed, losing his place in the novel, and grabbed for his motorcycle keys.

She cleared her throat, as if that would make him forget the panic streaking through him. "Nothing. I..." Leo stood still in the middle of his apartment room, waiting as his heart rose into his throat. "I just... Can you come over?"

"Aye," he replied quickly. "I'm on my way. Are you sure you're all right?"

"Yeah, I'm fine." Belle was doing a horrible job at hiding whatever it was that bothered her enough to ask him to come back to the farm.

"You're safe? Not hurt?" Leo was down the fire escape, taking two steps at a time.

"No, I'm not hurt... I mean... Not really."

Ice pierced his heart at the sound of so much brokenness and uncertainty.

"I'll be there as soon as I can," he assured before hanging up and cranking his bike.

As powerless as Leo was against the darkness, he knew there would be repercussions if any of this had to do with the influence of the demon. No one would get away with making Belle cry.

Breathe in six seconds, hold for eight, exhale for nine... Or was it six, seven, and eight? Four, eight, and seven?

Belle couldn't even remember the right counts for this breathing exercise. A million thoughts swarmed between her ears, all white noise and blaring out whatever rationality was left. Her hands trembled as she held the steaming mug of tea. She couldn't even drink it, despite her dry mouth, because her throat had closed up. From her place on the couch, she tried to recall the other exercise.

Was it smell three things, taste two, and feel seven? Or some-thing else? Smell, taste, touch, and hearing. I know that much. But what's the order? What should I do first?

So instead, she took ragged breath after ragged breath, the skin of her fingers and palm heated by the ceramic until they tingled. It was the only thing she could feel besides her racing pulse and insides quivering like jelly.

She heard the bike come roaring up the drive and it didn't take long for the front door to swing open. Leo stood there, staring at her, and she knew what he'd see. A frightened girl, wracked with tremors, sitting on the couch in her pajamas. Once neat curls and waves were now disheveled and matted after fingers had raked over her scalp too many times. Mascara that her mother accused of being clumpy was now smeared under her eyes after tears had ruined it.

Would he run? Would he think her a coward? Or would he be the grounding force she had needed ever since the red Malibu drove away?

Leo closed the door and took just two steps in before her weak legs somehow found the strength to stand. Her mouth, too, somehow found its voice and it wouldn't stop now that she knew he was here. Maybe he would listen.

"My mom just came to visit," she began in a panic. "Completely out of nowhere. I mean, sometimes she at least calls a couple of hours ahead of time, but this time she didn't. She just showed up two minutes before I was ready to walk out the door. And, of course, she was her usual critical self. She found something wrong with everything. My hair, my makeup, my clothes. She even got on my case about the stove not working! It's not my fault it's on the fritz! How can she blame me for a thirty-year-old stove not working right? Who does that? Who thinks that way?"

As her fervor began to build, she found herself pacing across the floor, around the coffee table and behind the couch in no particular pattern. Just to stay moving. "I cleaned this house from top to bottom before she got here. And guess what? She noticed! But in that snide way like, 'You must have expected company, because you never clean.'"

Her impression of her mother was severely exaggerated to the aim of mocking her, but Belle didn't care. The commandment to love thy mother and father was the last thing on her mind.

"Once she was done insulting me, my house, my job, my friends, my dad, and the farm, she started in on her usual negative rant that could go on for days." Belle dragged it out to get her point across, her knees bending as if she had been weighed down by a heavy burden being dropped onto her shoulders. "That woman could go to heaven and complain that it was too perfect. She can never be happy with anything or anyone and she doesn't even care! She doesn't care that she breaks me like this every time she visits. She doesn't care that I can't stand to be around her. She'll just guilt me into spending time with her, saying that she's all the family I have left. That may be true, but I can't believe I ever came out of that woman's womb! She didn't even come to dad's funeral!"

Fresh hot tears stung at her eyes as she replayed it all in her head one more time. "I may have her eyes, but I don't know how I could ever share genetics with her. She drains me, Leo. Out of all the things in the world that could drain me, she depletes me entirely."

He strode forward, slowly and cautiously like he was approaching a wild mustang.

"She just makes me feel so worthless, so useless. Like I can't do anything right and I'll never be good enough. Her opinion shouldn't even matter, but she's my mom. She's the one who carried me for nine months and went through so much pain to have me, but you know what? She's the one that left! She walked out on me and dad when I was just a baby. She left me at the daycare center and disappeared for a whole week! The next we heard from her, she was in Little Rock with some guy and already filing for the divorce. Said she couldn't be the wife of a church-going man and stay cooped up in a small town like Levi. She wanted to go places and dad wanted to keep the farm. She wouldn't even try to negotiate with him! She wouldn't try! She wouldn't try to make it work with her own family and we weren't good enough... I wasn't good enough."

Leo had taken the mug from her hand and placed it on the coffee table. Belle's sobs came out in wheezes as her very ribs felt like they would collapse in on her heart.

"How could anyone do that to someone they love?" she cried. "How could she leave us so broken and not feel a thing? I don't want to be like that, Leo. I can't be – "

She never got the chance to finish her sentence.

His hands, roughened by years of labor, had cupped her face and drew her up to meet him. Her hysterics were finally silenced as warm, soft lips connected with hers.

The static in her mind died away. Her red and puffy eyes drifted shut. His thumb tenderly slid across her cheeks, wiping away the tears that had been shed. All at once, her body went still and numb as her delicate hands rested upon his thick forearms. She felt like a newborn lamb in the embrace of a loving shepherd.

As the kiss deepened and his mouth moved in passionate ways against her own, Belle's head swam with a dizziness she had never known before. Her legs wanted to buckle, but he held her firmly in his grasp, instilling her with strength while he stole her frailty at the same time.

Not a single thought echoed in her mind, and the numbness of shock soon gave way to a euphoria that gushed through her core.

Her blood ignited for the first time in her life. Every nerve became disentangled. Her seams unraveled. The barred doors unhinged. Her brick walls shattered into dust.

Belle was reduced to nothing so that Leo could build her back up again.

He pulled away and his sweet, hot breath plumed over her flushed face.

"If you ever start to think that you're unworthy, that you don't mean anything to anyone, I want you to remember this..."

Belle opened her eyes and met the smoldering blue gaze, listening to the rest of what he had to say as if it were the very thing that would keep her alive for just a little longer.

"You were not made to fit a mold. You weren't made to be perfect. You were born wild and you should stay wild, no matter what anyone else says. It doesn't matter what your mum says, what your friends say, or what anyone else in this town says. The world and all its expectations of you mean nothing. What matters is how you see yourself. At the end of the day, if you're happy with what you've done and who you are, then that's the only opinion you ever need to listen to."

She blinked. "But I – "

"I don't care," he whispered fiercely, his fingers knotting in her hair. "You can't listen to any of them. That's what will kill you in the end if you let it. Don't try to be any less than the beautiful, witty, brave, and compassionate woman that you are. Don't dull your shine, just because someone else is blinded by you. You can't be someone you're not. Your mum... she didn't leave because of you. She left because she thought she could find something better somewhere else and she was wrong. And look at you." Leo brushed away a new tear as it rolled down from the corner of her eye. "You grew up to be an amazing person without her. You just have to get her voice out of your head and believe that you are so much more incredible than you give yourself credit for."

Belle's fingers squeezed over the tense muscles of his arms and she tried to grasp his meaning through the rapture of his touch and his kiss. Just when she thought he'd take her in another, he pulled her into a hug instead. A hug so tight that she could almost feel the broken bits of her soul stitch back together. She could feel his heartbeat, racing just as quickly as her own in that feverish, palpitating way. With her ear pressed into the hollow of his throat, she could hear him take each steady breath and synched it with her own.

It was her first kiss. Her first taste of what love would be like. Her first wakeup call to a new life free of the restricting worries that came with feeling too much for things that didn't matter.

But Leo was wrong about one thing. His opinion did matter. Whether he wanted it to or not, it carried weight like none other could.

Belle wanted to be better, to be happier and free. But she wanted to show Leo that she was worth all this trouble, all the drama and the tears. She wanted to prove him right, that she was brave and compassionate. If not to the world, then to herself.

Chapter 14

Leo's arms encased Belle, her head pillowed against his chest. His heartbeat and steady breaths became her lullaby. Dead to the world, she hadn't moved in her sleep for hours. He didn't mind. She needed this rest and time to recover. Her mother had become a catalyst for a downward spiral of hysteria and only his kiss could stop her freefall.

He wanted to think it was the kiss that brought the pieces back together. But while he cradled her on the couch, letting her sensibly tell him all of the escalating problems of her damaged relationship with her mother, the more he realized it went much deeper than that. The kiss was long overdue, but she had called him before they kissed, before they embraced and he felt her crash into him. That could only mean one thing.

Belle trusted him. She trusted enough to come undone in front of him, to expose her broken and jagged bits without limitation or fear. It had been a long time since anyone had blessed him with that privilege, and he would have been a fool to not recognize it.

But she had trusted him from the beginning, ever since she gave him a clean shirt and a meal. She trusted him when he asked her to the diner, when he wrapped up her sprained ankle, when he held that snake, and now as she slept in his embrace.

How could he ever make her believe that she had put her trust in the wrong man? If the darkness was even telling a fraction of the truth, Leo would be the reason for all her troubles in the days ahead. All because of a kiss. This episode would bring more evil into their lives than she could ever imagine. He'd need to give a blood payment soon, though he gave one recently.

His leg still smarted with that pain, even after she had cleaned it and wrapped it up nicely, he'd have to cut into himself again and again, just to keep her safe.

How long could he keep this up?

She did feel good in his arms, though. Warm, soft, like she was made to fit against him like this for eternity. And by the way she seemed to fall into him so willingly, so easily, she must have thought the same. He hoped with every fiber of his being that she wouldn't try to give him that delicate, tender heart that he so longed to hold. It would have been the next logical step. But his hands were too rough, too strong to ever keep something that could break. And he couldn't give his heart in return. It'd only add to the mountain of burdens she already carried. Hard, stony, covered in ice and thorns. He wanted to give it, but because he loved her, he couldn't.

Being careful not to wake her, Leo slipped off the couch and used the throw pillows to replace him. Belle stirred only for a moment, but then went still again as she dozed back to sleep. If only he could have been so rested.

Dawn was slowly approaching and the silvery gray sky outside seemed more overcast than usual. The coming morning would be dreary and bleak, a continuing theme from the night before. If only he could have rewound the clock. He would have stayed with Belle the entire day, just to guard her against visitors like her mother. If he ever saw the woman, there would be no end to the string of curses and insults he'd fling upon her. He'd break her just like she broke Belle countless times before.

For now, he needed some way to stay awake. He had dozed a few times while Belle slept, but he had been too afraid of his nightmares affecting her. There had been times in the past where he woke up on the floor with the mattress turned over, and he didn't want to risk anything disturbing Belle. That, and he didn't want questions if she woke up to find him sweating and muttering names she didn't need to know about.

His feet barely made a whisper of sound as Leo found his way into the kitchen and turned on the vent light above the stove. As soon as he flipped the switch, the light flickered and burned out. Leo sighed and checked the bulb, but it was nearly impossible to see if it had blown in the dark.

Risking the possibility of Belle waking up, Leo tried to turn on the kitchen light. Nothing.

He glanced into the living room and searched for the digital clock on the DVD player. The tiny green numbers were nowhere to be found.

Leo rolled his tired, burning eyes and leaned against the cased opening between the kitchen and the living room, mindlessly flicking the switch up and down, hoping for a different result each time. If the power was out, how long would it be out? Was there a line down somewhere or did he need to try the breaker?

All the while he carelessly fiddled with the switch, he watched Belle's silhouette and the way her back rose and fell. Peaceful, beautiful, perfect. A thousand curses prickled on the tip of his tongue, but he wouldn't utter a single one. How could he have gotten himself into this mess?

One more try did the trick and the yellow light from the kitchen fell across Belle's face. Leo waited, but she didn't awaken.

He turned it off once more and went for the stove light. As he did, he passed by one of the curtained windows that looked out over the field between the house and the barn. The sky no longer seemed the same dull gray but conveyed a slight amber hue as if the sunrise had already come.

Leo glanced once and had to look again. The golden light didn't come from the sun, but from the barn.

Belle's hand ran across the rough texture of the sofa cushion as a bit of her consciousness restored. The coolness beneath her was the first shock. Then came the sound of the back door opening. A gust of autumn air rushed through the house and grazed across her nose and cheeks. Then came the cries of her horses.

Her eyes shot open and she pushed herself up. How long had she been asleep? By the steadily brightening kitchen, she assumed it was morning already. But the same sunrise that streamed through the kitchen windows never touched the living room.

Looking to the digital clock on the DVD player, she noticed it blinked midnight. Had the power gone out?

Her groggy mind tried to grasp the situation as she swiveled her head around in search for Leo. He must have been the one to open the back door. Belle took a breath and rubbed at her shoulder, once more regretting that she had fallen asleep on the sofa in an unnatural position.

However, she couldn't regret whom she had fallen asleep with. She smiled when she thought of the way Leo held her close, how his mouth had felt against hers. Her fingertips came to touch her lips, remembering how her first kiss had unfolded in such an unexpected, but completely comfortable way. Her stomach fluttered at the thought of there being more kisses to come, more caresses, more intimacy.

But those hopes for the future were pushed out as another sound came from the field. The horses were going crazy and in the silence of the morning, she heard something like the snapping and banging of wood.

She rose to her feet and stumbled into the kitchen, letting the sun's rays light her way to the window.

As she pulled back the curtain, she understood why Leo had run out the door in such a hurry. It wasn't the sun's light shining through the glass pane, but the glow of a fire. She could see it dancing behind the thin cracks of the boards that made up the walls of the barn. The reaching flames lapped between the wider gaps and from the hayloft doors. Slowly, the fire ate through the roof in patches, keeping some bits intact while she could see the shingles buckle in other places.

She gaped at the sight of it and wondered if she were dreaming. She reached out and touched the cold windowpane. This was no dream. As more seconds ticked by, she could feel her body pulling out of its shock.

Almost at the same moment Belle knew she could move, she saw the barn doors burst open, the frame burning like a portal into hell itself. Leo came rushing out with two horses, their faces masked by a swath of burlap to keep them calm.

Just from what she could see of the inside of the barn, every bit of hay had combusted, spreading to cover almost every inch of the floor.

Belle, ignoring the violent way her body shuddered and shook, grabbed her boots and threw them on before following in Leo's footsteps to run across the field to the barn.

He was already at the horse pasture, releasing Chestnut and Snow when she felt the heat of the fire against her face. Her feet slipped a little on the morning dew as she slowed. But she couldn't stop. The sheep were still inside, and their screams were clearly audible over the roar of the blaze. She looked around the opening into the barn and found a shovel leaning against the outside wall that hadn't been claimed by the fire.

She grabbed for it and rushed in, vaguely aware that Leo called out her name from the pasture.

The heat scorched her skin and she could already feel the sweat building on her neck and forehead. The light from the inferno nearly blinded her, making her unable to see through the flames and smoke that flowed upward through the holes in the roof. To her left, Maggie wailed and knickered, her massive hooves pawing the air. Her stall was slowly being consumed, the partitions of fire penning her in.

Using her shovel, she swung for the latch that glowed red-hot. It snapped easily and the crumbling door swung open. Maggie bolted out, the tip of her long tail on fire. Belle fell out of the way, so close to a spot of fire that she thought some had caught onto her clothes. Upon quick inspection, she found none, and then scrambled up to make her way toward the sheep pen.

Their corral wasn't nearly as destroyed as the horse stalls, but she could see the fire creeping ever closer, climbing up the wood railing. The ewes within had panicked, stepping in circles, bumping around and knocking one another down in their futile attempt to escape.

Once more, she could hear Leo shout her name, but she couldn't turn back now. As with Maggie's latch, she swung for the lock on the sheep pen. It took a few extra tries before it gave way to her shovel.

Belle grabbed for a portion of the door that hadn't been affected yet, and threw it open. The ewes and ram came pouring out into the barn, headed for their nearest escape route through the only doors that hadn't been eaten away yet.

Belle coughed into her elbow and tried to use it to shield her nose and mouth against the congesting smoke. Standing between the stampeding sheep and the towering flames in the back of the barn, she heard the snapping and crackling all around her. Falling bits of wood and their embers fell on the sheep's wool and she feared some would catch. But Leo was there to receive them at the doors and extinguish the threat. He managed to steer them all toward the pasture with the horses. They were safe now, but the nightmare continued.

Her whole world would be reduced to ash in a matter of hours. Generations of memories and heritage would be gone. The Volkswagen would never run again. The hand-painted name plaques on the horse stalls could never be recovered. Thousands of dollars worth of food, animal feed, tools, and equipment devoured by the firestorm.

A rippling of cracks erupted above her and she staggered forward, but was stopped when a piece of the hay loft came crashing in her path. Belle screamed and shielded herself from the barricade of fire. Leo's shouts were hardly distinguishable now.

She turned in circles, just as the sheep did, hunting for a way out. Closed in on every side, she could find no escape. The heat became intolerable, her sweat evaporating from her skin before it had a chance to accumulate.

Belle stood still, gasping for air and bringing her arms in to avoid the licking tendrils of flames that reached for her. With her last good lungful, she screamed for Leo and prayed that he would somehow hear her and know that she was still alive, waiting for him in the chaos.

Leo gulped down breath after breath, willing his heart to stay beneath his ribs instead of exploding out of his chest as he thought it would. While his insides turned hard, his limbs felt weak and he had to keep his knees locked to remain standing, rooted in place. He stared, eyes wide upon the burning barn.

Belle was still inside, or so he thought. After that last collapse, he wasn't sure. He continued to scream her name, but his voice lost its essence and the longer he went without an answer, the more the plea softened until he couldn't hear himself anymore.

How could this have happened? The darkness hadn't even come for its next payment. He would have given it. He would have given anything to avoid this.

Through the hissing and sizzling, he heard her call for him.

Her voice, strong and loud, was enough to propel him forward. He didn't care that he'd be leaping through a curtain of flames. He'd take the burns. Let that be his payment to the demon who had wrought this destruction.

The fire slid across his bare arms, singeing the hairs and blistering his skin. He stomped over the smoldering boards and vaulted through what gaps he could find to avoid the blazes. Miraculously, a horse blanket draped over one of the stall partitions hadn't caught fire and he snatched it up to wrap across his shoulders.

Leo inhaled to call for her one more time, but the smoke choked him. She screamed one more time, her voice breaking through the din. Nothing looked familiar to him, and a once straight-in shot became like a maze of death.

He found Belle sitting inside a ring of fire, her knees drawn to her chest and head tucked low to protect herself. With one great burst of adrenaline, he dove across the neatly formed perimeter of flames and seized her. Her green eyes looked to him in pure fright while he swaddled her in the horse blanket, exposing himself to the devouring blazes again.

Retracing his steps through the wreckage, he heard what would come next. What was left of the hayloft would be coming down soon as it continued to shower more kindled debris upon their heads. The roof, too, would cave in and the rafters were already splitting, giving way to the hungry flames that ate away from both ends to meet in the center.

Just when he saw a bit of gray dawn up ahead, one stretch of timber wouldn't wait. It creaked and then broke free from the rest of the structure. Leo looked up and saw it tumbling from the ceiling.

Stop.

Unsure why, Leo obeyed and grabbed Belle to force her down. Between his body and the horse blanket, she'd be protected from any falling fragments. Leo, not so much. But his safety didn't matter. Not to him.

The rafter, which he was sure would fall across his shoulders and pin them both to the floor, landed just a few feet away, right in the path they had intended to take. Belle let out a tiny yelp and shrank into him. They were running out of time. If they didn't get out soon, they'd end up like everything else inside the barn.

Leo helped her up again and led her the rest of the way to safe ground. When the cool morning air hit his skin, it was like a balm to his burns. They both coughed and sputtered, gasping as they stumbled along, getting as far from the barn as they could before their legs finally gave out.

He threw off the blanket and discarded propriety along with it. Hands and eyes roamed everywhere over Belle, examining her for any injuries or burns. He could easily forget about himself and his own wounds. They were nothing.

She, too, seemed to have the same idea. Belle reached for his arms and whimpered at the sight of the scalded blotches. Her lips trembled uncontrollably, unable to make the question, but he answered anyway.

"I'm fine," he rasped. "Are you..." He could scarcely finish his own sentence without coughing.

Belle only nodded and squeezed her eyes shut, her face contracting as if she'd soon cry. He couldn't bear to see her tears. He brought her into his damaged arms and held her tight as he had the night before, hoping that somehow his nearness could bring her some peace. But nothing could undo what had been done.

As he turned his eyes to the ruins, the roof finally gave way. Fire and smoke billowed out, burning boards crumbling and breaking as the final blow was struck. Only one thought existed as he watched the flames rise higher against the gloomy morning sky.

This was your fault. All your fault.

Chapter 15

Once the fence had been doused with the hose for good measure, Belle and Leo set themselves to checking the animals. The sun had still not made a grand appearance, but the light from the flaming wreckage might have been enough to see by alone.

Leo inspected the horses, running his hand along their backs and haunches. It took a great deal to calm them down at first, and their flesh still shuddered under his touch. Maggie was the only one to sustain some burns on her hooves, but they were fine and healthy otherwise. Belle took charge over the sheep, and though some patches of wool had been singed during their escape, they too, were unharmed.

The weight of his guilt pressed upon him, almost heavier than the ultimate burden he had been carrying since he'd left Scotland. This rivaled everything he had done up to that point. The accidents, the fights, the numerous unhappy incidences across the states were nothing compared to this.

Belle's heritage was in that barn, her livelihood. Half of everything she loved about this piece of land and its history was destroyed. All that was left were her house, the chicken coop, and miles upon miles of fencing. The land itself was still hers, but what value did it have now?

Because of him, her barn was gone. There was no amount of water that could save it and by the time he had discovered the fire, it was too late. All of it could have been prevented if he had never decided to settle down in Levi. If he had never come back to find Belle, she would still have her barn and the darkness would have never pounced upon her land like a hungry vulture. And though no lives were lost, it could have been worse. He understood that much. And it would only get worse, just like the darkness said.

He ambled toward Belle where she meticulously cut away the patches of burned wool with a pair of kitchen scissors. A small flashlight was clamped between her teeth so she could utilize both of her hands for the task.

She didn't look up, didn't try to mumble anything, didn't even slow down.

"I think there was an electrical short. The power went out and the string lights in the barn must have blown. The spark would have – "

"Stop," she ordered as she rose from the ewe she had been sheering, the flashlight now in her hand. "I don't want to think about it."

Leo followed her as she went to the next ewe. "You have to think about it," he insisted. "You need to know what happened. You have insurance, right?"

Belle sighed and brushed back a bit of her hair that had blown across her forehead. "Yeah, I have insurance, but please, I can't think about it right now. Just let me do one thing at a time."

"We'll have to call them in a few hours. What was the coverage? Do you – "

She turned on him, eyes blazing hotter than the fire that continued to eat away what remained of the structure behind her. "I told you I didn't want to think about it, Leo! One thing at a time. I can only focus on one thing at a time. Please, I'm begging you, let's talk about this later when I can stand it."

Her tone might as well have chopped off his tongue. Leo stood and watched her continue to go from sheep to sheep, trimming away the scorched wool and flinging it into the grass. With his hands in his pockets, he waited for her to finish. If doing one thing at a time would help her to cope, then he would let her. But that didn't stop him from making a plan.

They would need to find the insurance records and cross their fingers that it would pay for a new barn. More than that, they needed to hope that such an accident as faulty wiring or electrical blowouts were covered. He would gladly be a witness for the record, and he resolved to help in whatever way possible. It was the least he could do to fix what he had done.

Barns weren't all that difficult to construct. He had done it a couple of times before and if they had a good crew, a new barn would stand in place of the old one within a month or two. The material losses she sustained could all be replaced. They could rebuild and move on, but the memories stored away in that barn had all burned away. The hayloft where she snuck away to read that book and the stall plaques that had been made for each of the horses. The numerous tools that must have belonged to her father and grandfather were now as gone as their previous owners. Every piece of wood that she had touched had been claimed by the accident and now, she'd never touch them again.

Leo closed his eyes and listened as the remnants of the building became nothing more than a jumbled pile of smoldering pieces. Past the sizzling of the fire, he heard something else. Another roar, but different.

He turned toward the house and saw two beams of headlights zooming down the drive. He didn't recognize the vehicle. Given the state that Belle was in, he didn't think she was ready to face visitors. No doubt the fire and smoke would bring curious neighbors.

Unsure whether Belle even noticed the new arrivals, he casually made his way out of the fenced off pasture and toward the house. He wasn't presentable by any means. His shirt had been singed in some spots on his shoulders and almost every bit of exposed skin was caked in ash and soot. Belle was no better with her tangled hair and smeared mascara that had never been washed off from the night before.

A couple climbed out of the truck, both staring with wild shock at the barn. The man, tall and thin, looked every inch a farmer. His thin and silvery hair was combed to the side, his tanned, weathered face creased with many lines that told the history of a man who had been in this profession all his life. His wife looked to be comparable in age, a head of white hair cut short for maintenance-sake. However, she didn't wear the typical cotton dress speckled with flower designs. She, like her husband, wore a pair of sturdy pants and plaid button-down shirt. Because of this, he could guess that their farm was run by joint-effort.

The woman hastened around the side of the truck and looked as if she were ready to rush the field toward the barn and Belle. Leo blocked her.

"We're all right," he declared before any questions could be asked. "There was an electrical shortage in the barn and – "

"Who the hell are you?" the old man asked.

Logical question. Leo saw the urgent plea in the woman's eyes, but he wouldn't be moved. Even if he had been overtaken with sympathy, Belle's constitution mattered far more to him. He introduced himself to the farmer but wouldn't offer out his hand to shake.

"My name's Bo Johnson. My wife and I have our own sheep farm up the road."

He remembered Belle spoke of them before and nodded. "She's mentioned you."

"Never heard of you," Mr. Johnson said accusingly as he folded his thin arms over his narrow chest.

"Of course, you have," Mrs. Johnson protested shrilly. "Remember when I told you about Drake Henson getting beat up outside Stacy's Diner? This is the man who beat him up."

If he were ever to become infamous in a small town, Leo was glad it was for that.

"Woman, I don't listen to your gossip." That didn't keep Mr. Johnson's gaze from sweeping over Leo with sudden approval.

"Is Belle all right?" she asked eagerly.

Leo nodded. "She's fine. A little shook, but she's fine."

"Oh, the poor dear. Where is she?"

"She's looking after the sheep right now. Best to give her some space."

Mr. Johnson finally came forward to tend to his wife. "Why don't you go in the house and fix her some of that tea she always drinks so it'll be ready for her when she's all finished?"

"While I'm at it, I'll call the ladies and let them know what's happened," she replied. "I'll get them all praying for her and I'm sure some will want to come over. Belle shouldn't be alone at a time like this."

Leo bit back the reprimand on the tip of his tongue, knowing it would do little good. Mrs. Johnson had already sped toward the front porch, leaving the men alone. But not for long. More headlights turned off the main road and were heading their way. He was sure that he'd be standing here for the better part of the dawn, explaining the situation to the other farmers and ranchers coming to investigate.

As much as he hated to face the baffled, worried stares of the men and women who only knew him as the town defender, Leo would have rather been with Belle to help her ease out of this crisis. He wanted to be there in the field when she was finally ready to look at what was left of the barn, when she chose to finally shed tears and let her mind think of all she had lost. He wanted to be there for her, but she didn't want him.

Maybe that would make this next transition easier.

Cleaned, dressed, and a fresh layer of makeup applied, Belle prepared the pitcher of sweet tea. The ladies sitting on her front porch didn't ask for refreshments, but she had to stay busy with something, otherwise she'd go insane.

As disagreeable as her boss was, when he heard the news about her barn, he granted her the day off before she even had to ask. Not only that, but he said he'd pass her name along to the people in his church so they could pray for her too. Belle had never been to Our Lady of Devotion Catholic Church, but if the congregation was anything like hers, they would pray for her and send along more casseroles than she could ever eat in a lifetime.

Though she appreciated their support, she could have stood for a little more quiet and less questions that she couldn't answer. Yes, she had insurance. Yes, she would call them. Yes, of course, she would hire Mr. Tale to do the work. The contractor at her church wasn't lacking for work, being the go-to man for any and all building projects and remodels in Levi.

But Belle didn't want to think about how she would build the new barn, how many stalls it would have, or where she would keep the sheep in the meantime. For all those details, she would need a calm and level head, ready to pour every thought and bit of rationality into the decisions that would have to be made.

She had none of that. Her brain could only focus on one thing at a time. *Stir in the sugar, slice the lemons, pour the tea into the glass pitcher of water, don't spill it.* And when she was sitting on the porch with the rest of the ladies and listened to them go on and on about their own barns or the barns of their friends, Belle let her mind go blank. Their words grazed over her. Neither her attention nor her emotions could find purchase in the moment.

For now, all she wanted to do was exist and take in the reality that her barn was gone.

She looked to where it once stood and saw only a stretch of blackened earth with a mound of ash and half-burned up beams. All around it, the husbands of the women on the porch sorted through the wreckage, salvaging what they could and discarding the rest. Someone had brought a trailer to load up the bits that could be taken to the salvage yard, like the metal hardware and parts from the Volkswagen.

She hated to see the body of that once beautiful, vintage piece of her family be hauled up onto the decking. It sat there, waiting to be carried to some junkyard where it would sit until judgement day. That wasn't the fate she had in mind for the Bug. She wanted to ride it around town with Leo in the passenger seat one day.

Instead, he was with the other men, soot still smudged across his cheeks, his once gray shirt now as black as the charred shingles and planks he dragged from the rubble.

They hadn't spoken since she snapped at him in the field. That was hours ago, and the sun had come out to shine upon this disaster. All the clouds from earlier that morning had disappeared, ruining her hopes for a bit of rain to help cleanse Ground Zero.

Part of her tried to search for meaning in it all. Leo had said it was an electrical short, and she could easily believe that. The string lights were old, and there were bound to be a few bad bulbs. Never in her wildest nightmares, though, would she have expected this to happen. She thought lightning would be the culprit of any fires on her farm, but even then, it hadn't crossed her mind.

Evidently, it had crossed her father's.

Along with a hefty insurance policy, he had stored money away for years and put it into a special account that she was to never touch unless something happened to the farm. It was to pay for emergency animal care or make necessary repairs. If the insurance couldn't pay for a new barn, that money could.

Maybe that was why she didn't want to think about all she'd have to do. She really didn't have to. Her father had made a plan in advance for her and it was time to put it into action, along with some of her own.

When she looked at the scorched site of her old barn, she not only saw death, but life. The preexisting barn had honestly been too old to remodel or add to. She would have had to build a completely new structure to house all the dreams she had secreted away in her heart. Now, she could, and it wouldn't cost nearly as much as she had thought.

Where there was a mass of broken timbers, she saw horse stables. Where the trailer sat, bearing the final pieces of her heritage, she could see a proper shelter and barnyard for all the sheep she wanted to raise, complete with a sheering station and separated pen for the lambs that would come soon.

Belle remembered the story about the phoenix rising from the ashes, and she realized that could be her and this farm. A scripture from Genesis came to mind, the story of Joseph when he reunited with the brothers who had sold him into slavery.

But as for you, you meant evil against me; but God meant it for good.

Now, the refashioning of her farm wasn't going to save lives as Joseph did for Egypt, but maybe it could remake hers. This could be the first day of many, the first step toward building back up what her forefathers had. She could bring this farm back to life.

"Are you all right, honey?"

From beside her, Mrs. Kendall's silvery voice reached Belle in that far off place where her mind had wandered. She looked back to see the other ladies staring at her.

"Of course, she's all right," Miss Bonnie crooned. "She's got that young man workin' for her." Such a comment shouldn't have been so startling coming out of the middle-aged woman's mouth. It was known for uttering such sly, nuanced things that made the other ladies' brows furrow with disapproval or mouths curl with scandalous glee.

Miss Lynn, the head of the sewing circle, leaned over her knitting project to listen closer. "What's his name again?" she asked.

"Buck, wasn't it?" Miss Julie suggested, crossing her long slender legs beneath her sundress that was too short for this season.

"No, it was another animal name," Miss Georgina replied with a flip of her hand. "Tom?"

"His name's Leo Thompson," Mrs. Johnson announced proudly, but she wasn't smiling like the others. "He was rather rude when we first came over. Wouldn't even let me go out to see you, Belle."

She began to recount the story to the others of how he had practically barred her from going to see if the young lady was all right. Of course, they all agreed with Mrs. Johnson's assessment of him. Rude, blunt, and unhelpful. Little did they know that Leo had saved Belle the moment he blocked the older woman from approaching her. It wouldn't have helped the situation at all.

Miss Bonnie, however, could always be counted on. "He can be rude to me anytime."

The sultry turn of her voice made some giggle and others reached over to smack the air between them and the obscene widow of fifteen years.

"Well, Annabelle," Mrs. Kendall began as she set her glass on the patio table between them, "what sort of a man is Leo?"

A little taken by the question, she thought for a moment while the others waited. Her hands shook and she laced the fingers together to keep anyone from noticing. "He's actually very considerate... Direct... Intelligent... He cooks a good breakfast," Belle certainly hoped that part wouldn't be misconstrued. "I'll admit that he is a little rough around the edges, but you can't always judge a book by its cover."

Mrs. Kendall, the pastor's wife, nodded in esteem. "Well said. I doubt anyone here could argue with that old platitude."

"Honey, that book has got a fine cover. You know I'm not arguing." Miss Bonnie ended her opinion on the subject with an emphasizing moan as if she had just tasted something delicious.

"Wasn't he the one who beat up Drake Henson in the parking lot at Stacy's Diner?"

The tiny, timid voice came from the young mother near the corner of the porch, whose toddler played in the grass at the bottom of the steps.

All at once, the women went quiet and looked to Belle again for an explanation; especially Mrs. Kendall.

For a second, Belle's mouth couldn't form the words. She stammered and then finally pushed out the honest truth. "He was just defending me. Drake came in and started bothering me, and Leo stepped in."

The pastor's wife reached and put her hand on Belle's knee. "With violence?"

All but Mrs. Johnson exploded with further gossip and speculation. Miss Bonnie didn't seem too terribly upset to find out that the attractive man had a darker side, but the others certainly minded.

Belle gave a helpless shrug and repeated what Ivy had told her. "Drake's a little thick and maybe he deserved a good thrashing to make him straighten up. I haven't seen him since."

Mrs. Kendall didn't like that at all and looked as if she'd take back her earlier praise. "I don't know. I don't think anyone deserves to be hurt like that, but I also know Drake... Has Leo been violent with you?"

"Oh, no!" Belle replied quickly, knowing what she must have been thinking. "He's never hurt me. I don't think he ever would."

"Has he hurt others?"

She couldn't bring herself to lie to her pastor's wife and only nodded. She didn't need to know about the prizefighting and neither did the others. The truth would evolve into something more sinister.

Mrs. Kendall frowned, but in the way that made Belle feel more convicted than offended. "Please be careful around him." Her voice lowered so only she could hear. "I wasn't going to say this, but something doesn't feel quite right about him. I can't put my finger on it, but he seems more troubled than he looks. I think there may be some wounds beneath his skin... If that makes any sense."

Belle listened closely, because she knew Mrs. Kendall possessed the gift of the word of knowledge. God spoke to her in ways that Belle couldn't begin to understand, but what she did impart made sense. She had seen those wounds too, but Leo wasn't showing them to her. Not anytime soon.

She nodded. "It makes sense, and I hope one day he'll tell me what made them."

Mrs. Kendall shook her head. "I know you care deeply for people, Annabelle, but please hear me out. Don't get too close. If he's as troubled as I believe he is, then he might hurt you. I don't want to see anything happen to you."

She extended her hand and patted her arm affectionately. Belle smiled in return, but she would promise nothing. Leo would never hurt her, not on purpose. And the only way to see those scars and know their stories, would be to get closer. Though, she couldn't help but give some credibility to Mrs. Kendall's admonishment. If Belle did get closer, would those wounds somehow transfer? Could someone who truly wanted the best for her ever become a poison to her soul? Leo felt like home. He was a safe haven and a port of rest when she had been sailing for too long across a sea of pretense. How could anything bad ever come from such a good feeling?

Chapter 16

Weeks came and went. Each one its own special hell for Leo as he helped to build the new barn for Belle. He quit his job at the lumber yard in favor of working with Jacob Tale, Levi's seasoned construction man, who eagerly agreed to take Leo on as a temporary employee. He, along with several other men came to Belle's farm each day to make her dream a reality.

In that time, Leo had made himself scarce. He arrived to the farm after Belle had gone to work, and left just before she came home. If he didn't see her, maybe he wouldn't be so tempted to reach out and mend the bridge he had burned. It was better that way.

In that time, he felt as if he were doing two jobs. The first was helping the other laborers with the barn, and the second was looking after the animals in the pastures, ensuring their well-being during this time of adjustment. But when it was all over, they'd have a new home, more luxurious and modern than the one before it.

After the fire, Belle's state of mind improved and with some collaborative efforts from Mr. Tale, she was able to draw up the final plans for her new barn. The most complex of the structures was the horse stable, complete with ten stalls for the horses she would board or breed herself.

The new barn was connected to the stables by a fenced yard where the sheep would be kept at night. Belle said she'd use the spacious floorplan inside the barn for lambing season and sheering, and erect collapsible pens to separate the massive flock she planned to raise.

With compensation from the insurance company and the funds her father had set aside for her before his passing, Belle was able to leave the work to the men and breathe easy until the hard part began. She'd need help growing her farm into the once lively, lucrative business it had been.

Unfortunately for Leo, he wouldn't see any of it.

The darkness had warned him and he didn't listen. Disaster fell on Belle's farm and he had been too stupid to leave when he was told. The darkness won this round and the only thing keeping Belle safe now was the small payments he made each day as he ripped at the scabs over his burn wounds. Those small doses of pain satisfied the demon enough to give her and the farm some breathing room. But he couldn't keep that up for long, since the burns were healing. He would have to stop at some point. And Leo's once stony heart did something he never thought it could do. Break.

With the barn complete, life could continue as it had before Leo came in and wrecked it all. All that was left was to put the finishing touches on the stable house. The latches and hardware had already been ordered and Leo elected to pick them up that morning. That would give him plenty of time to install everything, turn in his key to Blanche along with the last of his savings to pay for the final month's rent, and leave Levi.

His bag was already packed and sitting on his bed in the apartment, his entire world crammed into one duffle bag that he could strap across his motorcycle. It was more than he had arrived with, but Leo felt like he'd be leaving behind a piece of himself. When his heart broke, a chip of it had been left behind on that farm. It belonged to Belle, the only piece he could afford to lose.

As he crossed the parking lot to the only hardware and animal feed store in Levi, he heard the incongruent yips and barks coming from the entrance. He looked up to see an older woman sitting in a lawn chair with a massive cardboard box in front of her. Big black letters drawn with a marker on the side read, "Puppies for Sale".

Against his better judgement, he veered off his path to the door and approached the box. Inside were half a dozen furballs of marbled gray, black, and speckles of light brown. Little pink tongues lulled out as they pranced and pounced on one another, ears flopping with every step. Leo allowed himself a smile.

"Blue merle Australian shepherds," the lady said. "Two and a half months old."

"How much?" he asked, his interest piquing when he heard that they were a herding breed.

"They don't have any papers. They're not show dogs, but they come from good stock. I'm selling these for my son and his wife. They just don't have the time to look after puppies. Three hundred each."

Leo looked to the old woman with her mischievous gaze, a coy smile just touching her eyes to add to that simpering look.

"Of course," she continued, "I'd give you one for free for a kiss."

He laughed. "Really?"

"Yes, really. You're Leo, right? That man who's working for Belle Clearwater?"

Amusement faded from his expression and he nodded. "Aye... Well, *was* working. I won't be staying for much longer."

She adjusted the flaps of her long sweater to cover her body as a cold wind blew past them. "Then you'll have to make it two kisses.

Never know when I'll get my chance for another." As if to complete their unconventional introduction, she offered out her hand for them to shake. "Name's Bonnie McEntire."

"Were you serious about the kiss thing?" he asked when they released hands.

"Very serious. I may be selling them for my son, but he's only asking for two hundred for each. I've got some wiggle room for profit." The wink said it all.

Leo, once more entertained, shook his head and turned back to the pups. A few had taken notice, but rather uncharacteristically, had scuttled to the farthest corner of the box to avoid him. Even dogs could tell he was bad news.

He squatted and inspected them all, finding them rather similar to one another, a cookie-cutter litter. Only one stood out. The puppy rushed to the side of the box and propped up his big, awkward paws to bend the cardboard a little so he could be petted. He wasn't afraid of Leo at all, and he certainly was different from the rest. While the other puppies looked at this strange new world with big brown eyes, this pup had been born with one brown and one blue. It gave him a special look, and in its strangeness, it made him even more beautiful.

"That was the runt of the litter. I'm surprised he's taking a liking to you," Bonnie said. "He's been a little skittish of most people who've popped in for a look."

Leo smiled and petted the soft downy fur along his head and back. The puppy craned and twisted to nip at his fingers, but settled for licking them instead. Now that she mentioned it, this one did look slightly smaller.

"He's perfect."

"I'll take those two kisses then," Bonnie said a little too cheerfully.

Leo, willing to indulge a harmless elderly woman, bent over and gave her a peck on each cheek. She roared with laughter and slapped her knee. "Not exactly what I was expecting, but I'll take it. The puppy's yours."

"I'm sure Belle's going to love him," Leo said after taking one more look to the runt who cocked his head to the side in that cute, confused way that puppies always did. "Hold him for me until I finish my business inside?"

Bonnie grinned. "He's for Belle? Aren't you sweet! Has she been wanting a dog?"

Regardless if he should have or not, Leo told her about Belle's aspirations for building up her flock and one of the many things she would need to make that dream a reality, was a sheepdog to look after her farm.

"You may have picked a runt, but you picked one from a good litter," Bonnie told him. "His parents are both herding dogs. They work on different farms outside of Levi, but something of their training's bound to be passed down. Aussies are smart, too. He'll take to it like that." She snapped her bony fingers and settled back in her chair with a satisfied smile.

Leo thanked her again and assured the yipping runt that he'd be back. A dog might not have been the best parting gift, but it would keep Belle's hands full. And if his suspicions were correct, they would both need something to distract themselves when he left Levi. He still refrained from giving it too much thought or he'd go insane.

Leaving Belle would be the hardest thing he'd ever had to do. Leaving his great-uncle in Brooklyn was nothing. Leaving Scotland had been hard, but totally out of his control. Now, he was leaving out of his own free will, but he didn't want to. These people, this town, that girl, all of it had touched his soul in a way that could never be duplicated.

He saw the way the entire community rallied behind Belle after the accident. Casserole dishes were pouring in and many had to go to waste or be put in the freezer, because there was no room in the refrigerator. Donations from the church came to help pay for all the expenses of building the new barn, and those who couldn't contribute in a monetary sense, gifted bags of feed for the horses and sheep to keep them fed while Belle tried to replenish her own stock. Tools, also, were donated to replace those that had been lost. A rancher even gave her three saddles for Snow, Chestnut, and Maggie. Nothing had been overlooked.

But Leo could never forget what caused it all. While the town of Levi had helped Belle to get back on her feet, he had been the one to bring her to her knees. He'd never let himself forget that it was his fault, and that was why he had to leave. This time, it was the barn. Next time, it could be Belle.

And one thing rang true and loud in that echoing chamber of his lonely heart. He cared far too much about Belle to ever allow that to happen.

"You're putting the barcodes on upside down."

Belle started at Ivy's voice cutting through the silence. As if woken from a dream, she looked back to the book she had been handling. Sure enough, the sticker was on upside down. Grabbing for the pile she had given to Ivy, she checked them all to find the same.

She didn't care if there were other customers in the store. She groaned aloud and buried her face in her hands, propping her elbows on the work table.

"Are you all right?" her friend asked.

No, she wasn't. She hadn't been for weeks. Not since Leo had practically ghosted on her. He wouldn't return her calls, she never saw him on the farm, and he was never at home when she stopped by the sewing store after her shift was over. It was as if he had disappeared in every way. The only reason she knew he was still around was because the evidence of him was all over the farm.

At the end of the day, the chores were done, the animals tended to, and even the house looked a little cleaner each time she came home. No note, no call, nothing. She had even been accumulating his pay and leaving it on the front door each morning, but he didn't take it. The little envelope packed with cash remained untouched.

They had gone from sleeping on the couch together after an intimate, impromptu, but totally romantic kiss, to absolutely nothing. Belle had been cut off from Leo cold-turkey and she felt like she was losing a piece of her mind. Day and night, she couldn't get him out of her head. In church, she couldn't concentrate on the sermons, because she wondered what Leo was doing. At the bookstore, she thought about him working on the barn and stable with the other men. In the evenings when she ate her meals alone, in the ringing silence of her kitchen, she wished Leo was there with her.

"Yeah, I'm good," she mumbled to Ivy. There was no hiding any of her grief and she was done trying.

"Does this have to do with Leo?"

She only nodded, her ponytail bobbing.

"Isn't he still working for you?"

Belle dropped her hands and stared. "Yeah, but I haven't seen him."

This was the first time she had even mentioned Leo to Ivy in weeks since she first told her about the barn fire. That catastrophe had been dealt with and was well on its way to being nothing but a bad memory. This crisis with Leo, however, dragged on for weeks and there was little hope in recovery.

"You haven't even seen him?" she whispered, quickly taking a seat across from Belle and interrupting her view. "Like, nothing?"

"Nothing. Not in the morning, not at night, nowhere. I've been trying to reach him, but it's like he's just gone."

Ivy's jaw dropped. "I would have thought he was really the one for you. He came in, like, a month ago and bought one of your favorite books. I was sure he was totally into you from that moment. It was so cute and romantic. I just assumed you two were keeping it on the down-low or something."

Belle's brows shot up as her palms began to sweat. "He bought a book here?"

"*Anne of Green Gables.*"

Something within her snapped and she let her head fall over her arms. She might have looked pathetic, but her chest was too full, her heart too sick, and her mind too scrambled. Belle had fallen to pieces over a guy, and she never saw it coming.

How could he do this to her? How could he kiss her, buy her favorite book, save her life twice, and do an abundance of terribly romantic things for her and just drop her out of nowhere? What kind of man looks into her soul and tries to heal its wounds, and then leaves like this?

In the hours when she should have been sleeping, she went over every word she said, everything he had done for her in those final hours. What had she done wrong? Was there a clue hidden somewhere that she had missed?

"You have got to find him," Ivy insisted.

"Where?" Belle asked impatiently, lifting her head to give her friend a helpless look. "How am I supposed to find someone who obviously doesn't want to be found?"

She reached out and took Belle by the shoulders. "Would he be at the farm right now?"

"Maybe. The barn's all done, though, so the workers won't be there."

"But he's still working for you." Ivy glanced over her shoulder. "It's only two o'clock. I'll tell Ray you got sick and had to run home."

For a moment, she didn't think Ivy was serious. But when those dark brown eyes leveled on her, Belle straightened and looked frantically to the barcode task she had botched up.

"I'll take care of it. Go find Leo."

She didn't have to be told twice.

Belle slipped out the back door and sped home, her heart hammering out of her chest. She hadn't been this terrified in what felt like ages. Her anxiety had become somewhat manageable in the weeks since the accident, even while dealing with Mr. Tale, the workers, and all the people flooding in to look after her in this time of need. Maybe it was the overall numbing that came from missing Leo that kept her afloat. Or maybe she was truly recovering and becoming braver.

Whatever it was, some of it came undone on that drive home to the farm.

When she came to the front porch, there was no sign of Leo's bike. Not by the front steps where he usually parked, and not near the newly erected barn and stable complex. The structure never failed to startle her each morning she looked out from her bedroom window, expecting to see the old building still standing where it had once been. Now was no exception, but she was too desperate in her effort to find Leo to stop.

The horses and sheep were still in their pastures, happily ignorant of her troubles. She called into the empty stable and barn, just for good measure, but he was nowhere.

It had been worth a shot, and now that her pulse had soared through the roof, Belle decided to make the best of her unsanctioned break from work to fix herself some tea. She had been wanting to avoid the practice for some time, hoping to wean herself off the chamomile. But right now, she felt she needed it just to breathe again.

The moment she walked through the back door, she was met by something darting across the kitchen floor. She let out a screech at first, before she realized the bounding ball of fur wasn't some oversized rodent, but a puppy.

It yipped and barked, coming up to her with a wagging tail that moved its whole hindquarters with each swish. It sniffed around her feet and bit at her shoelaces. Tears of surprise stung at the corners of her eyes as she stooped down to pick the puppy up. She soon realized it was a boy and noticed his unique eyes. One blue and one brown, giving him a haunting, but absolutely precious look to top off his merle coloring.

Belle had seen puppies like these online and always admired their breed. Herding dogs were her favorites, but Aussies topped them all. She hugged him and stroked his soft fur as much as he would let her. He squirmed in her arms and eagerly licked her chin.

"And where did you come from?" she asked in that annoying baby voice she never thought she'd have to use in her life.

Searching the counters and tabletops throughout the house, she found no notes. Not even on the front door. A puppy pad had been set up in the kitchen, along with a bowl and bag of dogfood, but nothing else. A black collar and matching leash sat by the sink, still in the packaging.

She knew there was only one person who knew where to find the spare key to get into the house. This was all from Leo, but he took no credit for it.

With the puppy still totally enraptured by his new owner, Belle sat down and began to call every number she could think of. She called

Mr. Tale, Blanche, Leo's old boss at the lumberyard, the bar, the diner, and she even started to wrack her brain for the names of the men who worked on the barn, so she could call them or their wives. All of it in some effort to find Leo.

But she received the same news. Leo was gone.

Blanche said he had packed up his things and given her the key to the upstairs apartment hours ago. Mr. Tale said he had quit about the same time, much to his dismay, because he had been a fine worker. No one else had heard or seen him, but he had told them all that he planned to leave Levi.

When she had exhausted all of her contacts, she gripped her phone tighter, willing it to ring. She had tried to call him directly, but the generic disconnected message was read back to her, saying the number was no longer in service. She couldn't even leave a voicemail.

There was no goodbye, no parting word, nothing. Nothing but this puppy. Did he think that would have been enough?

The tears flowed in streams down her cheeks, curling beneath her chin and dropping to the scratched wood veneer. Belle heaved for air, feeling her whole world suddenly crash down around her ears. She hadn't cried this hard since her father passed and she never thought she'd have a reason to sob like this again.

She wanted to throw the phone against the wall or flip the table over or take Chestnut for a run into the field and never come back. No amount of tea or essential oils could fix this. No bubble bath or period of isolation would heal this hurt. So she let herself feel it. Every bit of this heartache and loneliness, knowing that she had brought it on herself for allowing her spirit to feel too much for someone that could never be hers. Leo had always said he was a loner, a wanderer. She should have seen it coming.

The puppy seemed to understand her sorrow and leaned against her leg under the table, its paw resting upon the top of her foot.

If she could have just done something. If she had any other way to reach him, to tell him everything she had been too scared to say before. Maybe it would have been enough to make him stay in Levi. Stay with her.

Through her gasps and whimpers and silent supplications to God for relief, she heard it. The roar of an engine coming down her drive. It was too loud to belong to any car she knew. She held her breath and waited, wondering if he would turn around since she was clearly home.

He didn't. Leo drove up to the porch as he always did and shut off the engine.

She quickly bolted from the chair and wiped at her face, hoping he wouldn't see that she had been crying, but what was the use? He had seen her cry before. He might have been the only person alive who had seen her shed tears so freely.

When he didn't come through the door, she went out to meet him, the puppy jumping and slipping across the floor behind her. Leo stood at the bottom of the steps, his thumbs hooked in his jean pockets. His expression was carefully neutral, but she could see a hint of some unaccountable emotion behind his eyes.

Belle had imagined she would be grateful to have him standing there in the drive, but her former misery was displaced by rage. Her hands tightened into fists and she could feel the outburst coming.

"Did you just think you could leave like that?"

The shadow of surprise passed over his features. "Leave?"

"I called Blanche... and Mr. Tale... They all said you were leaving town." Belle had to use all the strength she had left not to sound like she was ready to break down and cry again. "Were you even going to tell me? Or is that what you're here for?"

The puppy sat on the top step, his tail swishing behind him and obliviously happy to see Leo.

His gaze dropped to the dog for a second before drifting back to her. "I did come to say goodbye, but I hoped to beat you here. Did you get off work early?"

How could this man stand there and talk like they hadn't just been apart for weeks on end?

"Yes, I did. You want to know why? Because I came looking for you. It took Ivy practically shoving me out the door, but I came home, hoping you'd be here."

Leo took a few steps forward, but stopped when his foot settled on the bottom step. "I was going to leave without saying goodbye... but it didn't feel right."

Belle huffed. "Well, I'm glad you suddenly grew a conscience."

She didn't know where all this venom had come from, where all these unkind words originated. Maybe it was seeing him there, looking handsome and tragic with his duffle bag slung across his bike. Or maybe it was the puppy or all the storming emotions roiling inside of her. It all collided like two massive thunderheads, and as if it were an immutable law of physics, she had to be mad at him, as much as she didn't want to be.

"I told you a long time ago that I never stayed in one place for long. Levi was no exception from the beginning and you should have known that."

Yes, she should have, but she didn't want to. She couldn't accept it.

"Why have you never stayed in one place? Why can't you just settle down? Have a good job, make friends... Do you just not like it here?"

"No, no," he replied urgently. "It's not that. It's... It's complicated."

"Nothing's that complicated." She recalled that he had once said something similar to her ages ago, a lifetime ago. "You were starting a good thing here. Mr. Tale even said he hated that he was losing you as a worker, because you did such a good job on the barn. Blanche hadn't had a good tenant in a long time before you came along."

"It doesn't have anything to do with them."

"Then what is it?" Belle cried. "Why can't you stay?"

Leo's face turned hard, as if he resented the very question itself. "I don't have a choice."

Belle could feel her nails biting into her palms as she squeezed her fists tighter. "You always have a choice, Leo. You taught me that, remember?"

"That was different," he asserted.

"No, it's not. It's not different and it's not complicated. Who's stealing the choice from you? Who's making you believe you have to leave?"

She could see the flash of bitterness and rage in his stare as he looked away. "That's not an easy thing for me to talk about."

Belle wanted to laugh. "Nothing has been. None of our conversations have been easy, did you notice that? We were never shallow, never casual. It was always deep and meaningful. I've never had that with anyone and now you're saying that you can't talk about what's going on right now because, what? You don't think I'll understand? You forget that I know what it's like to be trapped inside your own head. I know what it's like to think that there's no way out. That you don't have a choice. That this is just the way life has to be, because it's always been that way." She took one step down from the porch deck. "But you taught me that it doesn't have to be that way. You taught me that I do have a choice, that I can change my life if I just made the effort to. And I have been. If you were ever around, you'd see that."

Leo lifted his gaze back to her and she caught a glimpse of that brokenness again, that vulnerability that she had been longing to see in him. Just a little something to confirm that she wasn't the only one hurting here.

"Are you leaving Levi, because you want to, or because you think you have to?"

They stared at one another. Nothing but the occasional cry of an ewe and the panting of one incredibly patient puppy to break the tension and remind them of where they were.

"I don't want to leave," Leo replied, his voice soft. "But I have to."

Belle shook her head. "No, you don't. If you want to stay, then you should."

"It's not simple like that. There are things... things I can't talk about."

She remembered a conversation similar to this one, one they'd had in this very spot. Only the roles were reversed. This time Belle was the one trying to pry the unsightly truth out of Leo instead of the other way around.

Suddenly, a thought came to mind that could have solved the whole mystery.

"Are you wanted for something? Like, is the law looking for you?"

Leo snorted and rolled his eyes. "No, they're not."

"Then why do you think you have to leave?"

"I can't tell you."

Belle bit her lips together and tried not to be offended. It wasn't as if they were dating or married. He didn't have to tell her anything and he certainly wasn't obligated to give up his secrets. She just wished, after all this time, that he would have trusted her so explicitly as she trusted him, even without the truth.

"If you think it'll make me mad – "

"I already know you're mad."

She shut her eyes and smoothed back a few stray hairs the wind had blown loose. "Fine. If you don't want to tell me, then don't. All

I'm asking is that you practice what you teach." Belle locked eyes with the man she knew she had been falling for since the moment they met. "If you want to stay in Levi, but something is trying to drive you away... then I'm asking you..." She swallowed hard. "I'm begging you... Don't go."

Leo's lips parted at her request and she could see the man finally reweighing his options. To her, it shouldn't have been that hard of a decision. If he just chose to stay, chose Levi, chose her, then she'd try to fix whatever had scared him into thinking that he had no choice. She'd try to expose those wounds Mrs. Kendall mentioned and heal him just like he had healed her. It was Leo's turn to be saved from himself, if only he would follow his heart.

After what seemed like a lifetime of waiting, Leo bowed his head and turned away.

Belle felt as if she would crumble, rejected and unwanted in a heap on the porch. But she stayed standing and watched him go to his bike.

Leo reached out and grabbed the black duffle bag to shoulder it. "Have you named the dog yet?" he asked as he strode back to the porch steps and climbed them.

She let out the long breath she had been holding and almost forgot his question. "I haven't had time," she muttered, wishing that the world would stop spinning for just a moment.

Leo stooped down and swept the pup up with one hand, little legs and oversized paws kicking at the air. "He looks like... Ranger. Call him Ranger."

Too overpowered by the relief that Leo had made the right decision, she almost laughed. "Ranger? Why Ranger?"

"Rangers look after something, right? He's going to look after your sheep."

Belle's jaw dropped. "Is that why you got him?" She greedily reached for Ranger and took him into her arms.

"Of course. What else do you use a dog like that for?"

"I don't know... I guess I thought he was some sort of parting present."

Leo gave her a weak smile. "That was on my mind, too, but the thought was if you were going to have a big flock, you'll need someone to look after it while you're at work."

Belle took a chance as they made their way to the front door. "What about you? You could look after them for me, too."

He pulled a face. "I could, or I could check with Mr. Tale if he'll take me back."

"And Blanche?" she questioned, a bit of panic streaking through her.

"Blanche is a keen woman, but I think my credibility might have been ruined with her. Now she'll think I might up and leave at any moment."

Belle stopped him with one severe look. "Will you? I mean, are you going to try and stick it out here?"

He didn't answer her for a few breathless beats, but then he nodded. "I'll try... I can't guarantee what the future will hold, but I can try."

Every tense muscle in her body suddenly released and Belle felt as if she'd sink through the floorboards. "That's better than not trying at all."

"I'll need a place to stay while I try."

She saw the way his eyes glided toward the newly built stables and barn.

On an impulse that wasn't so uncommon for her anymore, Belle ignored the rules of propriety and everything else that told her what was about to come out of her mouth was a terrible idea. "You could stay here with me."

Shocked by the offer, Leo stared at her and blinked. Once he recovered, something like amusement flashed in his gaze. "You're making it hard for me to say no to you."

"That's only if you want to," she stammered. "I mean, I don't want to be that other thing stealing your choice away, you know? If you want to stay here, I have a guest bedroom." Before she knew it, she was rambling. "I don't even really know why I have a guest bedroom. I never invite anyone to stay or visit. It was my old room, but it's been cleared out. I don't have stuff hanging on the walls. That'd be pretty embarrassing, so you won't see anything like old trophies or boyband posters on the wall... Not that I had those, but – "

Leo's fingers curled around her neck and tilted her head up to receive his kiss one more time. Their second kiss was as purposeful as the first, shutting her up and expelling all the anxious energy from her body. She went limp, but had some frame of mind to keep supporting the restless puppy in her arms.

When he pulled away, Belle lost all her words.

"I'd love to stay here with you," he said softly, giving her the first genuine smile she had seen on him in weeks.

Her mouth mirrored his and she nodded. "I'm glad."

Epilogue

L eo was scared half out of his mind. He'd never let on, especially not to Belle. He should have never come back to the farm, but something told him it wasn't right to leave without a goodbye, without proper closure. Those eyes, imploring him to stay. Her voice which followed him everywhere, begging him to do what he truly wanted. It all swayed him away from the logical choice he had to make.

She didn't know what she was asking. It wasn't just the choice between staying in Levi or going somewhere else. This was life or death. But how could she know that? How could he explain it all without losing whatever esteem she held for him?

He sat at the kitchen table, a cup of freshly brewed coffee in one hand while the other fidgeted nervously over the pitted and scarred wood. Ranger lay in the corner of the kitchen where Belle had set up a makeshift bed of old woven blankets. The clock on the microwave read that it was two in the morning. All was quiet on the farm, but Leo wasn't fooled. If he knew the darkness, it would come at any moment and he had to be ready. Ready to explain himself, his choice, and suffer the consequences.

Another hour passed before the temperature dropped and Ranger startled awake. Leo wondered if he'd start barking as clouds moved across the moon to plunge them all in a pitch blackness. But the pup only let out a shrill whimper and burrowed under a bit of the blanket to hide from the coming evil.

When the darkness came, Leo couldn't even see him.

"What do you think you're doing?" he snarled.

"I'm staying," Leo said boldly, minding his voice so Belle wouldn't wake upstairs.

The digital lights on the appliances flickered. "Did you forget what I told you?"

"I haven't forgotten." He took a sip from his mug, hand steady.

"Or maybe you've forgotten what happened to the barn."

Leo shook his head and swallowed. "No. I remember that too."

The kitchen began to shake, and he heard the glasses in the cupboards clink together with the force of the darkness' power. "You will regret this."

"I know I will, but so will you." He lifted up his mug as if to give cheers to the demon.

"Oh no, I won't." The darkness stalked closer and Leo could feel its influences tighten over his entire body, rendering him motionless. "Because I'll make sure you bleed yourself dry before all of this is over. I'll haunt you night and day until you decide you can't stand another minute. I'll make you kill her, if I have to, just so you won't have a reason to stay anymore."

Leo glared at the formless mist that covered the kitchen. "You can try."

This coagulating mix of foolish bravery and terror in his chest was just one of the things that told him he was making both a grave mistake and the best decision of his life. For the first time, he wanted to beat the darkness. He wanted to win back what he had lost so long ago; his freedom. For all of his adult life, he let the demon dictate where he would go, how long he would stay, and what happiness he could have.

Not anymore.

Leo would take his own advice, as Belle said, and decide to live the way he wanted. The darkness and this lingering depression over his soul would be destroyed. He might not have known how to break the curse, but he'd figure it out. One day soon, he'd know what it was like to walk like a man unafraid, a man who didn't constantly look over his shoulders. He'd live in fear no more, because she made anything seem possible.

Just when he felt the darkness' talons reach out to claim him in a fit of gloom, there came a sudden shift. The murky mist that had clouded the room began to shudder and seize. The moon's blue glow streamed through the windows again and Leo heard the revolting hiss from the darkness, as if it were being burned by the moon itself.

The fog swirled and dissipated with so little warning that Leo stood from his seat and searched for it, wondering if it had tried to materialize into something else or migrate to another part of the house. But the air didn't feel the same. Light, thin, serene. It didn't feel like the darkness was anywhere close by.

Leo went upstairs and checked every room, including the one that had been set aside for him, just to be sure. When he came to Belle's room, he risked a knock.

"Belle?"

He heard a tiny gasp from the other side of the door and didn't hesitate to open it without invitation. If that gasp had been born of something the darkness had done, he needed to be there. But, just like the rest of the house, her room was void of evil.

Instead, he found her sitting upright in her bed and her hands neatly laced across the covers.

"Are you all right?" he asked.

Startled to see him in the doorway, fully dressed, she nodded. "Yeah, I'm fine," she replied groggily. "I just woke up and... Don't call me crazy, but I just felt this weird dread. So, I started praying."

She was praying? That explained the hands at least. Had she felt the darkness in the kitchen? He had never known anyone else to recognize, see, or hear the darkness when it came to visit him. But, could she somehow have sensed his presence?

"Feel better now?"

Belle nodded and gave him a sleepy smile. "I do... You haven't gone to bed?"

After five cups of coffee, he couldn't even think about going to bed before she mentioned it. Now, a drowsiness hit him from nowhere and he shook his head. "Nah, but I'm going to... Goodnight."

She wished him the same and he closed the door but didn't release the knob right away. A wild thought occurred to him. If she could somehow know that the darkness was close by, did her praying somehow banish him? Leo had never seen the demon leave that way, and he definitely had more to say. He didn't even collect the blood payment that was due right about now. There was no reason for him to leave, unless he had been forced out.

Could praying do that? What did she pray? Could Leo do the same? Or was it only something a Christian could do? In that case, Leo was slap out of luck. Hopefully, whatever Belle had done – if it was her who had done it – the darkness would stay away just long enough for Leo to figure out a plan to get rid of him for good. Then, there would be nothing to stand in the way of him and Belle being together in the way they both wanted.

Afterword

Hello Readers,

I hope you've enjoyed this first part of the Redemption Duet. This story has been insanely special to me because it was the first book I ever wrote... Well, not this exact one. The original story was much longer, more convoluted, and trust me, this one is way better. But these are the characters that started it all for me. Part of myself exists in both Belle and Leo, and I hope you've found a bit of yourself or your loved ones in them as well.

We are all broken in one way or another. We all have thorns we wished we could trim and hide from the world. The thing is, they are what makes us unique and beautiful. If we didn't have them, we'd be another face in the crowd. We would be two-dimensional, plain, and boring. Life isn't cookie-cutter, it's not perfect. We all have our scars. And I wanted Belle and Leo to prove that. Though they're only book characters, they both represent mental illness that get either overlooked or stereotyped too often. I'm talking about depression and anxiety.

And though Belle's case is limited to just social anxiety, it's not less crippling. Thousands or millions of people suffer from these conditions that aren't completely understood by those who only see what's on the surface. It's my hope that through their story, the myths can be dispelled and if anyone out there is reading this and they, too, suffer from either anxiety or depression, I want you to know that you are not alone. You are loved and you matter.

The first book in the duet focused mainly on getting Belle and Leo together, but there is much more to come. The darkness is not vanquished quite yet and the journey ahead will bemjust as bumpy as the beginning. But the ending will be well worth it. Look for the finale of this duet in The Lion.

Happy Reading!
Sheritta Bitikofer

About the author

Sheritta Bitikofer is an author of paranormal and historical fiction. She lives for the deep, engaging stories that enthrall readers from cover to cover. As a wife and mother of eclectic tastes, she can be found roaming Civil War battlefields, haunting her local coffeeshop, or relaxing with a plate of chili cheese fries.

Follow her for upcoming novel releases

www.sherittabitikofer.com

Also by Sheritta Bitikofer

The Outlaw

The Deviants

The Unsinkable

Keeper of Light

Bulletproof

The Nexus

<u>Bewitching Brews Trilogy</u>

Bewitching Fire

Bewitching Darkness

Bewitching Hearts

<u>The Decimus Trilogy</u>

The Beast of Verona

Amber Ashes

Saving the Beast

<u>Redemption Duet</u>

The Rose

The Lion

<u>Standalones</u>

Escape

Clouds

Passions

Silver Screen

By The Book

www.ingramcontent.com/pod-product-compliance
Lightning Source LLC
Chambersburg PA
CBHW051538260626
47170CB00003B/995